The Secret World BEYOND THE

CHAPTER ONE

THE BEGINNING

Summertime has approached once again. I am Susan Bower, 35 years old and widowed. My husband, Rob, was targeted by an unknown assassin and killed four years ago; Now my heart is deeply saddened by this event. I have my two twin boys, Alex, and Peter, to help me continue. I am looking forward to their journey, seeing what life will bring to our family now and what lies ahead in their future.

Unknown to my boys they will soon embark on a magical journey which neither one will ever expect and takes them to a place that challenges their imaginations far, far beyond.

Alex and Peter just turned 12 years old last week and invited ten of their friends from the neighborhood for a camp out in our backyard with their telescope, stargazing at the skies above, looking at the twinkling stars that shine so bright, always wondering what is out there. My boys seem to be on a quest, searching the skies for answers to questions, which only the two know. I do not know what drives my two little guys, but if they somehow get fixed on an idea they will seek knowledge from the universe – they will not rest until they get a response. They both have high IQ's, which qualifies them as freshman in college starting this fall and they have studied Astronomy.

Our home is in northwest Washington State. Our home is a nice three-bedroom house with spacious areas throughout, like the kitchen, with its stainless-steel appliances and the living area with our oak fireplace and the beautiful detail trim and yes, the portrait that hangs above of my family.

The beautiful hardwood floors throughout leading to the staircase steps and the upstairs three bedrooms with the private baths in each where the two boys still share a room to this day. They would not have it any other way. I must admit the backyard is still their favorite place to be. Growing up they had countless backyard adventures hoping one day to find all the answers to the vast universe and beyond.

The party finally ends around noon the next day, after a hearty breakfast of flapjacks, sausages, and orange juice. In the living room, they play video games and wait for their friend's parents to come and pick everyone up. I will allow none of the kids to leave without being picked up by an adult – my home my rules.

Well, after a long day, Alex and Peter are in two bathrooms taking hot showers before dinner. I am fixing one of their favorites (that always puts smiles on their faces) spaghetti and meatballs with garlic toast and salad – they both love their vegetables – thank goddess for that! Just like their mother! Therefore, after helping me set the table, they both pour themselves a large glass of chocolate milk.

They go to the dining room, sit down, and say grace before eating and enjoying the meal. After dinner, Mom clears the table. The boys go into the living room to watch their favorite program – "The Universe and Beyond."

After the program, has ended, they set up their telescope on the porch to study stars in the backyard. As Alex and Peter takes turns looking through the lens, they see a flash that runs across the sky and heads straight down toward their telescope. Alex is yelling at his brother, "Peter! Are you seeing this! Looks like it's coming straight down close to us – Peter looks out!" As the light hits, them, and knocks them off their feet, onto their backs and the telescope falls off the porch – landing on the grass.

Peter asks, "Alex, are you OK?" "Yes," Peter replies "are you OK Alex?" "Yeah" Alex responds, "but I feel kind of foggy, like I am dreaming with my eyes open, how weird." "I know what you mean" Peter says, "I feel the same way, but we're both OK, so let us not say anything to Mom – you know how Moms can be!" Alex says, "You are right, Peter, it's not like we're really hurt or anything and no broken bones either! Let us go back inside the house.

I just heard Mom call saying its bedtime." "OK" Peter replies. As both boys headed up the stairs, Mom yells out "Find anything interesting in the skies tonight boys?" They both answered back "No Mom, not tonight." Just as the boy's head into their room, they could hear Mom saying, "Sweet dreams love you." Mom could hear the door closing to their room.

They both have memories of sharing a room – even when they were small. Being separated was never a choice for either. Even now, they still enjoy having that sense of comfort from being together.

Well, after brushing their teeth, finally getting into their beds, and saying their goodnights to each other – they head off to dream land, finally falling into a deep sleep.

It was 5 am the next morning and suddenly, both boys awoke simultaneously and stood straight up in bed. Peter looks at his brother and says, "Wow, I just had the most bizarre and weird dream!" "No" said Alex, "It wasn't – I had the same dream as you did!" "How do you know it was the same?" asked Peter.

"Are you kidding me or are you really are asking me that – I am your twin!" Alex responds, "I just know OK!" Peter asks, "All right then, what was it about?" Alex continues, "The universe sent us a message and I'm wondering why they did that. I think it's because they're waiting for us to open the white door." Peter says,

"Oh, you saw it too!" "Yes"-said Alex, "I also saw the numbers they sent us." "No," Peter said, "They were not numbers." Alex asked, "OK then, what were they?" Peter says, "I believe they were directions to the white door."

Alex replies, "Yes, I see that now. Do you still have the star map?" "Yes, I do!" Peter exclaimed. Alex continues, "Good! We should put those numbers in.

It will then tell us directions to where our journey will begin across to the secret white door. I am so excited the two of us were chosen to follow the stars that will lead us to somewhere that no other person has ever seen!

Now let us put in those numbers and see exactly where it will line up. Let us look and see what it will show us."

As Alex sits down at the desk, Peter is sitting right next to him; he opens a desk drawer and takes out a map of the universe. They both have looks of amazement on their faces, seeing all the constellations. An overwhelming feeling suddenly comes over both boys. "Wow, this is huge! Why do you think we were chosen?" asked Peter. "Well," said Alex "This is all we've done and all we know ever since we were small. The two of us have always been looking up at the stars.

The two of us have always known there is so much more out there, and we've demanded answers from the universe, so maybe this is the universe way of answering us back." Peter replies, "Yes, you are right! I agree the map is so far reaching."

Therefore, they take out a ruler and Peter calls out each number to Alex so he can line it up and place a dot next to it. He then reads aloud, so placing a dot by each number and they have finished. Soon the two can finally see where on their map the directions end up.

"Are you sure this is correct?" asks Peter. "Yes, it is." said Alex "you are standing right by me, aren't you?" "I just can't believe you asked me that! Yes" said Peter "just checking, OK?" Alex replies, "Well, we have both have been doing this for a long time. Alex – have you ever heard of this area?" "No" Alex replies, "I haven't heard of it.

I think we should put the information our computer program and see what comes up regarding the directions in that area."

"OK" says Peter "let us do that and look."

Peter sits down at the computer. They already had a program for the constellations and stars with map they both designed.

As Peter puts in the latitude and longitude, Alex turns to his brother and says "What sector, I mean what area is that? It looks like – Wow have you ever seen this area ever before? They suddenly both looked at each other in total amazement.

"No" said Alex "this can't be right. How do we even know these directions are correct?" "Well," Peter replies, "These are in the right sector area and the right directions, as far as we know - hmmm interesting.

Well, what do you think brother?" Peter asks, "Would the universe give us wrong directions?" "I don't think so" Alex responds, "Since the universe went to such unusual lengths to give us this information. "

Well," Alex continues, "Really, I think the area we are looking at is undiscovered. It is new AND the two of us are the first ones to see it! What happens now, brother?" Well, I think we should study these directions."

"Yes" said Peter then it looks like we are going to be in the building business! to go where no man has gone before!" Suddenly they both laughed aloud, and Alex said, "Did you just say that!" LOL "Yes, it might be a little funny, but you know we These boys may be smart and even understand like a 40-year-old man, but really, in so many ways they are just 12-year-old boys jumping up and down.

They both yelled "To the white door and beyond!" Peter and Alex spend their time researching their information and try to figure out exactly how far it is and whether it is practical.
If the directions are correct and this place is out there – they are both wondering how long, it would take to build the craft and how long it would take to get there.
re going to build a craft that will help

They look at each other when Peter said to Alex, I believe this adventure will take us some time." "Yes" Alex said, "I think the craft will take us the longest." Peter explained to Alex "Look, we are going to need some help building this craft – not to mention where we're going to build it and how long it's going to take.

Also, we need to try and find some outside help – someone we can trust in this process." Alex grew weary "Well evening is approaching, it's getting dark, and I am starving" "Yeah me too, Mom has to work late at the realtor office where she shows houses and, in any case, she'll be a little late coming home tonight. So, you know what means!" Yes, I do" Alex says with excitement, "pizza night!

You call it in Peter, OK?" Peter responds, "Brother, one extra-large cheese pizza on its way – don't forget to order the salads – you know how Mom likes us to eat our vegetables – got it?"

Alex reluctantly agreed, "OK." It's on the way" Peter responds, "and will be here in 30 minutes."

As both wait for the pizza to arrive, Mom's car pulls up in the driveway, opens her car door, shuts it, and starts to walk toward the house. As she opens the front door and enters the house she yells out, "I'm home, where are my boys?" In unison, they both respond, "We are right here in the living room Mom! Peter informs her, "We ordered pizza and salads for dinner. We're just waiting for it to arrive."

Alex asks her, "How was work?" "Good" she said, "Where you get the pizza at your favorite place, of course, Papa Murphy's!" she smiled. "Well," she adds, "where's the love for good old Mom anyways? Oh, right here!" Both the boys came into the kitchen and gave Mom a hug.

As Susan went upstairs to change her clothes and then came back down to join her boys for dinner, the doorbell rings.

The pizza man was here! Peter answered the door, gave the man money, gathered everything up, and set it on the kitchen counter. Peter reached his hand out to the pizza man, paid him a tip, and thanked him – then closed the door. Alex went into the kitchen to get glasses, paper plates, and forks for the salad.

Everyone entered the dining room, sat down at the table, and put food on their plates. Only then did Mom asked Alex to say grace. Afterwards they all enjoyed their dinner and talked about their day.

After dinner, the boys headed upstairs to change clothes, get ready for bed and work on their star charts. We are now trying to navigate our way to the far eastern part of the solar system. Peter said to Alex "These are in an uncharted area, which no one has ever seen before. If we are successful, we will be the first twin brothers to go to uncharted area of space.

"Yes" they both said. "Here we come to save the day!" they chanted as they had a wicked smirk on their faces and just smiled. "OK, shall we say it?" asked Peter. "Why not?" said Alex. "Raise your sword to the universe, the stars and beyond!" Both laughed aloud for minutes.

"OK - OK! Back to the maps and we need to find out about these uncharted courses."

Alex said. "Yeah" said Peter "Any ideas?" asked Alex "Yeah, why do not we go over to and talk to the local expert at the star gate, you know, – that new place that just open up last year. It's pretty big!" said Peter.

"Yeah, they study everything about the sky that's in the sky well – almost. Anyways, they should perhaps have some ideas about uncharted areas within the universe."

Peter continued. "Maybe" said Alex "The universe is big, and one can't see or know about everything, but for sure they do have one of the biggest telescopes in the world and we can kind of feel them out to see what they know about these uncharted areas."

"Yeah," replied Peter, "Good idea! Let us go there tomorrow." "Sounds like a plan – OK!" jumped into bed they felt good about what they were hoping to find out. "Good night brother" whispered Peter.

As Susan woke, the sun rose, and a new morning had begun. The boys were up early. They wash, get dressed, and head downstairs for breakfast before heading off to the Stargate, which is in the college district area.

They were waiting for Mom to come downstairs, grab her coffee, a piece of fruit, and head off to work.

As Susan comes downstairs and enters the kitchen, Alex and Peter are eating cereal and toast and drinking juice.

"What are your plans today boys?" Mom asks. "Well, Peter and I are heading off to star gate over by the college district we are trying to get some information regarding one of the classes we are taking this fall." "Oh" said Mom. "We will be heading back home afterwards, OK?" said Alex. "Well, I should be on time tonight. See you both later. Bye boys, have a good day," replied Susan. "OK Mom, bye!" said Peter.

As Susan leaves for work, the boys grab their jackets walk out of the front door and down the sidewalk to the bus stop to wait for the bus. As the bus stops, they both get on.

The bus takes them right to the star gate. They get off the bus and walk back about a block. While they were walking up the steps Peter asked Alex "What's the name of the doctor we are seeing? "His name is Dr. Alan Burnett. Yeah, I read something about him. He is a leading authority in this field," replied Alex. "Oh – how exciting," said Peter. "Well, the conversation should be very interesting to say the least," replied Alex.

While climbing the fifty steps to the main entrance of the building -- it is big on the outside, painted gray with huge columns on both sides of the entrances.

It also has a double door with an archway made from glass on top of the door, above of the entrance. It is the most beautiful stained glass, with a telescope within the glass and amazing twinkling stars!

They were just standing there and taking it in for a moment before entering. Suddenly, the front door opened, and they saw a woman sitting at a front desk. She looks up, says good morning to both boys and asked them to sign in.

"Yes, thank you" they said. We would like to speak to Dr. Alan Burnett," inquired Peter. "Yes" the receptionist replied, "he's at the top of the staircase first door to your right just inside." "OK, thank you" replied Alex. "You're very welcome," the receptionist says.

Alex and Peter make the climb up the large spiral staircase that leads to the top of the stairs and go to the door. When they knock on it, the good Dr. Burnett opens it and says, "Yes, how may I help you?"

The boys explain to him they are starting college this fall and are both studying astronomy "Oh really" say the doctor "You both look kind of young to me."

"Well," Alex says, "don't let that fool you, we are pretty smart boys!" They both smiled at the doctor, and he smiled back replied, "Well, come in. What would you fellow students of the stars like to know and how may I assist you in your craving of knowledge?" "Well," Peter explained, "We have questions about uncharted areas within our solar system. Can you help us with some information regarding these areas?"

"Well," Dr. Burnett said, "Some areas within our solar system have indeed been studied and researched, but you boys also have to remember that the universe is so massive, we only can study a small amount of space at a time.

I must have specific information regarding a peculiar area you are interested in." "Can you tell us about uncharted areas and places that have not been studied? Alex asked.

"Well," said Dr. Burnett "those particular areas are not being researched now, we would have no way of knowing exactly what is or isn't in those areas. There are uncharted places in the universe. I wouldn't recommend flying off to one!" as he laughs aloud.

"I'm just kidding, boys! Look, uncharted areas can be extremely dangerous simply because they have not been studied or researched.

Let me tell you boys something – let us say that a person has directions to an area in the universe they wanted to go and investigate. They would not be able to go unless they knew the directions, they have been real and confirmed. "Do you boys understand?" "We do" Peter replies. "Look boys" Dr. Burnett continues, "A person can't take off for parts unknown if they don't know it's there.

I mean, you must know if the place is there. "Say this place is real?" asked Alex "and the directions were validated?" "Well," Dr. Burnett replies, "I think rushing into something without research and study could very possibly cost someone's life, not to mention how extremely dangerous and foolish it could be.

"Well," Peter said "just one more question Dr., if you do not mind? "No, of course not – what is it?" "Have you ever heard of a door in space?" "A door in space?" asks the Doctor.

"Yes" said Peter. "No, I can't say that I have" replied Dr. Burnett "well, good luck with your studies. Drop by sometime let me know how the two of you are doing in school OK?" "OK Dr. Burnett, we will. Bye and thanks for everything. Thank you for taking the time with us," said Alex. "OK" the Doctor says, "bye and don't be strangers." They both left down the stairs and through the front door. "Well," said Peter "what did you make of that?"

"Well," said Alex "he doesn't know shit about uncharted areas, courses, or anything like the information we are seeking for our own journey to the stars. Really, what he had to say would not stop us from seeking our own answers from the universe?

Well," replied Alex "what did we expect? Really, I mean not as if we gave him all the information we had. I mean all the information the two of us have, the directions and the course we are taking.

What do you think would have happened if we gave him the information he needed?" Well," replied Peter "he would not believe us for one thing. I mean after all – the directions and the course we are taking is uncharted – it is not in the star maps. It would be like looking into empty space with nothing there! Only the two of us are aware there is a white door out there.

We will open up the door, now I am thinking we should get started on building the craft to take us there." "How long do you think it will take us, Alex, to build the craft?" asked Peter? "Well," Alex responds, "I'm hoping we can do it fairly quickly, say two years or less.

However, if must build it from the ground, up it may be closer to – like three years. The computer system must be built, installed and then there's the craft itself."

"But I have an idea" said Peter "instead of building the craft from the ground up, which would take years, I believe – if

I'm not mistaken there's already a craft built that seat two persons. It's old and everything would have to be updated but that would save us a lot of time."

"This craft you are speaking of, where is it?" asked Peter. "Well brother dear," Alex responds, "we are in luck; it was at the college – but I read something about it and now, I do believe it's being housed at the space center museum."

"Now that's a great idea brother" Peter responds, "and I do think you are right; it's going to work out just fine." "Well, yes – but do we have a plan for getting the craft from the space center to our backyard? Alex asked, "Well, no brother" said Peter "not yet, but knowing the two of us, it's only a matter of time.

For now, I am starving! How about going home and getting lunch?" "Sounds good to me to let us go! Alex agreed. On the way, home the two brothers talked about entering college as freshman this year and leaving and going into space.

Alex said, "I wonder Peter, do you think this is going to be the best adventure ever?" "Well," Alex looks at his brother and says with a smile on his face "To the moon Alice and beyond!" Alex laughs and says, "You know – you got that right!"

As the two board the bus, they are laughing all the way home – sharing this secret with this smirk of a grin – that only the two share.

As the bus slows down at the bus stop, the two get off the bus Alex runs down the block to their house with Peter yelling at his brother to wait up. Alex yells back – "come on, catch up – I'm hungry!" OK me too, as Peter took his house keys out to open the front door. They both walked in, closing the front door and went into the kitchen to make lunch.

"OK, now that our stomach is full, we have finished our lunch, I have an idea about how to get the craft out of the museum," said Alex. "Oh, really – do tell Peter."

"I was thinking that the two of us could go over to the museum" replied Alex "and talk to Peter Vanguard, "if I were not mistaken, he runs the museum, we could ask if they would consider loaning us the craft." "

Why on earth would he do that Alex?" asked Peter. "Well," replied Alex, "we could tell him it's for a school project called man in space then we could take test shots of us in the craft, do a short documentary called 'The Universe, Man, and Space.'

We must shoot on location plus we would be happy to compensate the museum for their time and trouble." "Wow" said Peter, as he laughs and putting his hand over his mouth and then says to Alex "I swear you could sell swamp land." "Well as far as the money how much do you think it would take" asked Peter? "Good question" replied Alex.

"Well, enough for them to hand over the keys!" said Alex. Peter laughs a little, then chuckles aloud. "Well, we'll see what he says – they just might do it for free!" replies Alex. "How do you figure that?" responds Peter.

"Well, we could tell them that they would be featured in the science journal and the local newspaper. What do you think?" asked Peter.

"Shit" said Alex "this might just work – we're doing well now!" They turned and looked at each other – they both saw the same thing on their faces – the biggest grin. Peter says, "I think we need to try and see if we could get the craft over at our house, if possible, before we start back to school at the end of this month."

"Yeah" responds Alex, "that would be great, it would work out really well – we could work on it before and after going to school – weekends too.

It would be wonderful to have it in our own backyard so we could spend 24/7 working on the craft."

"Well," Peter replies, "We will certainly be terribly busy – between going to school, coming back home, and working on the craft. We will have no time.

Time is something we could use more of. Matter of fact, we should burn the candles at both ends!" Alex says. "Well, Mom is working late again – and I'm tired."

Peter says wearily. I am too!" Alex says. "Well," Peter says, "I am going to take a shower and turn in, I'm tired tonight. "Yeah" Alex agrees "I'm right behind you brother!" "OK" says Peter "I will be upstairs in a second.

I will leave Mom a note telling her good night from the two of us. "Yeah, that's a promising idea" Alex replies. "OK" Alex agrees, "Then be up in a second – oh, you might want to leave the note on the coffee maker, for sure she will read it there." Peter replies, "Already done, you know great minds think alike!" "You are right about that," Alex says.

As the boys take their showers, get washed up, put on their P.J.'s, and climb into bed Peter says, "Well brother, we are on our way!" "We sure are brother – Goodnight!" Alex says wearily.

As Susan pulls into the driveway and walks into the house, she sees the note from the boys on the coffee maker. As she reads it, she realizes that the two had gone to bed for the night. She walks up the stairs and opens their door to check on her two special guys – in bed sleeping away and dreaming of what tomorrow will bring them.

As she walks into her room, she wonders to herself what they are up to. She knows those two boys are always up to or planning something. Well, she thinks to herself, I am just too tired tonight to give it thought – I will think about it in the morning. As Susan goes into her room, changes her clothes, and climbs into bed – she falls asleep – not realizing just how tired she is. Heading down for breakfast, Peter hollers back at Alex asking him "Are you coming?"

"Yes" Alex replied, "right behind you brother." Peter opens the cupboard to grab two cereal bowls and two glasses for Sunny Delight orange juice.

Alex is by the toaster making English muffins. "OK" says Alex "the muffins are down." "OK" says Peter as he walks over and stands by the toaster with his brother, waiting for them to pop up.

They grab their breakfasts, walk over to the dining room table, set their breakfast down, and ate when Mom comes down the stairs and into the kitchen. "Good morning "Mom. The boys tell her coffee is ready, "Would you like something to eat?" asks Alex. "No" Mom says, "but thanks for starting the coffee this morning!"

"Oh" the boys said, "no problem." As she is getting ready to put her coat on, she tells them "Well, I have to get going early today.

I am showing houses early this morning. So anyways, tell me what the two of you plan to do today."

"Well," said Peter "we are going over to the museum today." "Oh really, any special reason you both are going over there?" "Well, no, not really, they have a lot of really cool stuff and we wanted to look," says Alex. "Yeah" says Peter "really cool!" "OK then boys, have a good day and I will be home on time today even perhaps early," Mom says. "OK bye mom! Love you," both boys say at once.

As Susan heads out the door, the boys finished eating – then run quickly to the bathroom before leaving and catching their bus. "Are you ready?" Peter asks. "OK" Alex responds, "I am finished. Hey, do you even know if Dr. Iris Vanguard will be there?" "Yes" said Peter "I called, and they said that she keeps a 10 am to 3 pm schedule and will be in this morning." Well then we are off to catch the bus and go downtown," replied Alex. "Yes" answered Peter "but it's passed downtown, more like on the outskirts."

"Oh" Alex asks, "does the bus actually go that far?" "Well," Peter responds, "We are in luck my brother it looks like the bus will let us off right in front of the building."

"Wow" says Peter "it just keeps getting better and better for us, we are lucky." Alex replies, "Yes we are, so far so good." (LOL) "You got that right!" says Peter.

"OK" Alex replies, "Let us go and catch that bus!" As the boys both head out of the house, they close the front door and lock it – putting the keys in Peter's front pocket. Peter says to

Alex here comes the bus; you got your money out Yeah. I got it" replies Alex, "and you?" Peter says, "Yeah and stop worrying, OK?"

The bus stops and they both get on. Off they went to the museum. After time passes, they both finally arrive, and the bus lets them off right on front of the entrance to the building. Opening the door and going inside was exciting for both Alex and Peter.

They see the first room – which was huge and was one biggest room either of them has ever seen. The boys could not believe their eyes as all their imaginations of flight were in one room! There were no words, which could even express their amazement.

As they were walking around, seeing everything, and looking at what they have that involves space, the universe, and flight – "Oh my GOD! Now seriously!" says Peter, looking at his brother. "Alex, is this the coolest place or what!" "Come on Peter, we have to find Dr. Vanguard and Oh, by the way –

yes, it is pretty cool!" "Now where is our craft?" asked Alex as they both looked at each other and smiled.

"There is Dr. Vanguard," observes Peter to Alex "come on – let us introduce ourselves." "Hello Dr. Vanguard, I am Peter Bower, and this is my brother Alex.

We are students at the university." "Yes" Dr. Vanguard replies, "what can I help you with?" "Well," said Alex "it's about the craft, which was sent over here from the college, is it still here?" asked Alex. "Well," said Dr. Vanguard "it is but, in another area, being held."

"Oh good!" said Peter "Why do you asking about the craft?" inquires Dr. Vanguard. "Well, we are shooting a documentary for a school project called 'Man, Space, Universe, and the Stars Beyond.

"Oh really?" the doctor said, "from the local university?" "Yes"-said Peter. "We would like to know if you would consider letting us borrow the craft so we can shoot our documentary.

We would do an in depth write up on you and the museum itself for the science journal and the newspaper. Would you be willing to lend us the craft for our project?" "Well," the doctor answered,

"I think that the museum would have to meet with you both and discuss the project. Could you boys arrange for the proper paperwork to be in our office – say within 48 hours?" "Yes, certainly" Alex said looking at Dr. Vanguard he was excited. "OK we will bring everything that you request within 48 hours to your office.

Dr. Vanguard replies, "just put everything we have asked for in a large yellow envelope and write my name on it along with your names and phone number. Be sure to include all the necessary information inside and I will be in touch with you after I have studied and looked everything over – OK? I will talk to both of you very soon."

"Yes" Peter responds "and thank-you so much for taking everything under advisement. All right, we will get everything too soon and we look forward to hearing from you about your decision. We will remember to include our phone number too. Just one other thing" "Yes" said Dr. Vanguard. "Well," Alex asks, "since we are here – could my brother and I see the craft?" "Yes certainly! Come with me" Dr. Vanguard responds.

They all walk down the hall and into another area, which housed the craft. They walked toward this large door, turned the knob and when the door opened, they stepped through to enter this amazing room, which was large and opened in size. They all walked over and OMG there it was – standing right in front!

It was difficult the brothers, they were shocked and could not believe their eyes! Dr. Vanguard said "Well, I leave you two to inspect the craft and look around.

After you are finished, please close the door behind you." "OK, no problem" Alex answered, "again thank you very much." Alex and Peter walked around and inspected every side of the craft, trying to study the design – and opening the craft door that leads to inside the chamber.

"Are you seeing this?" Peter asked Alex. "Yes, it is perfect." Peter continues, "I am looking at the computer system, it looks intact but needs some updates and/or upgrades as well."

Alex agrees, "There is some work, for sure, that needs to be done on it." "Yes" Peter replies, "You are right. However, it does not look like we will have any problems.

I cannot believe it – look there are the helmets and visors. Hey Alex, what do you think of the condition of the craft overall? I mean, do you think it will hold up OK in space, even with the work we must do? "So, what are you asking?" said Alex "do you think it will fall apart in space?"

"Well, no" said Peter "no, I think it will be fine. It looks solid overall, and I think with a little work and adjustments we stand a particularly good chance at getting this craft ready in time for lift off."

"Yes" said Alex "I agree after looking at the craft, seeing everything on it and what needs to be done in time for the big day." They were at the museum for quite a while, checking the ends and outs of the craft, it is condition and taking digital pictures inside and out so they could study what to be modified and what to be replaced on it.

After leaving the museum, they both felt good about their chances and their ability to pull this off.

"We got a lot accomplished, but now we have to do the paperwork and we need to manage all of this in a short amount of time. It to make this happen, we now need to talk to one of our professors who is teaching a class for which we both signed up.

We need to convince him to go along with our documentary on the universe," Alex said to Peter. "Yes," Peter replies "if we can convince the teacher of our idea to shoot the documentary and using the craft as our pawn – then I think our teacher just might go along with the idea and sign off on the paperwork.

We can explain that it would be a two-year project. We would film the entire documentary and every six months we will bring in footage to validate our progress."

"Wow" said Alex, "you know Peter, we are only twelve years old!" laughingly said Alex "and really this should be the coolest thing in our whole lives the two of us has ever done, I do believe!

We will go down in history as the amazing twins of space!" "If we pull this off, we will be more than just amazing – you got that right!" Peter said laughingly. The boys left the museum and walked to the bus stop to go home.

They got there just as the bus pulled up and they both got on. Alex looks at Peter and says, "Why don't we call Mom to see if she's getting off work. Maybe we can meet her downtown for dinner?" Peter responds, "Oh, that sounds great brother – yes let's give her a call."

Therefore, Alex gets out his phone and dials Mom's office number. The phone rings and she answer, "Hi Alex, what's up?" "Well, Peter and I are downtown and we're wondering if you're planning to get off soon?

You could meet us somewhere in the area for dinner?" "Well," Susan responds, "you just happen to be in luck, I was just heading out the door as we speak, so why don't we meet at Robin's?" "Yeah, that sounds great Mom – they have such great burgers" Alex, replies.

"OK boys" Susan tells them "I will meet you there see you in a few – OK bye." "OK" said Alex "we are meeting Mom." "Good" said Peter. "I know." Do you know what?" said Peter "you are starving!"

Well, this is true. As they came to a stop and got off the bus, they both had a smile upon their faces. "Oh good," said Alex "there is Mom by her car in the parking lot." "Oh, okay cool Peter answers. As she sees her two sons, she walks over to the front entrance of the restaurant to meet them.

All three went in the restaurant together. The host came over right away, seated us at a table and we ordered our food both Alex and Peter had bacon cheeseburgers with mushrooms and a salad instead of fries, Mom had fish, coleslaw, and steamed veggies.

They enjoyed dinner and after they were finished, Mom paid the bill. They all left got into the car and head home for the evening. The boys were tired after a long day of wheeling and dealing, trying to make their dreams come true. They felt they were one-step closer to reality.

Alex and Peter headed upstairs, saying goodnight to Mom. They washed up and crawled into bed to wait for what tomorrow would bring for them. Susan locked up the house downstairs before heading upstairs herself to her room and turning in.

The next day, early Alex and Peter were once again already up and downstairs eating breakfast. They both were in a hurry to get to the college, so they could talk to one of their professors, to get him to sign-off on their project so they could hand the paperwork in by tomorrow.

After arriving at the college, they found the professor who would teach their astronomy class. Alex and Peter walked over to where the professor was standing and introduced himself to Mr. Kyle Mason." Nice to meet you," Peter said, "my brother and I will be taking your class later this month when fall classes start up."

Alex said to him "we were hoping for you had just a few minutes so we could explain a special project my brother and I are working on. We are hoping you would sign off on the assignment, so we could get started."

"Well," the teacher said "you have me interested – tell me more. What is the project called?" "Oh" said Peter "it is called 'Man, Space, and the Universe Beyond'." The boys go into detail about what they want to do and what they are hoping to conduct to get full credit for the project.

Afterwards, the boys said there would be a write up about the project in the newspaper and in the science journal, including mentioning everyone by name involved and aided them.

Afterwards, the teacher was excited about it and said an enthusiastic "Yes! Now what do you two needs from me?" Peter explained "Some forms need to be filled out for the museum.

We need this done today." "OK" the teacher said, "hang on – let me get that for you. Can you come back in an hour? I will have something written up for you both to take over there."

"Yes" Alex said, "we will wait and again, thank you very much!" "OK, no problem." Mr. Mason replied. "I will be excited to get your update on this project.

I think it's a fantastic idea and I will be looking for your report in six months with film, of course." After coming back to meet with them, the teacher handed them the paperwork to take over to the museum. When they were finished, Alex and Peter head back to the museum to turn in their forms and wait for a decision to be made.

Heading home after a long day of working on the details, which had to be done, the boys were tired. Tomorrow is registration day for college classes, which is another early day for the two Bowers boys.

After a good night sleep, they are up and eating breakfast before heading off to the university to register for classes. "Well, are you ready?" said Peter to Alex. "You bet," replied Alex "let us go!" "OK" responds Peter "we'll have a science class, a math class, and our astronomy class. Today we must sign up for three classes.

It is only part- time, but we have work that must be started – with the craft AND going to school fulltime. It is for us to do, but we have no other options right now.

We're just going to be too busy and won't have enough time to do anything else but work on our documentary project!" "Yes" said Alex "this is the better choice for the both of us. We can pass all three of our classes with little studying – it will not take much and in return we will have more time to work on our project at home.

This plan of ours will work out and we'll soon be on our way to the stars and beyond!" They walk down to the bus stop to head back to the college. "Let us get going so we can get back. We still are waiting for the museums' decision regarding the craft," Alex says.

"Yes, I know Alex, and you are right, we need to go back and wait for the phone call. Besides, we need to make room for the craft by cleaning out the garage" Peter responds. "OK" said Alex "let us get going and take care of business so we can get back home.

You know, it's a good thing Mom no longer uses the garage for anything anymore." "Yeah" said Peter "at least we know she rarely goes into the garage anymore – and I hope that it stays that way, otherwise we'll have a lot of explaining to do if we get caught.

I will just say 'What do I know, I'm just a 12-yearold boy! Alex looks at Peter and says, "It figures you would say something like that – leave me out to dry! Well shoot," says Peter (LOL) "someone must take the fall and you are two minutes older than me! Alex says, "I should sock you in the face for saying that! Hey Peter, you know I love you – I'm just fooling around!" "Yeah – OK. Peter says, "This waiting to hear from Dr. Vanguard is driving me crazy!

I just want to find out if they are going to let us use the craft or not. We'll find out eventually, they should let us know what their decision is." "Wow" Alex responds, "Do you see the line for the advanced math placement test?" Yes" Peter says, "well, we both took that test."

"Yeah, we did and passed it too," said Alex. Well, we still must take the last math class, which is more like graphics and lines – you know measuring time distance and space – well, that should be interesting! Besides, we need that class so we can understand how to put this information into the online computer system."

"Well, we got the classes we wanted. Yes, that is good," said Peter "sure glad they didn't get filled up." Alex asks, "What about the astronomy line now – that was unreal! Did you get a look at all the students signing up for that class?"

"Yeah, I did – we were lucky to get in" Peter, responds. "Well, that's done – let us head home" Alex, reminds his brother "we still have the garage to clean out!" "Yeah" Peter replies "and we better get started – time is wasting and we're burning daylight!" (LOL) Alex shakes his head, "did you just say that –

I think you've been watching too many Clint Eastwood movies! You know, there can only be only one!" Peter is on the floor, "stop laughing!" says Alex. "I can't!" Peter responds, "I think I just wet my pants!" "OK! OK! Let us jump on the bus," Alex finally said, "I'm dog tired, and I feel the need for a nap."

"OK" Peter replies, "We can start after a break, – it's still early." "Sounds good to me" Alex replies. The boys get home and go upstairs to lie down and dream of space, stars, and white doors.

"I am so tired" Alex said to Peter "I didn't even wake up at all last night, and not once did I wake up, not even for dinner. Wow – are you awake or are you listening?" "Yes, I am awake – yes, I'm listening!" Peter finally said, "I also slept all night. Damn, were we tired or what?"

"Well," Alex says, "we better get up and eat a hearty breakfast – we have a lot of work to do outside. "Yes, I know Alex" Peter responds, "but do you think the craft will fit inside the garage?" "Well, think that we are going to have to make some adjustments and take some more measurements"

Peter says, "you know – remove all the shelves and clear everything out of there." You know, Alex, it will take time to do all of that. If Dr. Vanguard calls to give us the greenlight; we should put the craft in the garage right away." "Yeah, I know Peter," said Alex "that's why we are starting early this morning.

Grab your gloves and let us hustle – we have work to do. Let us pick up the phone and set it on the back porch so we can hear it ring." "OK" Peter replies "I will grab it on my way out in a minute." Both brothers' head out to the garage and start the cleaning process.

"Wow, did you realize all of the junk that was stored out here?" "No, I didn't" Peter said to Alex "it's no wonder Mom doesn't park her car here!" "Yeah," Alex replies, she couldn't even if she wanted too!" "Boy, that is the truth – OK Peter, let us get started. Everything we are keeping – let us just set aside to be put it in the basement.

"OK" Peter responds. The two brothers finally agreed. Packing and moving the boxes where long-ago memories were held, stored, and set aside.

Alex said, "So the two of us could have and hang onto these someday. I am sure that Mom wanted us to have something from our childhood and memories from Dad too. "Yeah" Peter says, "but for now let us get these boxes set outside and let us keep it moving."

It was going slowly at first, but the brothers kept themselves busy and worked half the day moving all the boxes into the basement. I think we should take a break now it is lunch time – I am sweating! Peter takes his hand and brushes his forehead, removing the sweat that gathered there.

He looks over at his brother Alex as he was taking a breather. Leaning over "Yeah," he said, "Break and lunch sounds good to me too. How about sandwiches, we could order in, and have it delivered?" "Yeah, OK let's do it – I'm hungry."

Alex goes into the kitchen, takes out two glasses from the cupboard, and pours two glasses of iced tea for the two. "Now, that looks good and cold – tastes good too. Alex says to his brother, "All we need now is our lunch to be here!" "Well," Peter asks, "how about I make the sandwiches. You didn't you order already, did you?" "No not yet" Alex replies. "OK" says Peter "Yes, let us makes them then.

What kind are you making? Roast Beef and cheese on a whole-wheat roll? OK, but I want Pepper Jack cheese. "Yeah, OK me too!" Alex agrees with a big smile. "Peter, you get the barbecue chips and set them on the table along with the glasses.

I will take our sandwiches to the table." As they both sat down and ate their lunch, the phone rings – Alex gets up to answer it. Peter looks at his brother and says, "Who is it?" "Just relax, its mom checking in" Alex informs his brother "she wants to know what we're up to.

I was telling her we are cleaning out the garage. The first thing out of her mouth was – why are the two of you doing that?" "What did you tell her?" asked Peter. Alex replies, "I simply told her that we're getting ready to start a school project need the space.

She said that was fine, but then asked where we were we putting all the stuff? I told her we moved it to the basement. She said just be careful and do not get hurt, she then said would see us when she got home.

I said all right byes." Alex sits back down and finishes his lunch with Peter. Afterwards, they went back outside to finish moving the boxes from the garage to the basement. The boys went back outside to where they had stacked the boxes and one by one moved them all to the basement.

They went back, grabbed two more boxes, and took them to the basement. They opened the door, went down the stairs, and stacked the boxes in the corner. When they went back upstairs, Peter heard the phone ringing, He rushes back through the house to the back door, where the phone is, picks it up, and says "Hello Bower Residence."

"Yes, hello this is Dr. Vanguard from the museum." "Oh yes, Dr. Vanguard, nice to hear from you. Have you made your decision regarding our project?" "Yes, that is why I am calling" Dr. Vanguard responds, "the board has reached a decision."

"And that would be?" asked Peter. "Well Peter, congratulations, your project has been approved." "OMG – We can't thankyou enough! This is wonderful – I will be sure to give my brother the good news – he is right here with me! I think he has already had a clue – he is, after all, smiling."

"OK that's good Peter" Dr. Vanguard says, "We are all excited about your project." Peter responds, "Yes, we are too." Dr. Vanguard continues, "OK Peter, the craft will be delivered tomorrow afternoon around 2 pm, does that time framework for the two of you?"

"Yes, its fine thanks so much for your support! I can't tell you what this means to us both." "Well son, just make us proud. Dr. Vanguard says to Peter, who responds, "OK we'll do just that!" After hanging up the phone, Alex and Peter jump up and down, "OMG can you believe this!" "Yeah" said Alex "We are just two 12-year-old boys who told a lie to get a craft and now we get to go to space!

CHAPTER TWO
THE CRAFT

After hanging up the phone, Peter laughed and looked at his brother, "can you believe this, – I do not care how smart we are, the two of us just pulled off the most outrageous story! Now, we will have a craft in our backyard – thanks to a trivial lie we told! Everyone around us believes in a project we made up, all this to get the two of us into space."

"Yeah" said Alex "the final frontier we are boldly going where no one has gone before!" Then Peter laughed so hard, then finally said "I think we have heard that before, well – not, the final frontier but, for sure to a white door in space. We shall go to a destination in space no one has gone before." "Yeah," Peter replied, "we couldn't make this stuff up!" "Yeah – you got that right brother!"

Alex responded. "This is getting better and better! If you first fail – tell a harmless lie and get a craft that will launch, you into space!" The boys were laughing so hard. "I just can't believe it – Hey Peter! I need to be pinched!

So far, everything has fallen into place. Hi Ho Hi, Ho – off to build we go!" They laughed repeatedly as the two went back outside into the backyard to pack and move the rest of the boxes into the basement.

After Alex and Peter finished moving all the boxes, they removed the shelf and take down anything that would be in the way of the craft. The garage has two big brown double doors that open to the garage.

It is huge inside, so both Alex and Peter both felt the craft would fit easily. "I think we did a pretty good job," said Peter. "I agree" Alex said, "I think it's ready for the craft tomorrow." "I hope so" replied Peter "well – here goes nothing – full speed ahead."

The boys finished inside the garage, for tomorrow-big day arrives. Peter was sweeping up the floor and Alex was taking out large garage bags to the curb for pickup. "Well brother" Peter said, "I think we did as well as anyone could, now we wait for tomorrow to come!" With a smile on both of their faces, the boys go back into the house.

Just as the boys walk back in, Mom pulls up in the driveway, finally home from working all day. "Hey boys," Susan called out. "Hey Mom" they both replied.

"Did you get the garage done?" she asked. "Yeah," Alex responded, "we just got finished." "Well, I am so proud of you both you." Susan saw. "You are both doing such a respectable job!" Just then, she could see the smiles appear on both their faces as they walked over to give her a big hug and kiss.

"Now" Susan asks, "what would you like for dinner? How about chicken tenders and fries – not the most nutritious choices, but for all your challenging work I'll make an exception." They all walked back into the house and Mom started dinner for her for her boys.

As Mom started dinner, the boys went upstairs to take a shower before eating. Mom was in the kitchen putting the food in the oven and afterwards she went upstairs to get change her clothes.

As she headed back downstairs with Alex and Peter, Mom asked, "How did signing up for classes go?" Peter and Alex said it went well and the lines were so long – especially long today – but the good news is the both of us got what we wanted this fall.

"Well, that's good," said Mom. "Yes, it was" Alex replied. "Did either of you see anyone you know?" Susan asked. "No Mom," Peter said, "everyone our age isn't in college yet." "Yes Peter," "I know that, but you both have made friends your age and older."

"Well, yes I guess that's true, sort of" Peter said. "Well come on and sit down at the table – everything is ready and it's time to eat" Susan said. "Alex, can you please help Peter set the table for dinner?" "OK Mom" Alex responded.

As they all sat around, they finished talking about today's events at school. The boys rose when they were finished eating and helped Mom clean up and put things away.

They then went upstairs to relax, and Mom went upstairs to turn in early saying, good night to her boys. Its Saturday morning, the museum is bringing the craft over and the driver will aid Peter and I. Placing the craft on a platform with rollers, just if we must move it around.

They should be here around noon today. As the boys await the craft, they are in the backyard opening the two double garage doors. As they finished doing so, they could hear the driver (of an oversized truck) backing his way into the backyard and through the back gate.

"OMG!" Peter says to Alex "I just can't believe it! They are here!" As the men step out of the long bed truck, the boys could see the craft on it. The craft is strap down on rollers, so they could roll the craft off the truck.

The two men are getting started by removing the straps that tie down the craft, rolling the craft off the truck and onto the ground right next to them and the two big double doors next to the garage.

They got the craft off the truck, with help from Peter and Alex, and got the craft in position to go into the garage. They rolled the platform to the center of the floor and place it right where the boys wanted it to be.

Afterwards, the men headed back to the truck and the goodbye as they drove off. Alex and Peter went back into the garage and at once looked over and inspect the craft. They made notes of things.

They walked around the craft and checked the paneling outside just to make sure it was solid and safe. Peter was writing down everything that must be added to the craft Inside, the two boys could tell it needed electrical wiring for the online computer system and other electrical components.

While it does needs work and adjustments, Peter and Alex are very much looking forward to making the craft solid and ready by the launch date. They realized they must assess and retest all the equipment on board until they are convinced, they have a green light to launch their craft into outer space to the secret white door.

Their desire is being fulfilled, an invitation the two just cannot say no to. After securing the craft and locking up the double garage doors for the night, Peter and Alex go back inside the house.

After entering the house, Mom pulls up the driveway. The boys can hear her shut the car door, walk to the front door, and turn the knob – before opening it going inside.

"Hey boys!" She yells out her standard greeting, as always to her two twin's boys (or young men). After a long day of showing houses and setting up appointments for the coming day, she comes into the house and heads to the kitchen, wondering about dinner.

Peter and Alex come in the kitchen, stand next to her, and say, "Don't worry Mom! We know you are tired, so we ordered pizza and salad tonight." Oh" she says "Well OK that sounds fine to me tonight. I will change my clothes.

I will be back down in a minute."

As she walked upstairs, she turns around and says, "You know there's money in the drawer for the pizza, OK boys?" "Yeah" said Peter "We know Mom." After coming back downstairs, she sits at the table with her boys.

Talking over dinner with her boys has always been one of her favorite things and to. Today, it is still one of her favorite things! Especially now when the two are getting older.

Have so much more to say and to share. She thought to herself – they are only teenagers, now in college and very smart – did I say they were smart? I mean my boys are geniuses.

"Well, I'm sorry" Susan informs her boys "but I decided to cook – so I canceled the pizza order and decided to cook baked chicken, twice baked potatoes, buttermilk biscuits, a green salad (of course) and yes – your chocolate milk!"

As the boys go into the kitchen to grab the plates, forks, knives, napkins, and glasses.

As they sat the table, Mom finished cooking the rest of the food and put it on the plates. "Here's the chicken!" she yells out to Peter. "OK Mom" Peter replies – "Got it!" "Good, you can put that on the table. Here is the salad and the chocolate milk – OK? And those hot buttermilk biscuits – right out of the oven.

They were driving the boys crazy – "Wow, Mom!" said Alex "these biscuits are off the hook! I didn't think it was possible to get them on the table without Alex and myself eating at least one of them!"

"Well, she says, "I understand perfectly! I did, felt the same way when my mom cooked the same biscuits!" She smiles at her boys. After getting everything ready and on the table, they all sat down, Mom said the blessing and the boys waited patiently to eat. "Well – dig in!"

"Well – OK, you don't have to say that twice!" Alex responded as the boys piled on the food. Susan just smiled, she thought to herself – these boys are always starving! You would think I ever fed them – laughing silently to herself. "Well, how was your day today, Peter? You too, Alex" Susan asked her boys.

"Good Mom – it was alright." "Well, what did you guys do?" she asked. "The two of us – well" said Alex "Peter and I arranged for a craft to be delivered here.

We stored it in the garage. It is a part of our Astronomy class for extra credit. Just something that Peter and I produced and are working on." "I see," Susan replied, "but you two haven't even started school yet!"

"Yeah, we know" said Alex "but Peter and I went to the teacher, and he signed off the project. He thought a documentary was a promising idea."

"Well, it does sound interesting" Susan responded, "so the craft is in the garage?" "Yes, it is!" said Peter, who was just now speaking up. "Where did the craft come from?" Susan asked. "From the museum" Peter answers.

"Oh really, isn't it strange that the museum had a craft on the property?" Susan replied. "Well, yes" Alex responded, "They got it from NASA. It was built long time ago, now they have it on loan to be displayed for a period."

"Well, you two have been busy little beavers and if I know the two of you – you are up to something. I will find out about it – eventually – a mother will always find out the truth!

You just can't hide anything from me, so don't go thinking you can!" "Well really, Mom!" Peter says defensively "It's just a project for school – we thought it would be an innovative idea.

We presented it to the teacher, the museum and got the right paperwork together – and well - Shoot! Here it is in our garage!" Susan smiles, "Well then, how about we finish our dinner, and the two of you can show me this craft we now have in our garage?"

Alex replied, "You bet Mom!" "OK, let's go!" said Peter. "Alright, grab your jackets – hold up boys – I'm right behind you!" Susan says. Peter and Alex open the garage and –

really – the look on Mom face! Well, that was priceless! "OMG, it's amazing!" said Susan. "Yes, it is!" said the boys in unison.

Susan then just simply smiled and stared. "I am so very proud of you both and don't you ever forget that." "OK Mom, we promise we won't!" said Alex. As they locked up the garage and walked back into the house, the boys took off their jackets and went upstairs to study star charts. Mom went into the living room to relax and watch evening news before turning in.

As another day ends, everyone turns in and says goodnight. The boys are off dreaming of space, the great beyond, and the universe up above. The next morning is a new day at the Bower house. The boys are up, dressed and downstairs at the table eating granola cereal and a bagel.

Mom too is up early, drinking her coffee and getting ready to leave. She wants to start her day by being first to the office, return calls, and then off to show houses.

She eats yogurt quickly refills her coffee cup and she says goodbye to her boys "See you both later, OK?" They both said goodbye and have a good day as she is walking out the door. She turns slightly and says, "Love you – see you this evening!" Then the door closes behind her. After finishing breakfast both boys got up, put their jackets on and went outside to work on the craft.

They wanted to see what was needed so they could be worked on the craft. Peter made a list and Alex called out what to be done. "OK" says Alex, "electrical wiring." "Yeah" Peter replied, "we got that written down already." "What about the outside paneling? Alex asked.

"Well," Peter responds, "It looks pretty good!" "OK" Alex says, "then let us moves on, check the forward thrusters, the electrical system, and fuel cells."

"OK – I'm writing it down," said Peter. Alex continues "Write down nose gear, main gear, flight deck, space radiators, (inside door) check the nitrogen tanks, speed brakes, the main engine alt. control thrusters and body flap – have you got all of that?" asked Alex. "Got it all!" said Peter. "OK good" Alex replied.

"Let us make sure you got the landing gear wrote down. We need to check on the hydraulics and make sure they work so we can lower them." "OK – got that too!" Peter says. "Also" Alex continues "write down so we can check the fuel tanks, we need to make sure there's no leaks." Once again, Alex says, "Got that too!"

"Well brother" Peter asks, "Have you got any ideas on the subject – we need to get our firsthand some fuel as well, we both know that we are going to need it, but for now there's so much other stuff to keep us busy."

Alex says "Let us not think about or be too concern with that at this present moment – let us get everything else green light ready. Then we can kick around some ideas for getting the fuel for takeoff." "Yeah OK" Peter replies, "I agree we sure do have other things to get done, so let us concentrate on the check list first.

We must do before we can put in a flight plan into the onboard computer. "Well," Alex says, "It's lunch time and

I'm starving – go figure!" "Yeah, me too" Peter agrees "let us put a pizza in the oven." "OK – lets!" Alex responds. The boys soon realize they have been outside working away all morning. "OK" Peter says, "Lets close shop and lock the garage up." "

OK" Alex agrees, "After lunch, I think we should go to town and get some of the things we need to start working on the craft." "Sounds like a plan," agrees Peter "anyways, let us go in the house and eat some lunch – now that's a plan!" "Brother I am right behind you!" says Alex.

As they enter the house, Peter grabs a frozen pizza out of the freezer and puts it in the conventional oven, so it cooks faster. As Peter and Alex wait for their pizza to cook, they talk about the craft and how long it will take all the repairs to be done.

"Well," says Alex looking at his brother "between starting college next week and working on the craft too, we have to factor in just how many hours we can get out to the garage to start all the list of repairs we have to do.

However, right now I would say we might look at another three to 4 years. You know, that is a guess –factors consider. We must just see, but I think we should do everything within the period we both have in mind.

We should know more once we work on it." "Yeah" Peter replies, "you're right and then we will get to solve the puzzle of the white door in space and finally get to open it – OMG!" Alex says, "there is a part of us, you know, that just can't believe we're actually doing this! Shoot, I am so excited! I cannot believe that, first – only the two of us know a secret we are keeping.

The two of us are actually on a mission to solve a mystery in space and we were asked by the universe to come and seek out the white door and open it." Peter says, "Well, also it's the idea that we get to do this together side by side, us two twin brothers. It just doesn't get any better than that!"

As Peter was talking and looking at Alex, he knew their lives would change in such a way, neither of them did not understand at this moment. They did not know what would happen to them when they launch and got there, went to another world in a different galaxy and opened a door just hanging around in space waiting for two special twins to come.

"Well, you know my brain is on overtime thinking about all of this!" says Peter. "Yeah, I know Peter," responds Alex "but for our own sake, let us just take it one step at a time – OK because I think for reason, someone really wants the two of us and until we figure this out, we can't tell a soul.

I mean, who in the hell would believe us even if we are as smart as Einstein and have an IQ off the charts." "Well," replies Peter "let us just keep this information to ourselves and try to gather as much information as possible as we go along, study the star charts and ask a lot of questions.

"Well," says Alex "that's the plan." "Well, I like it," responds Peter. "Well, here's to us, to the white door in space and our journey to get there!" Alex replied. Alex heads into the kitchen to remove the pizza from the oven and pour two iced teas with lemon over cold ice into glasses.

The two boys got everything done and sat it on the counter in the kitchen, they sat down on the stools next to the counter and eat their lunch. As they ate, they talked about starting college and the repairs on the craft.

After lunch, Peter and Alex cleaned up their mess, grabbed their jackets, and headed into town to the electrical store so they could pick up things. "There – OK?" said Peter "I am ready to go are you, Alex?" Yes" replied Peter "let's get started."

As they head out of the house with their bus tickets in their hands, they begin to walk two blocks down the street to catch the bus. After the bus arrives, they get onboard and found a seat. They waited for their stop at the electrical store and hardware store, which in fact it was right next door to each other.

As there stop came closer, Peter pulled the cord, and the bus came to a stop. The boys got off the bus and walked down the street half a block to the electrical and hardware store.

They entered the electrical store first, they picked up the wiring they needed for the onboard computer system and other things in the craft. After they finished, they went next door to the hardware store and looked around to see what they needed to get that was on their list.

After picking up bags of supplies, the boys walked back down the street to catch the bus and go back home. After arriving back to the house, the boys went to the garage and unlocked the two double doors.

They unpacked their supplies, putting everything away. The boys stayed inside the garage to work for a while on the wiring for the computer system. Peter crawled inside the craft and sat down, getting the wiring out of the bag.

Peter crawled under the onboard computer system, Alex hands Peter the wires clippers, and Peter takes out wires from his bag and were wired up the components on the computer system, linking up the lights and all the switches.

Wiring everything up takes time, it is work. Two hours later all the switches for the computer system are now working. Wiring for that part is now finished. The boys looked at each other and smiled – no words were needed, just a look that the two were on their way to achieving something great.

One look – one glance and one laced up wire at a time. Peter looks at his brother and says, "You know, every now and then – we just have to say it!" with a big smile on his face, Alex "go ahead Peter, and say it!" "OK" Alex replies "I will," said Peter.

"TO THE UNIVERSE AND BEYOND! Just then, a smile came across both of their faces. As the locked up the garage and bolted the two double doors, they went inside the house for the evening. (Susan) Mom called and says she was on her way home. "Oh – OK – Good!" says Peter. "Also" Mon said, "I stopped at KFC and picked up dinner tonight."

"Oh really! "I love, love, love my KFC!" said Peter. "Oh yeah, so does Alex" says Peter. I will tell him." "OK" says Mom "sees you in a few minutes." "OK, bye!" After Peter hangs up the phone, he yells to Alex – Guess what! Mom bought KFC home tonight!" "Oh – Yummy!" says Alex. "Mom said for us to get the table ready.

She will be home any minute, OK?" Peter tells Alex. The boys go to the kitchen, get out the paper plates, napkins forks, and large spoons to dish out the potatoes and other fixings. They set everything on the table, with the glasses for their chocolate milk and ice water for Mom.

After the table was set, you could hear Mom's car pull up in the driveway. She walks to the front door and turns the knob. Within seconds, she was inside the house putting the food on the dining room table. The boys wait for Mom to go upstairs to change her clothes so they could get together.

As she comes back downstairs and goes to the dining room table, they all sit down. Mom picks up her glass, goes to the kitchen, pours out the water, and pours herself iced tea with lemon.

She then goes back to the table to join her two boys for dinner. Mom asks Peter to say the blessing tonight, and Peter says, "OK Mom." After the blessing, the boys pile the food onto their plates starting with the chicken – two pieces first, then mashed potatoes followed by a heaping tablespoon full of gravy to go over the mashed potatoes.

Coleslaw, the corn, on the cob dripping with warm melted butter, and the hot buttermilk biscuits – with warm honey oozing out of the biscuits.

The conversation begins when Alex and Peter ask Mom "Sell any houses today?" "Well," Mom said, "Yes I did, boys! I sold the house on Williams Street, which was a three-bedroom house with two baths. It had been remodeled, so I got a big commission check for that house when it went through. "Wow that's great!" said Alex. "What about you guys – how's starting the project to fix the craft?" "Well," said Peter we got the wiring done on the computer system today – you know it is a slow process.

Well, Peter and I made a checklist of things on the craft. We just take it one step at a time and check things off the list as we finish them." "Well, that's good" said Mom "all one can do is just take it one step at a time and work on only one thing – then move on to the next." "Yeah" said Peter "that's our thoughts, too."

"We have timing right," said Alex "that we know." After everyone finishes dinner, the boys help Mom clean up the kitchen and put things away. She tells them to please eat the leftovers for lunch tomorrow.

The boys agreed they would be happy to. Alex and Peter go upstairs to go through their list of things to do on the craft and to plan to do everything in time to have a – greenlight all systems go! Therefore, while the boys discuss their plan on what to do tomorrow, Mom says goodnight to her boys, wishing them sweet dreams.

The morning arose to another beautiful day. The sun is up, and it is another day Susan Bower will sell houses. A day filled with dreams and possibilities for herself and for her two twin teenage boys, whose life mission is to finish their craft and go where no one has gone before.

Mom is up early, dressed and in the kitchen to fix herself a pop tart with a cup of coffee and a glass of juice. She grabs her jacket and gets ready to leave for work to sell another house – her support her boys.

As always, she yells out to her boys – "I am leaving, goodbye, have a good day!" Shuts the front door behind her. The boys skip breakfast and head right to the garage, unlocking the two double doors, closing the doors behind them.

They will finish on the inside of the craft this morning. They work for hours connecting hoses to the waste tanks, wiring the rest of the panels, and connecting all the switches on all sides.

They work nonstop until noon, then lock everything up and go inside the house to eat lunch. Warming up the chicken with all the fixing to go with it. They grab the paper plates, forks, and napkins.

They filled their glasses with ice and get Pepsi. They took their plates with food and went to the dining room table to sit down and eat their lunch.

Peter looks at his brother sitting across from him and says, "don't you just love KFC on the second day?" Alex smiles and says, "You know I always love my KFC anytime on the first day or the second, it's always good!"

Both brother's smile and laugh a little, then continued eating their lunch. After finishing and getting their bellies full, the boys felt very tired. After cleaning up their mess, they both headed up- stairs to take a nap.

"You know, I am tired," Peter says. "Yeah, me too!" says Alex. "OK, well I will see you later." Peter answers. "We will probably get up when Mom get home."

Alex reminded his brother. "OK then, see you later brother" Peter responds as the boy's head upstairs, they lie down to rest, all is quiet in the house.

Mom comes home early in the afternoon, sees the house is quiet and the boys are lying down – but within seconds, they awake and hear Mom walking up the stairs. Mom yells out "Hey guys – are you awake?"

"Yeah" answered Peter. "Yeah, me too – just now" answered Alex. "OK" Susan said, "Well I came home early because I was thinking I would take you both shopping for clothes and anything else you might need for school."

"OK – cool Mom!" as the boys smiled. "Let's get going to the mall." Susan replies "I will you give you my credit card, just go and pick up what you need – OK? I will be at bed bath and beyond and will meet you in one hour at the food court – OK? Closest table to the entrance."

"Well, OK! Grab your jackets and let us get into the car." The boys grab their jackets and Mom gets hers, they open the front door, close it behind them, and lock up the house.

They all get into the car, and within minutes Mom is parking her car in the parking lot. Her and the boys enter the mall, she gives the boys her credit card and tells them one hour – no longer, and do not forget to meet by the entrance to the food court.

The boys agree and take off to go buy new sneakers, pants, shirts, socks, underwear, coats, and hats.

When the boys are finished, they meet Mom at the food court. Mom had just arrived and was sitting at the table, waiting for her boys. "Well did you get everything you guys need for college tomorrow" she asked. "Yeah – we did OK," answered Peter. "Well, I picked up some fresh fish at the store so I could make fish and chips for dinner – how does that sound to both of you?"

she asked. "Really delicious Mom" Alex says. "OK then – let's get home and start cooking!" she answered. "Alright Mom" said the boys "let us go." As they head back to the house minutes later, they arrive, pulling into the driveway and parking the car. Mom, Peter, and Alex get out of the car and head to the front door.

They unlock the door and go inside, turning on the light in the living room and kitchen. The boys head upstairs to put their new clothes away in the closet and dresser drawers.

Mom is in the kitchen deep-frying fish and making her delicious baked fries in the oven. The boys head back downstairs to the kitchen to help Mom to set the table and get ready to eat, as the boys were getting the table set up, they were waiting for everything to get done.

The fries, salad, and the fish had just been done; the boys were putting ketchup, tartar sauce and dressing on the table.

They all sat down at the table, Mom asked Peter to say the blessing, and afterwards they ate. "Wow!" says Peter; "This is delicious fish – I mean it's really good," says Alex.

"OK, well thank-you guys – just eat up!" Mom replies.

As they finished eating dinner and sharing stories about today's events – something they have been doing now for years now anyway – Mom asked both the boys, "Are you ready to start college tomorrow?

I can't believe you are going to be in college freshman, you're actually in college – Wow!" Mom says, looking at them both. "Well Mom" Alex replies, "we are not your little boys anymore and our birthday is just around the corner."

Mom answers, "Soon you both will be turning 13 years old – so are you both excited about school and the new adventure that it will bring you both?"

"Well," said Peter "I just really love the classes and Alex mentioned he thinks the teachers are very smart, we actually met the science teacher, and we do like him very much.

"Well boys" Mom replies "get a good night's sleep.

CHAPTER THREE

STARTING COLLEGE

Well, the next morning comes early, Susan (Mom) is up early to make sure her boys are up and ready for their first day of college and have breakfast. This morning, she decides on making breakfast for her boys. Alex and Peter are up and dressed, they just came downstairs to the kitchen when they saw Mom cooking breakfast.

"Wow Mom – are you making breakfast?" says Peter. "Yeah" Mom said, "I just want to make sure you both have full stomachs and clear heads, so you two can think clearly and concentrate today." "Well, that's great – thanks Mom! Alex said, "So what's for breakfast?"

"Well," she replies, "I'm making you two a couple of breakfast sandwiches. "Oh," said Peter "what kind?" "Ham and eggs with melted cheese on an English muffin, and orange juice as well." she replies.

"Well, you guys go ahead and have a seat, everything is ready." The boys walk over to the table and take their seats; Mom walks over, brings their food, and sits it down in front.

"Dig in and enjoy" she says, looking at them at both with a smile. After finishing their breakfast Peter looks at Alex and says, "Well brother, are you ready to go to our math class this morning?" "Yeah, I'm ready!" said Alex.

"OK, well after our math class" said Peter "the two of us will come back home and reheat the fish Mom made last night, warm up some tortillas and have a couple fish tacos."

"Oh yeah – that sounds good!" said Alex. "OK then" says Peter "sounds like we have a plan." The two brothers smile. "Well," says Alex "after we eaten our lunch, we have to go back to school and attend our afternoon class, which will be Astronomy."

"OK then" Peter replies, "Let us get started brother!" "Right behind you" Alex answers. The boys get ready to leave grabbing their jackets and walking out of the house – locking the door behind them. They walked down the street to wait at the bus stop for the bus to arrive, within minutes the bus pulls over; the two boys got on board, find a seat, and were talking away.

Soon the bus arrived across the street from the college. The boys walked over to the front entrance and made the climb to the front double doors to the main college entrance.

The boys walked down the hall to enter their first class and they later finished the math class, and walk down another long hall, around two corners and finally entered their science class.

They entered the room, found a seat, and listened to the teacher. Later, they both came out of the classroom, and were thinking how much they both liked the style and way the teacher taught.

The morning was over and soon they were heading home for their lunch of fish tacos. The boys each had their cells phones with them, Alex's phone rings, right away he could see it was

Mom calling to check in on them. "Yes Mom" Alex answered. "How's everything?" Mom asked. "OK" Alex responded. "Morning is over, and everything went well, we are both heading home, and we are waiting for the bus to go back to the home and have some of your great fish tacos."

"Oh, that's good!" Mom answered. "Well, I'm glad everything is going well. "OK then, I will be home this afternoon." Mom continued. "I'm showing a house later and will see you both then. "OK Mom, bye" Alex said. Mom is off showing a house for two new clients, Tom, and Betty Newman, who is looking for a four-bedroom house with an extra bonus room.

Susan looks over a list of homes that is available and finds one she thinks her new clients might like – a five-bedroom house on Acacia Street, with a big back yard and extras she thinks her new clients might like.

She picks up the phone to call Mr. and Ms. Newman and inform them both she believes she has found the dream home they are looking for. She asks them, "Do you have time to meet me at the residence to look?" Tom right away says, "We will be there!" He also asked, "What time do you want us to be there?" Susan says, "How about – say around noon."

"See you then." Tom says. Susan replies "OK, bye for now." As Susan gets ready to show a house, the boys fix their lunch of fish tacos. Peter is in the kitchen putting the final changes on their tacos and Alex is pouring two Mountain Dew over ice filled glasses, so they have something to drink with their lunch. They finish in the kitchen; they both grab their plates and sit down at the table and eat.

Afterwards, Alex looks at Peter and says, "Well are you ready for our last and favorite class?" "Yes, I am!" replies Peter. "Well, me too" says Alex.

"ASTRONOMY – here we come!" They clean up from lunch, grab a bottle of water, and head out of the house, locking the door behind them.

They walked down the street to wait for the afternoon bus to come and drop them both off at the college. minutes later, the bus pulls over and stops, the two boys board the bus and sit down to wait for their stop. They were talking and enjoying the ride.

They arrive at the college; the two boys get off and walk once again up the front steps to the double door entrance. They entered the college for the second time today and walk down the hall to finally reach their class

.

They found a seat and waited for a minute for things to get started. They both walked over to the third row from the front, by the teacher.

They sat down and watched the other students come into the classroom. One by one, the classroom was filled up and all seats were taken

.

The teacher walks in and says "Good Afternoon and welcome to Astronomy. I am your instructor Mr. Dennis Wetherbee.

Let me start by saying that the seat you are seating in will be your seat for the rest of your time here with me. OK, let us move on. In this class, we will be covering topics from the brightest stars to the occurrence of various meteorite types. OK, let us get started – in your books on page five you will answer the ten objective questions – right now in class before you leave.

You have 20 minutes to answer the questions then turn in your answers before the end of this class. Now, can anyone list the twelve constellations of the zodiac? Let me pick on someone; let us see how about Peter Bower.

Please stand." "Yes sir, I can." Peter responded. "Well – OK well, let's see that would-be Pisces, Aries, Taurus, Gemini, Cancer, Leo, Virgo, Libra, Scorpio, Sagittarius, Capricorns, and Aquarius."

"Yes, you are right, please sit down" the teacher replied. The teacher says, "Let us move on. What do astronomers mean by plain size? OK, let us pick out another student. OK, would Alex Bower stand up and answer the question." "OK, yes sir, the answer is how bright an object looks in the sky."

"Correct!" says the teacher, you may sit down. "OK, let us do another question: Explain why, in any given era, the stars may be found at practically the same coordinates on the celestial sphere, while the sun, moon, and planets change their locations regularly. OK, would Susan Moore stand up?

"Yes – the answer is the stars are too far from the earth for the unaided eye to see them move, even though they are traveling many kilometers per second in various directions. The sun, moon, and planets are much closer to earth.

We see them move on the distant stars" she responds that's correct," says the teacher, please sits down. "OK, here's our first quiz. Please take one and pass the rest out. Get started as soon as you receive the test.

After you have finished, please put the test paper on my desk and you may then leave. OK – get started."

QUESTION 1

For each used on a terrestrial globe, list the corresponding name on the celestial sphere:

Equator: Celestial Equator

North Pole: North Celestial Pole (c) South Pole: South Celestial Pole

Latitude: Declination

Longitude: Right Ascension

Greenwich England: Vernal Equinox

QUESTION 2

Which of the five brightest stars in the sky are above the celestial equator and which are below?

Above: Arcturus, Vega

Below- Sirius, Canopus, Rigil Kenta urus

QUESTION 3

Which of the brightest stars never appear above the horizon at latitude 40 degrees?

Canopus, Rigil and Kenta urus

QUESTION 4

Match where you might be on earth with the correct description

of the stars.

The stars seem to move along circles around the sky, parallel to the horizon.

The stars rise at night - angles to the horizon in the east and sets at right angles to the horizon in the west.

Vega practically crosses your zenith. (d) Acrux is always above your horizon. (e) Polaris appears about 30 degrees above your horizon.

QUESTION 5

Why do the stars appear to move along arcs in the sky during the night?

Because of earth's rotation

QUESTION 6

Why do different constellations appear in the sky each season?

Because of the Earth's revolution around the sun

QUESTION 7

What is the Zodiac?

A belt sixteen inch around the sky centered on the ecliptic having twelve constellations.

(Tropic of Capricorn)

QUESTION 8

If a star rises at 8pm tonight, what time will it rise a month from now: 6:00 pm

QUESTION 9

Why is a solar day about 4 minutes longer than a 9-side real day?

Because while earth rotates on its axis, it also moves along in its orbit around the sun earth must complete slightly more than one whole turn in space before the sun reappears on your meridian.

QUESTION 10

Arrange the following stars in order of decreasing brightest:

Antares (size 1), Canopus (Magnitude 1), Polaris (size 2), and Vega (size 0)

Canopus, Vega, Antares, Polaris

QUESTION 11

Why will the polestar and the location of the vernal equinox on the celestial sphere be different thousands of years from now causing your star maps finally to go out of date?

Because of the precision of earth's axis.

As Peter and Alex were done with the test, at about the same time, they got up, dropped the test off on the teacher desk, and headed out of the classroom to go home. Jumping on the bus, Peter looked at his brother and asked, "Well, what you thought of our first test?" Alex started laugh and said, "Piece of cake!" "Yeah" said Peter "my thoughts too."

Alex says, "Well I'm starving! "Yeah, me too – let's head home and see what Mom's cooking for dinner," replies Peter. The boys get off the bus and walked the few blocks home. They got to the porch, unlocked the door, and went inside the house Peter picks up the phone and calls Mom at work.

She picks up the phone and he asked, "When you are coming home?" "Well, she said, "I'm leaving now – you, OK?" "Yeah, we are starving!" Peter responds. "Well," Mom says, "I could pick something up – OR I could make spaghetti and meatballs when I get home – with garlic bread and salad." "Ooh – that sounds great!" Peter says.

"OK" Mom responds, "I'll stop by the store and get some hamburger, I have everything else." "Good" said Peter "See you in a few! OK – Mom, drive safe." "I will" Mom says "Bye." Alex and Peter go to the kitchen, start water boiling for pasta, and add the pasta in as soon as the water boils. They make garlic spread to put on the bread.

When they finished, they put the bread in the oven. "Well, the spaghetti is cooking, and the bread is just waiting to be cooked. Therefore, we just need Mom to get home, cook the meatballs, and make the salad. Therefore, as the boys wait for Mom to pull into the driveway, they wait and keep an eye on the pasta that is cooking on top of the stove.

Mom finally gets home, walks to the front door, and enters the house with groceries in her arms. She walks into the kitchen and sees the boys are cooking pasta on top of the stove and the bread is ready to be cooked in the oven. She yells at the boys "Hey, guys you sure been busy!"

"Oh, Hi Mom! Alex says. Well, we just thought we would help out, OK?" "Well, how nice! Mom replied. Well, the meatballs are already cooked just need to be warmed up."

She warms up the meatballs, drain the pasta, add a red sauce to go over it and make the salad. Then, she adds the warm meatballs to the pasta. The boys are ready, they have the table set, grab the pasta, and set it on the table with everything else they are having tonight.

Mom runs upstairs to change her clothes and put on her sweatpants before going back downstairs. They all sit down, and the boys go back into the kitchen to grab the garlic bread and slice it up before putting the bread on a plate and bringing it to the table.

The boys grab their chocolate milk and sit down at the table with Mom. Alex was asked to say the blessing – they all say Amen and eat. As the boys make their plates, Alex grabs the spaghetti to on his plate. Peter does the same, with bread and a separate plate for the salad.

As they enjoy dinner, Mom asked Peter and Alex "how was your day today at school?" Alex talks first and begins by saying everything was fine, "Mom, you know it's interesting, we love school – but for us it's kind of too simple.

"Well Peter" replies Mom "if you feel the same way too, then I think you should both go full time. I also believe you both should talk to your professors and see if you can take your final exams now – even though school has just started.

I think they will make exception for both of you because of your high IQ." The boys listened careful to what Mom had to say. "Well Mom" said Peter "you are right. Alex and I have been talking and we agree that we should go full time because of our IQ being so high.

I think we must take acceleration classes. They have different classes for individuals very smart. You even must take a test just to see if you can apply to get in the program. If you are one of the lucky ones, that gets high scores, and by amazing high scores – I mean high scores – just to get their attention to get in.

The best part is if you are one of the lucky ones allowed to enter this program, they have offered full scholarships to right people. "Well," Mom replies, "That sounds great, and it would offer you both another amazing advantage, not to mention you both would have your master's degree in record time as well."

"Well," says Alex "that's something we both like and that's where we can work as fast or slow as we like to earn our degree. We hope, in just years, the two of us can make that happen. We both feel it is possible for us because we understand things differently than most and we need little study time.

We are going to school tomorrow to talk to someone in the fast class program." "Well, OK" Mom replied, "let me know what they say. Would the two of you must take a test to get into the program?" "Well yes, said Peter "we probably would have to and besides, we would want to – the sooner the better!"

"Well," says Alex "and there's the scholarship potential – wouldn't that be nice!" "What about you, Mom" asked Peter "how did your showing go today?" Mom responds, "The new clients love the house and – yes, I sold it and it's another check for us!"

As Mom was saying this, she was smiling from ear to hear. "I can't tell you Mom," Said Alex "just how proud we both are of you! You have showed both Peter and I that if you work hard enough, treat others with kindness and a positive outlook always helps – then the possibilities are endless."

"Well thank you boys!" she responded, "I love you both very much and I'm happy I could give you the gift of never giving up." "Well, you did Mom!" Peter replied. "OK, well what do you say we finish eating this delicious dinner that – well everyone here helped to make so we can start the process of cleaning up the kitchen and putting the leftovers in the fridge."

Well OK Mom, no problem" says Alex. They all finish eating dinner and help clean the kitchen they cleared off the dining room table and the boys helped load the dishwasher – it was filled tonight.

The boys turned on the dishwasher and turned off the light in the kitchen, as the evening hours were coming. They gave their mom big hugs and kisses and the love you more than all the stars in the universe combined.

"You know I never get tired of hearing that from either one of you guys or this mom love you more than the stars in the heavens!" The boys smiled as they said goodnight, went upstairs, and as the kitchen was closed for the night. Mom grabbed the newspaper and went to the living room turned on the television watched the cooking channel for a while.

The boys are upstairs talking, going through their star charts, and studying the directions and course, they would take. "Well," Peter says, "We have another big day tomorrow and not only that but now we can try to change our course and get our education done much faster."

"I believe we will" said Alex "I can feel it in my heart – yes it's amazing, isn't it?" said Peter "what we feel to be known is what's going to happen – I mean it really feels like the two of us are on this amazing path that's already map out for us.

We are along for the ride!" "Well," said Peter "I couldn't have said it better myself!" "Well brother" answered Alex "let me ask you something." "What is that?" asked Alex "OK, so why do you think we were chosen?" asked Peter.

"Well, for one thing I know I have never brought this up before but, for some weird reason, I can't help but think that Dad has played some kind "OMG really!" said Peter. "Well, you know," answered Alex "Dad was working on something pretty amazing,

I believe, before his mysterious death." "Yeah, you are right about that!" Peter answered, "what if he found the same thing?" "But Peter" replied Alex "we didn't find it – the door found us!"

"In any case" answered Peter "it is possible Dad could have been the first one to find it. It's possible – just possible – he might have been killed for this information, rather someone else killed him to try to get it."

"Well," Alex responded, "There's something to this – I mean we – meaning the two of us – should be careful what we do." "You mean" Peter answers "if Dad was killed for this, and the person or persons responsible didn't get the information they wanted, then they could be just biding their time."

"Why would they do that?" asked Alex. "Well," Peter says, "to see if we are, in fact, our father sons!" "OMG!" Peter says in amazement, "I get it I totally get what you are saying – so this person you think – might be waiting to see when we get older, if we follow in our father's footsteps and find or locate this information for ourselves.

But you know it's kind of funny we didn't really stumble onto or find out anything until it found us!" "Yeah," responds Alex "it just might be that the white door wants us to follow in our father's footsteps. Maybe finish what he started those years ago;" Wow!" responds Peter "do you think all this could be even remotely possible?"

"Yeah," answered Alex "if we could find out what Dad was working on before he died!" "Well," Peter says "we could ask Mom where's his office paperwork is at – I don't know Peter. We should do our own digging for now and leave Mom out of this. It could be too dangerous.

"Yeah, OK Alex." Peter responded. Alex answers, "I just can't believe we haven't talk about this before or discovered this until now." Peter then says, "Well look, we really were too young to know anything."

"OK" Alex said, "I'll give you that – so true! Well, we have a mission and hopefully we will have the time to figure this out." "Well – OK – for now let's just leave it on the back-burner cause" said Peter "with school this year, we have so much else going on.

However, we will get back to this mystery and solve it. Dad deserves that!" "Yeah, I agree," said Alex "I just realized that everything is tied to that white door, "Yeah, I can see that," said Peter. "Yeah" said Alex "looks like Dad might have discovered it and the door wanted it.

Now the two of us will race to open it in Dad place OMG!" What is next for the two Bowers boys – mysterious invitation from the universe and the secret white door and beyond?

"Well," said Peter "I guess the two of us will just have to stay tuned, because we just can't make this stuff up. As the evening was getting late, the boys turned in saying goodnight to Mom and to each other.

The next morning arises; the boys are up early and dressed. Heading downstairs and out the door, grabbing only a water bottle got something to eat along the way.

"OK" says Alex "let us get this show started." Then, as soon as said that they were both out the door with their jackets on and at the bus stop.

Within minutes, the bus appears and the two boys board sitting in the middle of the bus waiting for their stop at the college. As they get closer to school, the boys stop at Subway to pick up two breakfast sandwiches and two juices to eat before first class this morning.

After finishing their sandwiches, the two brothers cross the street and walk to the long steps out in front of the college, making their way to the double doors that stood in front entrance of the college.

As Peter and Alex enter and walk to the admission office, they ask where the fast class/accelerated program for testing. The woman looked up at Peter and said, "That would-be Mr. Thomas down the hall first door on the left."

"OK" said the boys, closing the door behind them. As they walked out of the admission office, they continued walking down the hall until they got to the door on the left side which read "Testing for Fast Class."

As they both entered, there it was a man standing behind a desk. They said, "Hello Mr. Thomas, I am Peter Bower, and this is my twin brother Alex.

We are here to evaluate for the program. We are two of the smartest kids, as you can see by our ages. We are young, but"

Peter said, "don't let that fool you – we are extremely smart.

"OK" said Mr. Thomas "are you taking any classes currently?"

"Yes, we are" said Alex "How many?" asked the teacher? "Three" says Alex Astronomy, Science, and Math, but to tell you the truth – the classes are too easy and a bit boring for us, we feel the fast class would be a better fit.

Well," said Mr. Thomas "you would have to attend full time it is required. "No problem" said the brothers "but we would have to have scholarships." "Well, that might not be a problem. It will, of course, depend on how high you both place and score.

OK then, let us get the two of you signed up for testing and get you dismissed out of your currently classes." "OK" said the boys "and when does the test start?" "In a few minutes across the hall" replied Mr. Thomas.

"It should take most of the day to complete. When you finish, just leave the papers on the table. Someone else will pick them up."

"OK" said the boys, as they signed up and entered the room to start the test. After just 3 hours, the boys they were done and left the test papers on the table.

They both got up and walked to the door, closing it behind them. "Let's go next door and get a sandwich at Subway," said Peter.

"Oh yeah, that sounds good – let's go – right behind you" replied Alex. As the two brothers left, Alex had a smile on his face. Peter looked at his brother and asked, "What are you smiling about?"

"Well, I think you already know!" answered Alex. "Oh," said Peter "Yeah, the test wasn't that hard – it looks like we'll get those scholarships!" The two brothers smiled. "Well now! That wasn't hard!" Alex said "LOL – yeah" answered Peter "Now we'll get our degree sooner –

a lot sooner than we thought!" "Yeah" said Alex "we'll have our master's degree sooner than blast off!" "Wow, life is great!" "Yup" said Peter "sooner than we go to space – and that's the truth!"

"Well," Alex says, "Let us pick up our food and head home. We are getting up early in the morning. "Well," answers Peter "I know you're tired!" "Yeah OK – so what!" responds Alex-I am tired too.

"Yeah well, we can start working in the garage later." Peter responds. "OK" said Alex, as they both walked down the street with their sandwiches in their hands.

They walked to the bus stop, the bus pulls over, and they get on board and have a seat while they wait for their stop. When they get close, the boys pull the cord; they get off and walk toward their house.

Alex gets his keys out to the front door, as they turned the knob to enter the house, the two sit down and eat their lunch at the table with two cold root beers. After lunch, they both head upstairs to lie down and take a nap to recharge.

These two boys were only 12 years old, and they both needed their sleep. After sleeping, they both got up – feeling rested. They go downstairs to get two water bottles from the fridge to drink.

They hear a noise, as Peter yells out "Hey Mom, are you home?" "Yes" Mom replies "I am home sweetie, be down in a second – OK?" As Mom came down the stairs, she asked the boys "How about dinner and a movie?

"Hey, that sounds great!" said Alex. "So, what do you want to see?" As the boy's smile – "is there anything else besides sci fi?" answers Peter. "I guess not!" replied Alex. Well, anyway, just as the boys started too laughed, Mom says, "grab your jackets and let us take off and just relax for a while – OK? "Sounds good Mom, we can talk about things later," answered Peter. "OK – let us just enjoy ourselves for a while and, of course, watch the new Star Trek movie, because I know it's one of your favorites – and you two been waiting for it.

CHAPTER FOUR

THE FAST-PACED LIFE

After everyone got back from going to the movies, and out to dinner. It was after nine clocks in the evening, and everyone had an exciting time but also very much sleepy so off to bed Alex and Peter went up the stairs saying good night to Mom as the two made their way to their rooms.

Mom made her way to hers all closing their bedroom doors. Well, the next morning Alex and Peter are up early since college life is on hold until their test results come back from the fast class testing placement center waiting a call from Mr. Thomas who runs the program.

The boys work on the craft today while the two waited for the phone call. The boys head to the kitchen to pour a couple bowls of cereal and make bagels to go with the cereal and two glasses of orange juice.

As the two set their food on the table to get ready to enjoy their morning breakfast and Peter grabs the honey for their bagels and their juice he poured and set them both on the table. As Alex goes back into the kitchen to take the milk, out of the fridge and pour enough into the picture for their morning cereal.

As the boys are enjoying their morning cereal and bagels Mom comes down the stairs and says good morning to her boys sitting at the table as she walks into the kitchen to pours herself a cup of coffee and sit down at the table with Peter and Alex and says, "so what's the plan today?"

"Well since we are on a break from school," says Peter. "Why is that well" said Alex Peter continues, "we took that fast class placement test yesterday and now we are just waiting for the results and a phone call."

"Wow that is wonderful! So how do you think the two of you did on the test?" asked Mom. Peter answered, "
The instructor said to us the test would last most of the day but Peter and I both finished the test in about three hours.

So, Mom to answer your question we both thought it was a piece of cake and now we are just waiting for the instructor to give us some good news and offer us two full scholarships." "Wow really? Says Mom. "Well of course Mom it wasn't hard at all we get it," says Alex. "Well, that's wonderful boys! You know you get your common sense from me.

I have to admit you both get your smarts from your father and damn not only was he a very handsome man to me – but boy oh boy was he smart!" "Oh, really Mom?" says Peter. "Yes, and the two of you take a lot after him god rest his soul.

Well maybe one day the two of you can figure out how to reverse time and bring him back for not only for me but for all of us." "Well one might be able to do that through space," says Alex.

"What do you mean?" asked Mom? "Well, I mean that it might be possible to go in space and reverse it, so you come back in a Moment in time that Dad is here." "Wait really?" said Mom. Alex answers, "Peter and I believe it could be done." "How?" Mom asked. "Well, it's-complicated, but I do believe you would have to find a hole in space – a time hole, and they are not always visible very often and it's hard to find but very possible.

Well, it's a proven theory shared by others." Peter replies, "well we feel that it just might be possible that the two of us can just prove this theory if we put our minds into believing the facts that the universe holds many answers to questions that we haven't even begun to ask it if one can ask one might receive the question and much more."

Well," Mom says "you boys! We might have a surprise for you one day!" Mom smiled and gave just enough hope for future possibilities to believe in. Alex says, "Well Mom's wishes really can come true especially when you have two very smart young boys at home like us."

"Well, you are both smart and that's for sure and you are my two shiny stars from the universe above" Mom replied. "Well, I have some paperwork at the office to do but I will be back early today so I will see both later." "OK Mom" Peter said to her. "Also, there's money in the drawer in the kitchen so if you guys want to go out and pick up lunch for yourself, OK?" "All right!" says Alex as Peter and Alex look at their mom get up and walk away.

"OK" Mom replied, "I am going to grab something out of my room and get going – see you both later!" "OK" said Alex "bye Mom." The boys pick up their cereal bowls and stuff on the table and cleaned up their mess.

"Well, I guess we should go and work on the craft, OK?" said Peter "let us put the phone on the porch outside by the back door and the garage doors will be open so we will be able to hear the phone ring if the instructor calls regarding our placement test scores, OK?"

Alex and Peter shake their head as they both agreed. They sat the phone down on the back porch and walked out to the garage opening the two double doors and leaving it open so they can hear the phone. "OK let's hook up the waste tanks and other the other tank also you work on the one and I'll work on the other?" Peter asked. "OK" said Alex "the hoses are on the table over by you Alex," Peter stated. "OK I'll grab them both," replies Alex. He walks over to the table, gets the hoses, and gives Peter one with a clamp to lock it in place.

They both worked minutes go by and they both finish with hooking up the hoses. The phone rings Alex runs out of the garage to the back porch where the phone is and picks up the phone and Peter is right behind his brother.

"Yes hello," said Alex. "Yes, hi this is Mr. Thomas the instructor from the test you both took." "Yes" said Alex. Mr. Thomas continues, "Just got your results back and your score we're off the charts.

What I mean is I looked at by our scores, both of your scores were so high it actually was off the charts!" "WOW!" replied Alex. "Einstein doesn't have anything on the two of you.

I mean really I would like to congratulate and welcome both of you and your brother to the fast class and give you both full scholarships here at the college." "Well thank-you very much from me and my brother Peter and we accept the scholarships OK good. Well, what do we did to do now?" asked Alex. "Well," Mr. Thomas replies, "You both need to come in. Can you come in within the hour, and sign papers and get your class schedule?"

"OK" Alex responds, "My brother and I are on our way see you. OK bye. Well brother lock up the garage we must get to the college at the placement center." "OK" said Peter. They both locked up the garage and the house and walked down the street to catch the bus and head to the college minutes away.

The boys are filled with excitement as they both stepped off the bus and walked across the street to climb up the steps that lead to the front entrance door. As they reached the top step, they reached for the door, push the door open, and walked down the hall to the first door on the left.

When they went inside Mr. Thomas, the instructor was standing in the room. As the boys said hello so did the instructor "how are you guys today?" Mr. Thomas asked.

"Very good thanks" responded Peter. "So why didn't you both tell me you both were geniuses?" the instructor responded. "Well, we haven't known for very long and really we have seemed to have gotten smarter as we aged"

Alex said. "Well, in any case, this school is honored to have you both here with us. OK so you will study and getting your PHD in Astronomy?" Mr. Thomas asked. "Yes," said both boys. "OK then, the harder you work and the faster you work you will have your degree within no time at all especially with both of your IQ being so high, I don't think it going to a problem for either one of you.

OK so your books and everything the two of you will need to get your degree has been paid for!" the instructor told them. "OMG! That is great thank-you so much!" Peter exclaimed. "OK" the instructor continued. "It works like this you go to your class, and when you take all of the pretests and pass them, you can take your final exam, and move on to the next subject and do the same thing.

You are freshman now, but you can start your sophomore's classes and then junior and then finally your senior class. OK questions? No, the boys said, "We understand fully. OK then Mr. Thomas states, "You both start tomorrow at 8am."

As the boys leave, they go to the bookstore and just mentioned their last names for payment issues. "OK cool!" says Alex. They pick up the books they will need for tomorrow's classes. The boys are so excited; they realize that they can take their final exam at any point, if they score high on the pretests and really for the two-no problem.

"Hey brother do you realize that we don't even have to study very much? We can just take all of the pretests and pass those, then take our final exams!" exclaimed Peter. "OMG, do you realize what this means!" asks Alex. "Yes, I do" said Peter "we can take our entire tests one at a time.

After we have passed all the pretests and, at the end of the month. – Yeah, if we take a month – we might do it less than that, OK well anyway – after that we will be ready to take the final. I think it might be possible for us to be sophomores in maybe 5 months." "Yeah OK" says Alex "we will see Peter. OMG!" "Alex, we are going to be able to graduate a lot sooner than we both thought" says Peter. "Yeah" said Alex "it looks like it, doesn't it?" "Yes, it does" Peter responds.

"Well, we had better step up the craft we still somehow have to get the rocket fuel; yes, I figured that out already" Really?" said Alex. "Yeah, I know a guy who has a contact through the underground and I believe he can get our fuel, but he did mention that we have to have cash." "Oh well!" responds Peter "did he mention how much it would cost?

"Well," says Alex "you know that it's going to depend on how much fuel we order. "Well, OK" replies Peter "that makes sense. "OK" responds Alex "how about the rocket suits, we still are going to need that as well!" "Yeah – well we can't get that online!" laughed Peter.

"No" answers Alex "but I have an idea. We can call the museum they loaned us the rocket so just they might have the suits too!" "Well, that is a great idea" says Peter "and makes perfect sense." "Yeah OK" answers Alex "well I give the director a call." "Good" answers Peter "see what you can find out." "OK" Alex responds "I am on it brothers and you know I have a good feeling about this it's going to work well – cross your fingers! Here's to getting our suits from the same place that loan us the rocket!"

After finishing their discussion on rockets, suits, graduating, rocket fuel. The boys left the bookstore, with all the books in hand and now they are ready for tomorrow's classes. "Well, let's head home Peter."

"OK Alex and let's tell Mom the good news!" As the boys walked down the street to the bus stop. The bus was already pulling over as they walked up to it as they both board the bus and find a seat they wait for their next stop as the bus Moments later comes to the final stop the boys get off and walk the couple of blocks home as they approach their house Alex gets his keys out and unlocks the front door and they both go inside.

The boys go upstairs to put their books away and come back downstairs and Mom pulls into the driveway, shuts her car door, walks up the house, opens the door, and yells as she enters the house, I am home boys. Peter and Alex come and say hi to Mom hey boys and they ask her "how was your day?" "Well Mom says,

"I sold a house I was working on wow Mom that is wonderful. How was your day today?" "Well," said Peter "Alex and I both did so well on the placement test that the school offered us a fast class accelerated program and gave the two of us full scholarships everything for our degree is paid for."

"I can't begin to tell you both just how much I am proud of you both." Mom told them. "Well thanks Mom that means a lot," Peter said. "Yeah Mom" said Alex "it really does." "Well, I love you both," Mom told them.

"Well, we both have five classes and we figured that in just a few years or sooner we will have our masters." Peter said to her. As Mom is looking at her boys, she is surprised that it will not take them both long to achieve their goals and happy for them both. "OK" Mom says, "get it done and don't forget to have a little fun too."

Well, Mom is in the green! So, boys grab your jackets – we're going out to dinner!" "OK Mom that sounds great" Alex said. As they, all head out to dinner and the boys wanted steak they went to their neighborhood local steak house and had a steak, medium well with all the trimming the boys could want and after dinner, the boys enjoyed having dessert one of their favorites chocolate cream pies.

After dinner, they head back home, and the two boys was full and happy thanking for Mom for the delicious dinner they had tonight. "Well good night, Mom" the boys said, "tomorrow is going to come early for us two, so goodnight"

Peter told her. Mom said good night to them both as they headed upstairs to their rooms to turn in for the night. Mom locks up the house and head off upstairs to turn in for the night. The boys changed their clothes and put their PJ's on and jumped into bed and saying good night to each other as they both closed their eyes and drifted off to sleep. Peter says, "we are about to have the most amazing adventure very soon."

"Yes"-said Alex. Peter smiles and says, "To the Universe and beyond!" as they both chuckled a little then slowly drifted off to sleep.

The next morning the boys are up early and downstairs putting their books and other items they will need for school in their backpacks. The boys ate a bowl of cereal and grab a muffin on the way out the door with an energy drink in their hands.

The boys walked down blocks to catch the bus and, on their way, to school this morning. The bus pulls over across the street from the college as the boys get off the bus and across the street walked up the steps to the front door and down the hall and through another door to reach their accelerated class

. As the entered the room, the Peter and Alex had already taken all their pretest for math and after passing them all, they both plan to take the final math exam and moving on to the next subject and doing the same thing. The boys feel that their classes they have is just information they already familiar with so passing these classes right now is first on their minds so they both can move on quicker to other subjects.

The boys worked on all five subjects the day until around three pm. The gathered up their belonging, left out of the classroom, walked down the hall, out through the front entrance, and walked down the street to catch the bus and go home for the day.

Peter looked at Alex and asked him "how many of the pretests did you get done today?" He answered, "Well I believe finished 10 out of 30 tests, and so twenty more to go until we take the final exam, then it should take us maybe 2 more days until the final exam."

As the next few days passes quickly the boys wake up to take their final exam and that was one test down, we got rid of. The brothers looked at each other "well" said Peter "just four more exams and we will be sophomores." "Well really" Alex responded, "its thirty pretests for each class, and we have four more classes – plus the finals for each class." "Well, you are right," said Peter. "Piece of cake! Said Alex. The boys realized the bus had already stopped and they were home before they knew it. The two boys stepped off the bus, walked down the street, entered their driveway, and walked up to the front door.

Alex got his key out, unlocked the front door and went inside. They went into the kitchen and grabbed two sodas, made themselves two roast beef and cheddar sandwiches and Lays potato chips they took their food to the table and sat down to eat.

"Well today was a long day!" Alex said. "You got that right!" said Peter. "Well, we are home now, and it is time to see if we can find those rocket suits. About the fuel, I think we should deal with that later-OK. It is much too early to have fuel just lying around the garage," "

Yeah" responded Alex we can place that order right before we get ready to go. OK so the suit?" said Alex. "I am on it," said Peter. "OK, what You are thinking?" Alex said, "Well like we discussed earlier, I think we should talk to Mr. Vanguard at the museum. Peter responded, "If he's not in, I will leave a message asking him to get back with us and explain we need the suits for our project and just how much it would help in every aspect, especially visual, for our presentation project."

"Yeah" Alex said, "I agree as well. I called and left word so I am sure he will call us back about this matter so we just must wait and see." "OK then" Peter agreed.

The boys head outside to work on the craft when Peter hears the phone rings, he comes in to answer it. He picks up the phone and says, "Hello yes is this, Peter."

"Yes, well hello this is Mr. Vanguard from the museum." "Well good to hear from you, how are you?" Peter asks. "Well Peter I am fine. I got your message and thought I would get right back to you as soon as I could." "OK thank-you" Peter responds."

Well, when is your first presentation to the college taking place?" Mr. Vanguard asks. "It's going to be on Friday at the end of the week," Peter answers. Mr. Vanguard continues, "Well for one thing, I called to ask you if you both wouldn't mind if I attend? I would love to be there when you show your first video. "Yes" Peter replies "please come. "Good" said Peter.

Mr. Vanguard then asks, "I was also wondering, the museum and I would like you both to have something we feel just might help you put your presentation over the top." "OK" says Peter "that sounds wonderful."

Mr. Vanguard continues "Well Peter, are you both missing something that would help your project?" "Well," says Peter "my brother and I are looking for two rocket suits with helmets.

I left you a message explaining everything." "Yes, I received it. I thought it would be a particularly clever idea to let you borrow the suits for your project." "OMG – that is wonderful! Oh, thank you so much Mr. Vanguard" Peter replied.

"I had them both packed and they are in route to you and your brother as we speak. So, I will be looking forward to seeing you and Alex on Friday," Mr. Vanguard says. "OK" Peter responds, "see you there, Mr. Vanguard, and thank you once again." "No problem" Mr. Vanguard replied "I am glad I can help, and the museum and I are really thrilled to be in your corner. OK Peter, we will see you and Alex on Friday bye for now."   Peter got off the phone and the two yelled and jumping up and down "Damn! Can you believe that WOW! Today is one day neither one of us will forget," said Peter. Alex had a grin on his face – he simply looked at his brother and speaks

"TO THE UNIVERSE AND BEYOND!"

As they held their hands up in the air and smiled, laughed a little and Alex said aloud "well then it should be here anytime!" "Yeah" responds Peter "and it will be delivered at the back entrance by the garage just like the craft was. The driver will honk his horn when he pulls in back."

The boys are on cloud nine as they wait for their delivery and they both realize now that the only thing they will need is only one item and that is the rocket fuel and when the time is right, we will call and place our order. Well, after their discussion, an hour passes by before the boys hear a honk in the backyard and realize that their package has arrived.

Alex and Peter go outside to meet the driver and move the Peter got off the phone and the two yelled and jumping up and down "Damn! Can you believe that WOW! Today is one day neither one of us will forget," said Peter. Alex had a grin on his face – he simply looked at his brother and speaks

driver got back into his truck and the boys thanked him as he drove away. The boys grab a crowbar to lift the top off the crate open and look inside.

They are both are in total amazement of the two rocket suits that are inside the crate. Peter yells out "OMG! I mean WOW! This makes it very, real, doesn't it?" Alex looks at his brother and says, "Yeah, it does and soon we are going to have one magical journey of which the both of us will never forget."

Peter reaches down in the crate and pulls out one of the suits "OMG Alex it's so amazing just look at it!" "Yeah, I am brother, but look – now that we have the suits, we need to shoot the video for the school project. You know the fake project we made up – remember – to get the craft in the first place!"

Yeah, I remember," says Peter. "Well, I'll go in the house and get the camera and the stand so we can make the video. We both have a terribly busy week ahead and I don't think it's a clever idea if we wait much longer to shoot it after all people are expecting to see something by the end of the week on Friday." As Peter goes into the house and gets the video camera and stand carries it back out to the garage. Alex helps set up the stand and puts the video camera on top. Alex adjusts the camera toward the craft. Peter says, "OK, first we need a script."

"No, not really – why don't we just wing it. I mean" Alex says "we are just going to let everyone who is watching that this is the craft, the work we have done on it.

and we will say were we going to take it in space we would take it to the closest star one and then shoot the video. We also would explain how to adjust make this a reality. The two of us then would explain about wearing the rocket suits, how it would benefit us by providing oxygen and keeping us alive while we were outside the craft shooting a video at the space, universe, and beyond and what magic can happen if you work hard and believe deep down inside that anything is possible including going into space and beyond if you believe and want it."

"OK" says Peter "press the stop button for a second – wow this is really good, but we just need to explain how when inside the craft, we put the directions in the computer and how those directions will take you where you want to go." "Yeah" replies Alex "to the nearest star! OK I will get the video set up, run it and you explain about the directions. "OK" said Alex.

Peter climbs into the craft and points the camera at Alex and then Alex explains how to put the information into the system, and he explains by showing star charts and pointing to where you are now and where you want to go.

Alex explains by pointing it gives you numbers and by taking those numbers you can enter it into the computer, and it will spit out directions and line that will light up in straight line to where you are now to where you will end up.

"OK got it!" says Peters "that will work. Wonderful – we're finished." "OK – good" says Alex "now all we have to do show our project on Friday." Peter answers, "Well it's good, and everyone is going to love it. We won't have a problem, for sure, after this from anyone." "Well," Alex says, "Let us go inside and put the camera away.

Mom should be home, and I don't know about you, but I am staving!" "Well, you know" Peter smiles "that's nothing new!" "Oh" Alex laughs, "you are so funny – but I know you are starving too." "Well," Peter answers, "Let us head inside." "Yeah OK" Alex responded.

As they locked up the garage double doors, they both walked back to the house through the back-yard door and put the camera and stand back into their bedroom closet. The boys headed downstairs and saw Mom entering coming through the front door.

"Hey boys" Susan says. "Hi Mom, how's everything?" Alex asks. "OK – you know well!" Peter answers, "Alex and I just got done shooting a video for science class project." "Oh – really!" Mom answers.

"It has been a very long day Mom Alex and I am starving!" says Peter. "Well now, tell me something I don't know!" laughs Mom. "Hey, is that food I smell? Looks pretty heavy, let me help you" Peter responds. "OK, funny man – set the table and gets the glasses, silverware, and plates." "So, what did you pick up?" asked Alex.

"I stopped by China Palace" Mom replies "and picked up some shrimp, fried rice, beef and broccoli, prawns, egg rolls, wanton soup, hot and spicy chicken!" "Wow Mom!" answers Alex "that sounds and looks incredibly good!" She smiles and they all sit down at the table and said their blessings.

"Well Mom who turn is it anyway?" asked Alex. Mine" Peter said. "OK then, 'sweet Jesus hear our blessings and our prayers thank-you for this bounty we are about to receive Amen." "Well, that was very nice," Mom said to Peter.

"OK let's eat!" As they dish the food onto their plates, they began their evening conversations at the table. "Well boys, what is going on in your fast class?" Susan asked. "Well yesterday." Peter replies, "Alex and I got full scholarships and now we go to this special program they have at the college called Fast Class.

We work as fast as we wish to get our degrees. It looks like we will have it sooner than we thought." Susan says, "The both of you are working so hard to achieve your dreams and make something possible for the two of you.

You'll take it where you have never been before, especially at the age the two of you are." Peter responds, "We can't wait to fulfill our deepest dreams. Really, we are just along for the ride in this amazing possibility that the universe has given us."

"Well," Susan says, "Let us clean up the table – Oh and boys and put the leftovers in the two plastic containers with lids for lunch tomorrow. You can take it with you to eat." "OK" the boys nod their heads as they packed up the food for school.

"Well," said Peter "I am going to take a shower. I won't have time in the morning before I must leave." "Right behind you!" said Alex "you and I are on the same page and tomorrow will come early once again. The both of us have finished our pretest and take the final exam and one more step to be moving on."

The boy's heads upstairs to take their showers. As they walk up the steps, they said goodnight to Mom as she was locking up the house for the night and heading upstairs herself to her room. "Goodnight boys!" she calls out.

The boys finished their showers. Crawled into bed and slowly closing their eyes. Thinking about their possibilities of flight into space and beyond the milky way, streaming passes the brightest star in the heavens above oh how great it will have an imagination that will take you anywhere you want to be especially if you have a rocket ship in your backyard that will take you to the corners of your own imagination.

Well, the morning is here, and the boys are up, awake, dressed, and ready for school. They both headed downstairs to grab a muffin and a bottle of orange juice to take with them both as they head out the door with jackets on to walk down to the bus stop. As the bus pulls over and the two boys board the bus and find a seat.

The two take out their muffin and OJ and eat their snack before they get to school and give the two energies before class this morning. The bus stops at the college across the street the boys get off and walk over crossing the street to the main entrance and climbing the steps that once again leads to the front doors of the college.

They head straight down the hall to their fast class to work on twenty more pretests to get to where they can take the final exam. The boys figure if they do ten tests today and 10 tomorrows the two can take their final exam on Thursday morning and be done with math.

After the ten pretests, the boys worked on their other subjects and start the pretest for science and astronomy. The boys want to get a jumpstart and move up to sophomore. They are working hard every day they know they will achieve this goal soon.

The boys worked until five pm today on the subjects they needed to are done and are now early. They go home and relax – thinking their birthday is coming up soon and they will turn 14 years old. They both board the bus and wait for their stop to come. Afterwards, they get off at their stop and walk the couple of blocks back to the house. As the get closer to the house, they can see Mom's car in the driveway. The boys are happy to see Mom home.

.

As the turned the doorknob and opened the door – in walks Mom and she yells out "boys are you home? How nice." "Yes Mom, we're home!" answers Peter. "I'm always happy to see my two young men," answers Susan. "Well, are you both starving?" she asks with a smile on her face. The boys looked at their mom and Alex says "always Mom!

"Well," with a smile upon her face she says, "how about a thick steak, medium well done, stuffed twice baked potatoes and a lobster tail with warm melted butter dripping on top – with a strawberry salad on the side?" "Wow – are you kidding – really?" Peter responds, "That sounds amazing!" "Well," Mom answers "don't forget the dessert of course, a coconut cream pie."

"I can't believe – are you really cooking Mom?" Alex exclaims. Mom answers, "You don't have to ask me that and the only thing you both need to be concerned with is where your jackets are my boys?" As the boys looked, confused Mom looks at them and finally says, "Mom sold another house – grab your jackets boys! Mom sold another house, and we are in the green!"

They all laughed as they grabbed their jackets, locked the house up, and went to dinner. After enjoying their delicious meal, they all headed home, Susan was feeling tired after another day of selling houses. The boys were also exhausted after all the paperwork at college. They all said goodnight as they climbed the steps to their rooms, crawled into bed and dreamt a little dream of what tomorrow might bring.

CHAPTER FIVE

SCHOOL AND HOME

The boys went to school early this morning to finished working on their pretest for math. The boys were done fast and took the final exam, and they took finals on English, Science, and passed all three. Astronomy is the only class left which excites Alex and Peter.

Tomorrow is the presentation for their Astronomy class, and it will count for 50% of their grade. Therefore, they are ready. They shot the video last night in the garage and are ready to show their project Space, Beyond, and the Universe.

"Well," said Alex "it's a nice trade off. We got the craft and in exchange we must shoot this documentary for a class project, and it's graded for half our grade." "But Peter" said Alex "we did get the craft – oh and don't forget the rocket suits, thanks to Mr. Vanguard and the museum and those suits are in our garage now."

As the brothers looked away, they just knew they were both smiling at what they had achieved so far and really, it was amazing. "OK" said Alex "you can say it." "OK I will say it.

TO THE UNIVERSE and BEYOND!

Well, come on – we have a test in Astronomy." "Yeah" said Peter "it's on light and telescopes – piece of cake! Come on let us do it!" "Right behind you," said Alex. The boys sit down, and the instructor hands out the test paper and tells them they have 60 minutes for this test and "you may begin" he says.

QUESTION 1:

Explain why looking at stars is a way of seeing how the universe looked years ago.

Starlight is radiated by electric charges in stars. Light waves transport energy from stars to electric charges in our eyes. Light waves travel fasts about 300,000 km per second

(186,000) miles but trillions of miles separate the stars from earth and the journey takes years. We see the stars as they were years ago, when the starlight began its journey to earth.

QUESTION 2:

List the major regions of the electronic spectrum from the shortest wavelengths – highest energy to longest wavelengths – lowest energy.

Gamma rays, x rays, ultraviolet radiation, visible light, infrared radiation, radio waves.

2. (B) State what all electromagnetic waves have in common.

All electromagnetic waves travel through empty space at the same speed the speed of light about 300,000 km (186,000) miles per second.

QUESTION 3:

Write the general formula that relates the wavelength and frequency of a wave.

c=for wavelength=speed of wave frequency

QUESTION 4:

Suppose you see a bluish star and a reddish star. State which is hotter and explain your answer.

The bluish star is hotter. The shorter the wavelength at which a star emits its maximum light, the hotter the star is according to Wain's Law of Radiation. Blue light has a shorter wavelength

than red light.

QUESTION 5:

List the two windows (Spectral Ranges) in the earth's atmosphere for observational astronomy. Optical (visible light) including infrared and radio

QUESTION 6:

What are the two main parts of a telescope used for stargazing, and what is the function of each?

Main mirror or lens (objective) to gather light and form an image eyes piece to magnify the image formed by the main mirror or lens.

What are the two main advantages of giant telescopes used for research? Superior light gathering and resolving power

QUESTION 7

Which telescope is described in the chart above?
(a) 1 (b) 1(c) 2

QUESTION 8:

What two factors are the in telescope performance?

Size and quality of main mirror or lens a stable mount is essential

QUESTION 9:

List three advantages of a radio telescope.

reveals radio sources; show radio sources that are hidden from sight behind interstellar dust clouds in the milky galaxy works in cloudy weather and daytime shows radio sources that are found beyond our power of optical viewing.

QUESTION 10:

Craft takes the telescopes beyond earth's obscuring atmosphere, and it is possible to see gamma ray, x-ray, and ultraviolet sources that cannot be seeing on the ground.

There is no atmospheric blurring or radio interference so a space telescope can work at its practical limit of resolving power. Finally done "let us turn it end and get out of here," said Alex "OK let us go home" Peter responded.

The boys were finished with college today, so they walked down to the bus stop to catch the bus and go home. They board the bus when it stopped and pulled over. They sat down and talked about today's events. They both sit and relax and wait for their stop near their house. "

Well," said Alex looking at his brother Peter "we might sound alike, and we even might think alike, and we might act alike, but one thing is for sure we do good exactly alike because we are identical twins – the bowers brothers!" and they both smiled oh yes.

"Well, OK" said Peter "so the two of us stand about 5ft 8in tall and are still growing our hair is brown, straight and kind of long just past our ears with our beautiful brown eyes, so our mother says. Medium built and handsome boys, so our father said.

We have small lips, a beautiful smile, and straight white teeth and our shoe size is twelve. Well, this is who we are Alex and Peter Bower genius at large."

"Well today was a busy day. "Yeah" said Alex evaluating all day."

"Yeah, but we are done and only have one class left.

Astronomy" said Peter "there's a lot to cover still in the book and quite a bit of testing still to do before the final exam." Yes, Alex replied "but we will find out tomorrow. How we did on our other test we took? "No problem there," said Peter. "Yeah, there never is," said Alex. "Well," Peter replies "tomorrow is our documentary in our Astronomy class at noon – let us get there a bit early so we can set up the stand, video camera and the projector slide."

Well at least we get to sleep in a little bit! "Yes" answered Alex "that is going to be heaven for both of us brother." "Well, we are home – let's get off the bus," said Peter. As they walked up to the front door, Mom opens the door and says, "hey boys!" "Hey Mom, how was your day?" Alex asked. Long evaluating all day but it's over now and we are home Sweet Home and that's our favorite place!" Mom laughs and says, "you sure boys?"

"Well," Peter replies, "other than space, yes well now I believe that's the truth." "Come in and take off your jackets," Mom says to them. "I have been cooking." "It smells delicious!" says Alex. "Yes, it really does Mom!" adds Peter. "Thanks boys." "What are we having tonight for dinner? Peter asks. "Well, I made some homemade chicken noodle soup with buttermilk biscuits and fresh green salad.

Mom replies, "How does that sound boys?" "Well Mom" adds Alex "you are a fantastic cook and anything you make we already know it will taste delicious!" "OK then boys" Mom replies "glad to hear it, now if you could help set the table with bowls, spoons, napkins, knives, butter, set the glasses on the table too and small plates for our salad." After setting the table, the boys go into the kitchen to grab the biscuits, and honey, milk and the chocolate and Mom took the soup set it on the table with the salad next to it. "I'll say the blessing tonight" and afterwards she poured the soup into the bowls for herself and the boys.

They all eat quietly at first, then conversation struck up and Mom asked, "How was your day?" "Long" said Peter "Yeah we had evaluated all day in all our subjects." "Oh really?" Mom answered. "Yeah, but the good news is Peter and I already finished 4 of the classes and we just have 1 class left."

"Wow that's amazing!" Mom said. "Not really" answered Alex "do you know Mom? "Do I know what?" said Mom. "Just how smart Peter and I are?" "Well, I know that you both are very smart" Mom answered. "NO Mom – we are extremely smart," replies Alex. "What do you mean extremely?" Mom asked. "Well," said Peter and then Alex looked at Peter and shook his head to his brother not to tell Mom the truth. "

Nothing Mom, we are smart that's it and we both love you." "Well maybe you will get the one thing that you have been wishing for and maybe it will come true," adds Alex. "Well, I don't wish for anything boys – I have the two of you here with me." Mom answered. "If you could have Dad, back, would you?" asked Peter.

"What a strange question to ask me. Look I miss him to the point that sometimes I feel like he is here in the house sometimes and with me and it has been years since his death. I have only his heart in mine and sometimes it feels like I am waiting for him to come back, I know that is impossible, but why is his things all over the house, like his books and his pipe, his sweater that still to this day hangs on the back of the chair.

I mean why his stuff still all over the house. I know it looks or seems strange but for me even after four years it still does not feel time to get rid of any of his stuff. I feel like I am waiting and not sure why, I just know that it is not time, I am waiting for a sign- that is all I can tell you both. "Mom, just do something for Peter and I that follows your own instincts about Dad," Peter said. "Really, why one can't make the impossible happen?" "Well, who?" says Alex. "What are you both trying to say to me?" Mom asked. "Nothing – just never give up on wishing that Dad was here at the table with us, OK?" Susan (Mom) looks at her two boys and as she is looking at them both, she still thinks about him, her beloved husband, friend, father, and lover Rob Bower.

The anniversary of his death is approaching again and once more for Susan things are different for her or her two sons. After all these years, later, and no matter what she is told she just knows in her heart that he is not dead. I mean she says to herself. A person would feel it would not they well I do not that is why I still to this day have all his belongs that I just cannot seem to part with after all there is a tombstone with name on it, but there is this mysterious connection I just cannot explain to myself or to my two sons.

Well after finishing dinner, the boys help Mom clean up the table and put things away. The boys walk up the stairs looking back to say good night to Mom, and she says love you too good night.

The house is locked up and as Mom turns out the lights and heads upstairs to go to her room to get ready to turn in and gets sleep. As a new day, will approach and the boys have a presentation to deliver for astronomy class tomorrow? "I think after our presentation, we can get out direction mapped out and get ready to enter it on the onboard computer system.

You know it's going to take time to map it and figure out the universe code," Alex said. "Yes" said Peter "we will work on that and get a hold of your friend. He will get a hold of his contact for the fuel. We must set up a time to meet but we have a few more things to do before than so hopefully by the time we get ready to arrange the meeting our contact will be still available."

"Well, we can't be concern right now," said Peter. "Yeah" answered Alex "let us move on and stayed focused. OK brother "Goodnight slept tight," Peter answered. Well Mom is up early this morning; she is downstairs in the kitchen brewing her coffee. As she is waiting, she starts cooking apple chicken sausage for Alex and Peter and buttermilk flapjacks with warm maple syrup. As the delicious aroma starts to fill up the house. The boys wake up, go downstairs, and say, "Wow Mom that smells delicious!" "You both up from a dead sleep! Well good! Go sit down.

I made you apple chicken sausages and flapjacks with warm maple syrup and orange juice." "Wow you are the best Mom ever!" said Peter. "Why yes I am!" Mom answers. As she smiles, then leans in, and gives both her boys a gentle kiss on the cheek

. "Eat Up! You got a presentation at noon!" "Right – yeah Mom we do and thanks for the breakfast!" says Alex. The boys go upstairs to get ready for their noon appointment at the college. Alex and Peter came back downstairs; gather their backpacks they had notes in, pens and things that the boys will need for the project. Alex and Peter go into the garage and get the stand, video camera, and projector to take to school.

Mom will be home today, so she told the boys she would drop them off and park the car. Since she would stay and watch their presentation, she would meet them both inside. The boys told her OK and mentioned what room they would be in and see you inside as they both opened the back door to get their stuff out for the presentation Alex and Peter go inside their Astronomy class and set up the stand, video, and projector. They take out from their backpacks the rest of the items they will need for this project. minutes later, the professor who teaches the class and the instructor from the fast class program came into the class.

The rest of the students taking the class all came in. Alex started by showing the picture of the craft, and Peter explained what the project was all about, what their plan was in shooting the documentary and how it would benefit themselves and others in learning all about the Stars Universe and Beyond, including how important this would be in educating and teaching and how they both felt this project would be a learning tool regarding the understanding of what is out there and beyond.

They showed through the video how the craft was originally being designed and how they rebuilt the computer and other aspects of the craft to bring it up to date. The class of students and teachers were impressed – they could not believe how much they were done in a short amount of time. At the end of the video, they should show the rocket suits and how both the boys looked wearing them. The teacher went over to both boys and told them "Congratulations you both got an "A" on this project."

The boys thank the teacher, packed up everything, and left through the door. They both headed down the hall to the double doors that lead outside. In addition, there was Mom was waiting for them both "Well, now that was one fabulous presentation! Are you ready to go home?" "It's good to be backing home – yes, it is! Said Peter.

After walking into the house, Alex and Peter took off their jackets and hung them on the hooks next to the front entrance. They went upstairs when the phone rang. Peter walks back down the stairs and answers the phone in the hallway, "Hello" says Peter "this is your teacher from your fast class."

"Oh yes," said Peter. "I am calling to tell you and your brother that we got your test results back and it is really remarkable – you both scored one hundred on all the tests!

Well, there's something else to tell you, "The teacher said. "Oh really, what's that?" said Peter. "I have talked to the other teachers and professors, and we all agree.

We have decided to promote you both from freshman to juniors." "OMG really?" answers Peter. "Yes, tell your brother too. "Oh, I will and thank you! "Alex! Alex! Where are you?" "Upstairs Peter-what is it? "Our instructor called from our fast class" Peter replied. "Yeah – what did he have to say?" asked Alex. "He said because our scores were so high, we are now juniors!" Peter responded.

"You're kissing up really worked!" laughed Alex. "Yeah – did you see that coming?" Peter replied. "No" said Alex but we'll take it!" Alex and Peter ran downstairs to Mom. "What Peter?" Mom asked. "Our teacher called, because of our scores on all four of the tests, he and the college have given Alex, and I a promotion to junior am status starting tomorrow!"

"Oh, my, that is amazing! I am so proud of you both. The journey that the two of you is on is one filled with amazement, excitement, and beauty and I feel that the best for you both has not even begun yet and the journey is going to be to the universe and beyond."

After a good night sleep, the boys get up and go downstairs to the kitchen. They started the coffee for Mom, knowing she would be up soon. They both thought it would be nice to have it ready for her. Alex and Peter toasted bagels and poured two bowls of granola cereal. Peter pours orange juice into two small glasses and then butters the bagels.

They sit down at the table and eat their breakfast. Mom is up, walks downstairs, and says, "Oh my – I can smell coffee! Thanks boys!" they both welcome Mom as she enters the kitchen and pours herself a cup of coffee, then walks into the living to watch some news. The boys finish breakfast and head to the garage to work more on the craft.

CHAPTER SIX

CRAFT 101

Peter unlocks the garage double doors. They both walk in, and Peter got their list of what was left to do. Alex looks at his brother and says "well, what are we starting on, Peter?" "Oh yeah – sorry I am checking out the list" Peter answers. "Yeah, OK the next thing on the list is the movable antenna for communication."

"OK" Alex responds, "Let us work on that afterwards. We have the Astronauts Portable Life Support – this supplies air, water, and radio communications. We also have the ascent fuel tank for engine used to blast ascent stage back into lunar orbit. So, let us check on these and see where we are from there OK?"

The boys worked throughout the day trying to get the craft ready for their adventure in space.

Mom walks out to the garage calls out to her boys "Hey!" They answer, "yeah Mom, over here what's up?" Mom answers, "well I thought you would like to come in for lunch." "Yeah OK" the boys said. "I picked up some subways sandwiches and drinks!" Mom tells them "Come inside and have something to eat." "OK right behind you" Peter replied. The boys walked out of the garage and locking up the double doors behind them.

They follow Mom into the house for lunch. They all sit down at the table and boys ate. They both look over at Mom, she was having a salad, and the boys asked, "Is that all you're Eating?" Yes" she said "but thanks for your concern but your mom is doing fine. "Well," Mom continues, "You boys have been working hard today on the craft." Yes" said Alex "we must do still. You know -for the project "right" said mom "well I am sure the both of you will work it out.

I have no doubt in both of your abilities in what you can do. I have always known just how smart the two of you are you know. The two of you can't fool me." Well mom replied to Alex "why would we want to "Look Mom told them "I know and will always know the truth in just how smart my two men really are and don't ever forget that when you both are thinking of hiding something from me remember you came from me, and a mother always knows.

"Alex and Peter look at their mom and realized that she might not know what the two or might be up too and what their plans are, but Mom knows we are doing something even if she is not sure what that is or might be, still she knows something is up with her boys. Alex and Peter finished eating their lunch, got up from the table and headed upstairs to look at star charts and work on their constellations and mapping.

They still have work to do on the charts and both realize that mapping out the correct destination must be perfect. Not one mistake can take place, or they could end up somewhere over the Milky Way and beyond to a shiny star. The boys thought about their destination, what would it bring, and what would happen when the universe asked the boys to open the white door. An invitation such as this has brought on sleepless nights and, as always, brings them back to what lies beyond the white door? There course is a journey like no other before and they realize that the course they put into the craft onboard computer system from their dreams must be put in the same way.

The boys wonder how to know if those numbers were real and would lead them both to a place that no one has been before.

I think" Alex said to Peter "we need ask the universe for a little proof just to make sure that numbers are real directions what is the white door".

"Yes, said Peter we need to ask for a little hint that would allow us to continue on the journey.

"Well," said Alex "how do we ask the universe?" "We need to go outside" Peter answers "remember when we first were looking up and the universe sent us our first message in the form of a dream." "Yes" said Peter "I do recall that so maybe we need to go back where it happened in the first place." "OK" replies Alex "we'll let us give it a try and see what the universe has to say. "Well, OK" Peter agrees.

The boys head outside, look through the telescope and waited until they found a shooting star, then asked the universe for a little more clarity in what their journey will bring. As they ask, Alex and Peter wait for the flash to end across the sky. The boys go into the house, go upstairs, and crawl into bed.

They both hope the dream will come down upon them both and they might get answers to questions that the universe only holds. The brothers say goodnight to each other and say good night to Mom. They are in their beds and hope they will dream of a little dream and the sky above will hear their cries and give them visions of clarity that will ease their minds so their paths to the door will open and inside they will go.

As the night ends the boys wake up and look at each other. Peter said, "Did you dream last night? Did you ask Alex?" "Well," said Peter "what I saw were the numbers the same as before but with one exception, after the last number there was an arrow,

and it was pointing up like someone was saying go this way – but the crazy part was what I saw next yes said Peter I saw the same thing and what I saw was after the arrow pointing up was some letters. "Are you sure it was letters?" asked Alex. "Well, no – not exactly letters. More like – and this is creepy – but I saw were initials.

It said 'Initials R.B. Lives Here.' "Well," said Alex "that is what I saw too, but what the heck is going on? Are we crazy – or is that our dad initials?" "I think it's Dad," replied Peter "and they are trying to say something to us. But if Dad is there than that means what?" "Well," Alex says, "We better find out for ourselves. What else did you see?" "We'll let us see . . ." Peter replies, "OK, well – we both saw an arrow which appeared to say, 'Go This Way'" "Yes," agrees Alex "that is what I saw too." "The arrow I saw had a last number then the arrow went in a straight line past the last number and then pointed up.

"Yes" said Alex "that's what I saw too. "So, it's saying," Peter continued, "after we follow and put in the last number in the computer, it will lead us straight up to find the door." "Yes" Alex agrees, "it showed us that once you go straight like an arrow to the last number, we will find the white door."

"Yes" said Peter "it showed us that once you go straight, the door appears along with a docking station." "Yeah" said Alex "it looks like a parking space, but more like a platform to dock next to." "What about the door?" asked Peter "did it give you any signs of what was beyond the door?"

"What I saw" Alex explained "and what the universe allowed me to see – was the door openings up like a crack." Peter asked Alex "did you see that the door was open a little?" "Yes" Alex said "it was opened a crack, and it looked like I could, in my dreams, peek in." "Yeah, me too," said Peter. "I was able to poke my head in and what I saw confusing," said Alex. "Really?" said Peter. "What did you see?" Peter asked Alex.

"Well at first I heard laughter – then I saw what appeared to be a guard standing in front of the door," said Alex. "Yes, that is what I saw too" said Peter "but what did the guard look like?"

"Well, I will tell you "Said Alex "it looked human in the face but the rest of him looked robotic – very strange indeed – not like a robot or anything else I have ever seen before. The face seemed so real – so human. It is strange his eyes were piercing dark like chocolate, small mouth and lips, the hair was very dark in color, and I remember seeing the hair was long, hanging straight down, like it flowed down on the wiring on his hands. There was no skin on the rest of him – and there was one more thing I can recall?"

"What's that?" said Alex. "Well, there was a sign on the door." "Oh yes, I remember that too!" said Peter. "Yeah, but do you recall what the sign said?" asked Alex. "Yes, it said 'Searching for the Truth' see you soon R.B. After that I woke up and that is all I can recall." Peter answered.

"Well, that is amazing! So, what are we to make of all of this?" Alex asked. "Someone is trying to tell us what? That Dad is not dead and buried here. Are we supposed to believe that! Somehow, he is now inside the white door – a door he discovered! I do not understand this! Why all the lies and secrets?" "Well," Peter responds, "We have more questions than answers and I'm not going to rest until we find Dad and the truth behind the white door."

"Well," answers Alex "he's supposed to be buried – maybe that's where we should start." "Well," Peter says, "I need a break – my brain needs a break from this! Let us go downstairs and get juice to drink." As the boys were walking downstairs, they both had going on, their heads filled with aching questions to answers they did not have. All they had was swirling around and around in the mist of their brains.

They know they had to search out the truth and the mysterious secret of the white door and the initials they knew now were R.B. one knows the truth. Mom was already up and, in the kitchen, making French toast. She had the table set and the glasses filled with Sunny Delight. French toast on their plates – four each with powdered sugar and fresh strawberries preserves, topped off with whipped cream.

On the side, as well was Jimmy Dean sausages. Mom knew this one of her boy's favorite breakfasts. The boys walked into the dining room and saw the great breakfast on the table for the two. They looked at their mom and said to her "Mom, you know the two of us would be totally lost without you!" The two then reached over and gave her a gentle kiss on her cheek.

"Well now!" Mom said, "I am the lucky one because god has blessed me twice!" She smiled at her boys, with a twinkle in her eyes, and said, "OK, please sit down and enjoy your Sunday breakfast."

As they sat down and ate, Alex and Peter were second-guessing their dreams from last night and were wondering what it all means – really. The laughter, the Robotic Guard taking his post in front of the white door and what was the universe trying to tell the two bowers brothers. Sometimes in dreams, it is not what you think but what you do not. The boys were trying to figure out the message. They played it back slowly in their heads and aloud together, to understand what they thought the real message could have meant. "Well," said Peter "the arrow represents directions, the course that we are planning to take, but those initials – that is really puzzling and an interesting new development. I just wonder. "What is that?" asked Alex. "You know, why now the universe would tell us?" "You mean about the initials?" said Peter.

"Yeah" Alex replied, "why would they tell us now and not before?" "Well," Peter answers "maybe the universe wanted to be sure that we would see and investigate for ourselves – and do you know what?" said Alex "someone or something wants us there really bad." "I wonder why?" asked Peter.

"It seems that someone or something is willing to say or do just about anything to get us there," responded Alex. "You think?" asked Peter. "Yeah" Alex responds, "I didn't before . . . but now that they mentioned those initials – almost to lure us. I wonder just what it is the universe wants us to see?" "Well," said Peter "there's that . . . in everything they are saying there is some sort of truth in it, and they need our help. Really we will not find out unless the two of us blast off and find out the answers to all."

"Well," said Peter "the directions we are planning on going with "Yes," said Alex. "Well," Peter continues, "I don't think the place we are going to is a planet. I'm thinking it's more maybe like a gateway to another world – within a whole other dimension." "Yeah" Alex answers, "something for sure that no one has, up to now, discovered.

Except for R.B." "Oh yeah" Peter responds, "we don't know about that and up to now there hasn't been any proof yet, so I guess it's better if we wait on any judgment call until the time comes and the two of us see with our own eyes." You know like Mommy used to say when we were young," said Alex. "Oh yeah" said Peter "I know that saying –

the proof is in the pudding and well what can you say Mommy was right!" Alex says, "Well what can one say, this is huge, and it really makes you wonder what type of world it's going to be and just how different from our world it is – and of course the people – are they human or something yet to be discovered?"

"Well," Peter says, "in any case, we've already had our minds made up for us on the day that the two of us received that invitation inviting us to go where no man – or two boys – has gone before LOL!" "Did you just say that?" Alex laughed. "Well – yes!" Peter said, "don't you find it fitting?" "OK Peter, I give you that!" said Alex.

"Well, I guess the two of us will find out – and see – soon enough for ourselves" Peter says. "Look," said Alex "we're not crazy; we are two very smart young men, and apparently the only two on our planet (besides, you know who)!"

You mean said Peter "with those initials that we our curious about . . ." "Yeah," replied Alex "those are the ones that has begun to figure out the mystery of the gateway to the white door beyond time and space."

"Well," said Peter "I was wondering, Alex – do you think that we are correct regarding what our dreams shown us?" "Well," said Alex "one can never be certain and really we can go around and around all day on the subject, but until we get there, solve the mystery and see for ourselves we will always have questions.

I mean this is the biggest adventure of our lifetime. Two teenagers are going to another world to a gateway outside our own universe! We are the biggest nerds, the smartest, and who ever sent us that invite – well shoot . . . someone is expecting us and that sign on the door see you soon!" "Well," Peter answers, "Let us give this whole conversation a break for now.

We must concentrate on our schoolwork!" "Yeah" said Alex "I agree – OK! "Well," Alex says, "Since we have completed all of our assignments, we are now sophomores. Our direction is clear, brother; we are now heading straight from 'getting our education finished' to 'getting on with parts two.' Our second part is plotting our course into space.

Well, this is Sunday – back to school tomorrow." "Yeah" said Peter "I love going to school!" "Me too!" said Alex. "Well," Peter adds, "we need to call your contact and get ready to go and pick up the fuel." "Yeah OK" said Alex "let us get ready to pick up the fuel and get ready to store the fuel in the garage. It must be stored in a cool environment." "OK" Peter agrees, "We can go outside to the garage and start working on that, but when we finish, we can call your contact, place the order and meet him to pay."

"Yeah" Alex replies, "that money is the money that Dad left us." "Yes" said Peter "but we are not spending all of it." "Yeah, I know," said Alex "but we'd better hope we don't have to explain any of this to Mom." "

Yeah, I hear that!" said Peter. "OK" agrees Alex "let us fix the storage issue and make the phone call." "OK" said Peter "let us get started brother." As Peter and Alex go outside to the garage, Alex takes out his key to unlock the garage doors and open it up they stand in the middle and ask themselves – 'where should we store the fuel?'

"Well," Alex says, "We can dig a hole in the corner, put the containers with the fuel in the dirt hole and cover with the cooling panels to keep the temperatures regulated." "Sounds good" Peter agrees. "OK let's get started digging," said Alex.

After digging to make the holes for the containers filled with fuel, the brothers had the cooling panels already bought. Therefore, they will put the panels around the containers – once they get them – and put the fuel in the holes and secure the cooling panels around the fuel tanks.

They continued digging and finished. The boys went left the garage, locked the two double doors, and went back into the house. They mentioned to Mom that the two were starving and asked what is for dinner. "Well," said Mom, who looked at her two boys and said, "how about Enchiladas?"

They looked at her and Peter said, "wow that not only sounds good, but smells delicious!" "Well," Mom said, "Why don't you get your brother and have him help you set the table?" "OK" said Peter "no problem, Mom!" Peter calls aloud for Alex asking him to come and help set the table for dinner. Alex yells back "on my way Peter" Peter replies "OK." They set the table with the plates, silverware, napkins, and the glasses with the brother's favorite chocolate milk and then Mom took the hot Enchiladas dripping with warm melted cheese and sauce out of the oven and set it on the table and her salad filled with veggies and Thousand Island dressing. The three sit down at the table, Peter says the blessing, and they ate. After dinner, Alex and Peter help Mom clear the table, put the leftovers away and load up the dishwasher. The boys finished cleaning up the kitchen and went upstairs.

Peter looks at his brother and tells him "Well I think we should go ahead and make the call to the contact so we can get the fuel we're going to need. We should place our order now." "Well, OK" Alex replies "but you are going to have to sit down and produce the right amount of fuel we're going to need to get us there and back – if that's what we decide on doing." "OK" says Peter "I will figure that out. I already have an amount in mind, but I will run the numbers and make sure it's correct and – oh, make sure it's right."

"OK" Alex replies, "We don't want any mistakes or problems later. "Well," Peter said "Alex, when you are 100%

sure your right, let me know when you have that done and I'll look it over to make sure that I produce the same figure."

"OK" said Peter. "Well, I should have something written down on paper by tomorrow" Alex replied. "OK Peter says, "I am tired, and I am going upstairs to bed. "Right behind you Peter! Alex agrees. "Goodnight, Mom!" they both yelled out, just as Mom yelled back "sweet dreams, good night – see you in the morning."

Another morning rises and the sun brightly shines through the bedroom windows as Peter and Alex lay sleeping in their beds. The sun beats down warm against their faces. The boys toss and turn as the sun awakens up both. They sit up in their beds and look at the curtains hanging on the rods, as the sun was glistering through. The boys yawn, stretch and sit up in their beds with their legs hanging over onto the floor, slip on their brown slippers and go to wash up in the bathroom.

They put on their blue jeans with a light blue button-up shirt, tucked their shirts into their pants, and wore a black vest over it before heading downstairs for breakfast. Mom was up and, in the kitchen, making ham and egg with cheese breakfast sandwiches. They both enter the kitchen and say good morning to Mom.

They took out the large picture of orange juice and poured themselves a large glass. They walked into the dining room, sat down, and ate their breakfast. Afterward, they said goodbye to Mom and headed off to school. They walked down to the bus stop as the bus just arrives and pulls over.

The boys board the bus and wait for their stop to come. Once there, they both jumped off, walked across the street to the college, walked up the front steps to the front entrance door and down the hall to their fast class. Opening the door and going inside to once again study on the subjects for today. The instructor comes over and starts them off in Astronomy. The boys worked on their subject for the day.

After studying, they both worked on space and the universe until four pm. After that, they shut things down and go home. Peter worked on his figures for the fuel to be ordered and Peter showed Alex the figures he had produced, asking him "let me know if this looks right to you and if there needs to be adjusted made before we put the order in."

Therefore, Alex took the paper, folded it up, and put it in his pocket to go over it later once he is home. After getting off the bus, they both walked down the street to the house, then up the driveway and finally they open the door to the house. It was unlocked and Mom was home.

Alex goes upstairs to the desk, sits down, and figures the correct fuel it will take traveling to the white door and back home. While Alex is working the numbers to need the correct fuel, Peter is downstairs talking to Mom about what is for dinner, which is Peter's favorite subject, especially since he is always starving. Mom looks at Peter and says, "You know –

I cook most of the time." "Yes, said Peter "you do." "Well tonight is not the night, OK?" she says as she is looking at her son. "Well," said Peter "I will order something." "OK" Mom said "Peter, just order for you and Alex – OK? I don't feel like eating tonight." "OK" said Peter. He picks up the phone calls in his favorite pizza parlor just down the street, calls in his order and waits for the pizza man to bring it. Thirty minutes later, there is a knock at the door. Peter opens it and pays for the hot pizza with two sodas. He takes the pizza and drinks upstairs to their bedroom where Alex is still working on the fuel numbers. "OK" says Peter "take a break and eat some dinner." "Yeah OK" says Alex. Alex puts down his pen and paper and joins his brother on the bed and they have pizza for dinner.

CHAPTER SEVEN

SEARCHING FOR THE TRUTH

The boys talk about Mom and Alex says, "I don't know what to say." "Well. I don't know either," says Peter. She really does not want anything, but really, she looks sad, a little. Mom tries not to show it." "Yeah" says Alex. "I believe her heart is broken, well maybe we should try to make her smile." "No, that won't work – Mom won't date even after all these years later – she wants Dad back."

"Yeah" said Peter "for sure Mom misses him but won't talk about the accidents and you know she's never talked about the accidents, not to you and certainly not to me either." "Well," Peter replies, "Especially now that we suspect that Dad isn't dead or possibly not even in the grave! Even though we have no proof yet, Dad left and went to the white door. How could he pull that off?" "Well, he had a plan, if it happened and what about the craft?" Well, he must have had one," said Alex. "OK" asked Peter "we need to think – where would he have kept it?" "Well," Alex replied, "I think the only place could have been the cabin. You know he must have had a secret hiding place and you know if it was there then that means he also had fuel too!"

"Wow you're right!" Peter exclaims, "That means that there could be more fuel." "Well," asks Alex "Mom does act like it's too painful – or do you think it's something else?" "What do you mean Alex?" Peter responds. "Well for one thing, she kind of acts like she is waiting for Dad to walk through the door most of the time."

"Yeah" said Peter "she does act like that. I mean it has been four years and for her it still feels like yesterday, but still something it not right and I think we should find out what is going on with Mom and why does she act like he is still here even after these years gone by. Well Mom is stuck on yesterday. Well," Alex answers back "I don't know but most move on after four years, but she acts like it just happened."

"Well," said Peter "Mom has not moved on at all." "Clearly" replies Alex "Mom either doesn't want to or she can't. "Yes"- said Peter "but why?" "Why indeed!" said Alex. "I think there's something the two of us don't know and I would like to find out what it is."

"Look" replies Peter "could it be that, simply put, Mom was in love with our father to the point that there is no one else for her and really she doesn't want anyone else. "Yeah, it could be," said Alex. "Yeah" said Peter "maybe there's just something!" "What?" said Alex "I am not sure, but I just get a feeling."

"I'm sick of this!" said Peter. "What the hell are you trying to say Peter? "Alex exclaims. "Look" Peter replies, "Do you think that it's normal to get an overwhelming feeling like if you turned around and Dad would just be standing there?" "Yeah sometimes," said Alex. "Well, OK" said Peter "but really after four years – for me – I don't think it's normal. You know in your heart that he's dead and not coming back."

"So why on earth do we feel this way, better yet" said Peter "if we are having these feelings then do not you think Mom is after these years, what does mean?" "I don't know" Alex replied but one thing is for sure if we're having these feelings then don't you think Mom feels the same way?" Just think said Peter "most move on, especially after four years, but for us it still feels like he could walk through the door and really I want to know why," said Alex.

"Well then, what we are saying is neither one of us believes that Dad is dead. We only have the message from the white door with his initials and the sign saying see you soon. Now, because of the message from the universe, we think Dad went to the white door because he is keeping others from finding out the truth about the door. Not to mention we were told that an assassin killed him. Really, it could have been that someone from the state found out what he discovered."

"I don't know," said Peter. "What?" said Alex? "Looks like someone tried to shut him up, you know Dad, – he was a man of principle there is no way he would sell out his work" Peter, replied. "Well," responded Alex "in any case something is going on that is bigger than the two of us. You know Dad was supposed to be buried." "Yeah right – OK" Peter questioned. "Well," Peter continues, "Let us see and not tell Mom.

Let us just wait until afterwards and see what the two of us find out. "OK" said Alex. "One other thing" adds Peter "you do realize what will happen if the two of us get caught." "Well, we better make sure we don't" Alex reminds him. Peter and Alex go to the backyard and grab two shovels and a flashlight. "Let's go and see if Mom is sleeping?" says Alex. "Why" said Peter.

"To take the keys out of her purse!" Alex exclaimed. "The keys!" said Peter. "Yeah" said Alex "you know – to the car." "OMG!" responds Peter "you want to take the car! How on earth do you expect to get to the cemetery?" "I don't know" said Peter "but shit Alex, do you really want to take Moms car? Well, she usually sleeps all night and if she's sleeping . .

." The boys go upstairs, crack open her bedroom door and investigate her room. Both boys saw Mom was fast asleep. Alex and Peter leave her bedroom, go back downstairs, get her purse, and open it up take out the keys to the car. "Hey" said Peter "are the house keys on that chain?" "Yeah" said Alex. "OK let's go!" Peter responds. They both leave the house and close the door behind them.

The boys approach the car unlocked the door. Alex puts the key in the ignition, puts the car's gearshift into reverse and the boys pushed the car backwards out of the driveway and onto the street. The boys got into the car and drove away. minutes later, they arrived at the cemetery and parked the car. Both got out and grabbed the shovels and flashlight. "Well," says Peter "thank goodness it's not completely dark yet."

We'd better find Dad's grave in a hurry while it's still light out," observes Alex. They both walked at a fast pace until they got to the gravesite with the tombstone marking with his father's name on it. The cemetery was quiet with no one around so both dug through the dirt. An hour went by, and they were still digging, creating quiet a pile of dirt next to the grave. They both did not stop until they finally heard the shovel make this clanking noise.

They knew they had hit up against the casket. They stopped and looked at each other. "OMG Peter!" Alex said. "Yeah, I know," said Alex. "Shit – look!" said Alex. "Just hurry up, get down there and open it up" Peter exclaims. "OK" Alex responded. Alex jumps down into the grave standing next to the casket and slowly opens the dark wooden cold box lying in the earth for the past four years now.

He opens it, slowly as first, pulling up on the casket door with all his strength. Then finally with one hard pull up on the casket suddenly popped open, exposing the coffin and its contents inside. "OMG!" Alex said, "I knew it – I really knew it. Peter, you are not going to believe this!" "Never mind, Alex" Peter responds "is Dad in there or not! For God sake hurry up, close the casket door and let us put the dirt back!"

"Peter – OK!" as Alex closes the door to the casket and they pile the dirt back onto the grave, covering up any signs of any disturbances. They grab the shovels and flashlight ran out of the cemetery to where the car was parked.

They both got into the car. Alex hangs his head on the steering wheel, and started to talk to him "Are you kidding me?" Peter asked him "come on let us go! We can talk about it at home, we need to get Mom's car back." The brothers drove back to the house, parked the car back where it was in the driveway, went into the house, and put Mom's keys back into her purse.

They headed upstairs to their room and closed the door. They looked at each other and stood in silence for what it seemed like a long time, but it was only seconds before Peter broke the silence and said, "so was Dad in the grave or not?" Alex looks at his brother and says, "It's time to wake up Mom. No wait!" says Peter "you and I must talk first. I'm not convinced Mom will tell us the truth."

"Well," said Alex "maybe not before but now, things have changed. You and I know more than we did before." "Well yes, that's right" Peter replied." We got a message from the door, and we believe its dad." "Yeah" answered Alex "sending that message to us, now we know he's not in the grave and not only that – he was never in the grave!" "Yes" Peter responded, "so what happened when he died?

You know only Mom knows the truth." "I know that Mom has the answers we need" Alex replied "but she has, for whatever reason, kept Dad secret for four years now. You and I are not children anymore and well, have you ever thought that Mom knows nothing – could that be possible?"

"Well," says Peter "let us wait and try to find out something, without asking straight out, to see if she knows." "OK" said Alex "but I'm not playing any games with Mom. If I think for a second, she knows – game over. I will tell her what we did and what we know. "OK" said Peter by next morning, both Alex and Peter slept little with everything whirling around their heads, they both thought they would burst and explode in flames. They were both very anxious. They finished getting dressed, went downstairs, made coffee, poured juice, and waited for Mom to come downstairs. They wanted to dig a little on their own. An hour went by, and the boys grew restless waiting for their mom to wake up.

Finally, she comes downstairs to the kitchen and pours herself a cup of coffee. Alex and Peter go into the kitchen and Peter says to Mom, "I would like to ask you something about Dad." "OK" says Mom "what is it?"

"I was wondering - did Dad die right away?" he asked. "Well," Mom says, "Your father is not here, and I don't really feel it's healthy for any of us to dwell on it. Really, it will change nothing or bring him back to us." "Alex and I both understand that Mom" responds Peter "but we still have some questions regarding the death of Dad, really – there are a few things we really don't understand, and we would like you to help us understand."

"What is there to understand? Mom asked, "He's dead and there's nothing I can say that's going to bring him back. "Oh" said Alex. Mom replies, "What do you mean by that? The two of you explain yourself right now!" "Look Mom" Alex answers her "we're just wondering why you decided to bury dad, instead of the other choices, of spreading his ashes?

" "Well," Mom responds, "I didn't make that choice your father did long ago. I only followed his wishes – OK. Understand? I would like to know – what is going on? What are the two of you trying to understand anyways? Your father is dead; there is nothing, I can do to bring him back – no matter how much I want to.

We just can't and there's nothing you or I can do about that." Alex looks at Mom – he cannot tell if she is being truthful or if she is hiding something from them. He also looks at her face to see if she is shaken up by the conversation they are having in the kitchen.

Well Alex whispers to Peter "she doesn't look upset. No said Peter "but she does look a little bit pissed off and annoyed at us for bringing up the subject. "I wonder why?" asks Alex. "Yeah" said Peter "me too." "Well," Mom said, "If there's nothing else, I have to get ready for work." "OK Mom" replies Peter. "Hey Mom" said Alex "Peter and I were wondering could we take off this weekend and go to Dad's cabin and spend some time."

"Yeah" she said, "that's fine. We could leave early on Friday. Have your bags packed with what you will need OK?" "Cool, thanks – no problem. It will be good for us to get out of town for a couple of days" Alex responded. Mom headed upstairs, with her coffee cup in her hand, and walks into her bedroom closes the door. minutes later, she walks out of her bedroom, down the stairs, grabbed her purse and keys.

She says goodbye to her boys and heads out to her car to start it up. After minutes warming up the car, she backs out of the driveway and takes off later. "Well now" said Peter "what do make of that? Does she know something about Dad's whereabouts or is she in the dark?"

"Well," said Alex "I'm not sure, but maybe this weekend will give us some clues when we get to search the cabin and try to find a hidden room or something. I know it is a gut feeling I have that dad was hiding something there. The two of us will find it so we can solve this for the last time. "OK" answers Peter "but what about Mom?" "Well," Alex says, "Let us leave her where she's at for now."

"And where's that?" asked Peter. "Oh, in the dark until we can figure this out and have more clues to go on" Alex responds. "For now, we'll wait to say something to Mom." "OK" Peter said, "I agree with you. "Well," Peter continues, "Let us get ready for school and learn something new today

. It will be a nice distraction for us both." They head upstairs to change their clothes and then came back downstairs to grab their backpacks. They stuffed the house keys in their pockets, opened the front door, and walked down the street to wait for the bus to come. As the bus stops and opens the doors, both boys board the bus, find a seat, and wait for the thirty-minute trip to school.

Once there they got off the bus, walked across the street and up the main entrance steps to the front double glass doors that lead them to a higher power of learning. They look forward every day to embracing the knowledge of what their instructors must teach them and what they will take into their minds. They were looking forward to asking questions and learning, mostly, on their own in the fast class.

They have learned to love and embrace this program and going to school for them is a gift. After studying for half the day, the boys talk to someone, they knew who worked for NASA. His name was Mark Wheeler.

He had a small office next to the college. As they walked over to where his office door was, they turned the doorknob and went in looking for Mark. "Hey Mark," said Peter. "Hey Peter and Alex – how's it going – huh." "Good" responds

Alex "thanks how you are doing? "Well, I'm good and keeping myself busy, you know" Mark responds. "NASA is always having me work on something. What do you need?" "Well," responds Peter "a favor really."

"OK how can I help?" Mark replied. "Well," Alex responded, "We need you to not say anything about what we're going to tell you for starters." "OK" Mark says and asks, "What is it I'm not talking about?" "Well," said Peter "it's about our father, Rob Bower."

"Yeah" Mark responded, "he died years, back, right?" "Yeah right" said Alex "but what we would like to know is – were there any unofficial reports of a craft leaving air space around 4 years back?" Mark replies, "You want me to look and tell you something, not to mention that NASA is keeping it under wraps?" "Yes!" said Peter. "Why?" asked Mark.

"First, tell us please," asked Peter "was there a craft which orbited into space four years ago, without NASA's permission?" "Look" asked Mark "I need to know, first, what you boys are talking about?" "I wish we could explain" said Alex "but we can't – and really you could, as well as the two of us, be in danger for just mentioning it." "OK" Mark explains to them "but if I look on this computer it would be a problem." "Why?" asked Alex.

"Because its every keystroke is watched," Mark responded. "Yeah, everything I touch is recorded by NASA 'because they are always watching me." "I see," said Peter. "But let's see what I can dig up without drawing attention to myself" Mark said "if I am looking for something that someone else asked for then OK, I just might be able to get take the attention off myself and make it look like just a normal workload day.

Regular stuff I'm doing." "OK" said Alex "the last thing we need is for NASA to find out understand? No! But I will take you at your word." "OK then" Mark responds, "let us see, unofficially looking back to 2009, if there's a report mentioned here concerning a craft that was witnessed by several people in the area, out of town – in a country area not too far away." Mark continued, "They reported seeing a craft shooting into the sky above. It looks like NASA tried to shoot the craft out of space and that's all that I know."

"OK wait" asked Peter "did it say they were successful in shooting the craft. Or did it make it into orbit?" "Well," Mark answered, "It looks like they were not successful in shooting it and it blasted off to parts unknown." "OMG!" said Alex and the look on Peter's face was total amazement. "OK, well thanks for everything. Look, do us one more favor, if you could Mark?" "Yeah sure, what's that?" Mark answered.

"Back track everything" Alex responded. "Look, don't worry." Mark assured them. "I will just say I was doing research for a Doctor Martin, and he asked me for some information. I will email him the pages we looked at and he will know what to do. OK? Do not worry. He owes me a favor, but tells me what's going on?" "If we discuss this with you," Peter tells him "It could put your life in danger."

"Look" Mark tells them "Don't worry about me I can cover my tracks simply fine. It looks like you two need information and a friend that might have answers." "Well, look," said Peter" our father was not in his grave. I mean my brother and I dug him up. He is not there and furthermore; our mother does not know what we did. After all these years, she still thinks Dad is dead.

We do not know if she is telling the truth or if she knows something, but Peter and I discovered something. We believed that it is the same thing our father discovered, if that is not enough, we think our father left in a craft four years ago; I tell you this; there is no way our dad would abandon or our mother.

Their love is like a made for TV movie. We are his sons; he would not just leave us unless he had no choice and he thought we would be killed. It was the only way; he could think of to save himself. What he discovered and found. Well maybe he had no time to tell us or take us." "To leave without notice it doesn't sound like your father would do that," said Mike. "So, what are you saying?" said Peter. "He left something behind for us both to find" Peter explained." It would explain more about the decision he made to leave something for us to find him."

"OMG – you're right Peter!" said Alex. "I get it – he's been leaving us clues!" "What kind?" asked Mike? "He's been contacting us through another world we believe, but only though our dreams" answered Peter. "Really?" replied Mike. Peter continues,

"How that does work is hard to explain, but he has been sending it down though light beams – like a flash in the sky. It hits us and then at night when we dream it leaves us visual messages that we can see and remember in the morning." "I don't think it's your father doing that to your dreams." Mike answers, "If you two are getting messages, it's got to be another source sending them.

Your father was on a very hush, hush project with NASA. He found something out about the project, and he wouldn't reveal what he knew," Mike explained. "Yeah?" Peter said. "I get it!" Peter continued.

"NASA told someone to get everything he had on the white door and when whoever came to look for it, they couldn't find anything." "It was because your father took everything." Mike replied. "He probably hid it – I'm guessing. I thought he was killed because they sent someone to talk to him and your father would not play ball – so to speak. I will tell you this. I know he had some help."

Really?" said Peter. "Well," Mike continued, "How did he pull that off? I know your father is one smartest man in the world. NASA has been underestimating him until now." "I understand very well," said Peter. "I think he was probably very scared back then"

Alex said "and if I know my father, he probably started wearing a bullet proof vest to protect himself. So, when the person or persons came to talk to him and could get nowhere, they shot him, buried him, and forgot about him – until Peter and I opened up the complex issue." "I think your father was scared not only for himself, but for his family" Mike responded "and his only concern was to protect his family. He would be better off dead – and so he was – better off dead."" Yes" answered Alex "until now."

"If NASA finds out about this" Mike warned them you two are in danger and so is your mother. Okay, whatever you are planning, you had better step it up. I will not say a word but look – these agencies – well let us just say they have been listening in on your family for years, just waiting for you to figure this out and to lead them to your father and whatever he found. NASA wants this information bad enough they would kill anyone, including the rest of your family and anyone else who helps you or gets in the way.

Hope you two understand what's at stake and do whatever's necessary to protect yourself and your mother." Mike continues, "Well, you better find those bugs – or maybe leave them and just watch what you say. Now that you know, what is going on and what is at stake for you, your brother, and you are Mom. You better leave now."

"Okay" says Peter thanks for everything. Mike responds, "If something happens, I will give you two a call and use a code word 'turtle.' It will mean you have to get out now." "Okay" says Alex "thanks for the information, Mike." "Okay" Mike replies "no problem. Bye." As the boys left, walked outside and down the street to wait for the bus – they talked about what they had learned

"So, Dad found the white door and – really because of his work, was being monitored by his employer," said Peter. "They also found out what he had discovered" Peter replied "and wanted all his paperwork on the white door. Our Dad wouldn't give it up." "I think our father didn't feel he could trust the people he worked for" answered Alex "and he was afraid they would launch their own craft and put the new world in mortal danger. He was afraid they would kill first and ask questions later. "The agency tried to talk to Dad at first" replied Peter "and when that didn't work, they couldn't get the disk, and other information Dad had on the white door.

He also erased everything on the computer, so they resorted to having him killed." "Yeah" answered Alex "and that mostly had to do with the fact the agency probably found out Dad was launching his own craft into space to locate the white door on his own. They would not let him do that." "Yeah, so they killed them," said Peter. "

Well so they thought," Replied Alex "but when Dad launched his craft, they didn't figure out he was alive right then." "Well, maybe" said Peter "but at that point, it was not likely they could admit to anything – or let anyone else find out so . . . yes, they let it go." "

Well," answered Alex "that's where we are, brother . . . Dad alive and headed to the door." "Yeah" said Peter "but that was four years ago; and we have a lot of catching up to do . . . and we have to leave." "Yeah, hurry up Peter," said Alex "we have to get home and tell Mom now! Look out Dad – Alex and Peter are coming!

CHAPTER EIGHT

ALL SYSTEMS GO

Well after a lengthy conversation with Mike and finding out Dad left this planet and is now sending us messages from the white door and the agency, he worked for is also linked to NASA, meaning that Dad answered to someone over there and they know now they tried to have Dad killed. However, when Dad launched his craft, the agency was let he know was alive and trying to enter a different world.

When they could not stop him, they bugged on our house, and then waited for Dad to get a hold of us, figuring we would follow his example. They would stop us at any cost to get the directions we now hold in our hands.

"OMG Peter" Alex said, "I can't believe all this." "Well," Peter asks, "Should we tell Mom? We have little choice now do we?" "Come one" Alex responds, "We've got to catch the bus. Hurry up!" "Yeah" Peter says, "No telling right about now – the agency probably already knows because of the computer.

They know it all – big eye in the sky and all." "Hurry up!" says Alex "and stop talking the bus is here." Alex and Peter board the bus; they sit down and take the thirty-minute ride back to their house. They both try to gather the thoughts swirling around in their heads. The boys realize they are now in danger and time is not on their side. The bus finally got to their stop just two blocks away from the house.

As tired as they both were, they ran all the way home. The boys saw Mom's car parked in the driveway, they open the front door and went inside. Mom was standing there talking to a man named Thomas Wolf. The boys opened the door and entered the house. Right away Mom said, "Hi boys, how was your day?

Oh yes, this Mr. Wolf from the institute where your father used to work. He just stopped by to check in on us – wasn't that nice of him? This is Peter and Alex my two sons." "Yeah – of course" said Mr. Wolf "genuinely nice to meet you both. Wow, you boys sure are all grown up now. I hear good things about the two of you, like going to college and both ending your third year now – that is impressive! Yes, it is you are last year – well not, you are last year – right? I mean you're both in the fast class, so one year left – is that correct?" Peter looked at the man and said, "Well, more or less – yes we're doing well in school. Thanks for asking. Mom, what is for dinner? We are starving!"

"Now boys, there's time, the two of you are not starving! OK – OK I get it! I picked up mushroom cheeseburgers and chili fries. They are in the oven on warm." "Oh – OK, good." Alex says. "Well, Mr. Wolf" Mom says to her visitor "it looks like I better get my boys fed – it's dinner time. Thanks for stopping by. OK, good night."

As Mom closed the door, Alex reaches over and puts his hand across Mom's mouth. She made a sound, but Peter comes over and whispers in her ear "Mom – don't. The house is bugged and has been for the last four years. Please don't say anything – they are listening."

As Alex took his hand off Mom's mouth, she quietly followed her boys to the backyard Alex looks at his mother and says "look we need to know the truth now. Peter and I know everything, including the fact that Dad took off in the craft and had been at the cabin. Yeah Mom, we know. We want to hear it from you! Tell us!" "Alright" Mom responds "it was four years ago, when your father was working. He came across a flash – like the ones the two of you did. Yes, I know about that. Anyways – like yourselves, the flash hit your father one night as he was getting off work, walking to his car and he said so.

He flew up in the air then fell hard back down. He hit his head and back hard. He was knocked out for a while. When he finally opened his eyes, he touched his head and noticed it was bleeding a little. He went back to work, grabbed a wash towel, and washed down the spot on his head bleeding.

Afterwards, he walked back out to his parked car, got into it, and drove home.

When he walked through the door, he told me what happened. I cleaned his head; he took a shower and went to bed. The next morning, your father saw what the two of you did – the directions to a world beyond your father's imagination and cannot be seen through any telescope lens. Well, what happened then was your father put the directions he saw into the computer at work. It showed him a line with an arrow initially and a line that went straight up passed any point your father knew about, into a different solar system. I mean it was off all the charts your dad had or knew about. It was then your father got threats from his superiors and from other sources.

He did not know who it was – only that it was from high up. They knew your dad had found information leading him to what we now know was the white door." "OK" Alex asked, "but how did his superiors know that?" "Well," Mom told them "Someone had been going through your father's work.

It was he deleted his work so no one could track anything." "Well OK so they found out enough information" Peter responded. "Yeah" Mom said, "I guess your father couldn't erase everything. "Therefore, they eventually found out what he was working on. When your father refused to turn the information over, they plotted his death.

Only your dad was ready for them. He knew what they were up to, so he wore a bulletproof vest. When they came after him and shot him, he laid down and died. I had a friend who worked in the morgue. He removed the vest and temporarily stopped his heart. When they came to check on him, it looked he was dead. The doctor gave me a death certificate; I had a coffin and a phony funeral to cover everything up. Look, I did not have a choice. I had to protect your father and my husband and don't forget – the rest of us were in danger at that time."

Well, we get it and understand that saying something – anything would have resulted in certain death for all of us," responded Alex. "I mean are you aware that for the last 4 years our house was being bugged?" asked Peter "No, I didn't know and to tell the truth I am glad really." "Why?" asked Alex. "Well, if they thought we knew, they would have given us away," Mom replies "besides, for the last four years it really sounded natural.

"Well, that is true," said Alex "so at least they don't think we know anything." "OK" says Peter "Alex and I get it.

We understand, mostly, what happened and why." Mom replies "but I know what you're going to ask – look no! We could not have gone for reasons. Your father needed you both here. Now you're ready." "OK – yes we are," said Peter. "He sent you the directions" Mom replied. "Yes, we have them" Alex said. "OK" answered Mom it is time to leave. I have been ready for this day for years now. OK, what do we do first?" "It's already done," said Peter.

"We have gone back inside" replies Mom "but first you two need to put the craft on the trailer now and cover it up.

OK, let us move!" As they, get attached the trailer to the car, backing up the car and rolling the craft from the garage to the trailer. They secure it down and lock it with straps on both sides. The boys finished, they got the cover out and threw it on top of the craft, tying it down with ropes to secure it in place.

Alex pulls the car into position getting ready to leave. They both go back in the house and see what else to be done. "Mom!" Peter calls out. "Hey in here!" she yells out. "Where's the cabin at?" Peter asks her. "Well, it's about fifty miles from here" Mom responds. "Don't worry – the house is not in our name – it's our house, but so that it can't be traced, we put it in our friend's name."

"Alan?" Alex asks, "Oh – is he there?" "I don't know" Mom answers him. "We should call now! OK, both of you go and pack what you're going to need, and I will make the call." As Susan calls Alan at the cabin, the boys throw clothes in bags, including their laptops.

They loaded the car and truck with everything they will need on their journey. Mom is yelling out to the boys "are you done? Hurry up! What about your stuff?" "OK" says Peter to her "I'm packing now! As Mom runs upstairs with bags in hand – she throws her clothes in and the rest of her things.

She runs back downstairs and puts everything in the car. Mom gets ahold of Alan and says, "Are you home? Are you there at the cabin?" "Yes," Alan says. "It's time," Mom said. "Are you sure?" Alan responds. "Yes, we need your help and we're leaving now" Mom replies.

"OK bye" Alan said. The boys move the car to the front of the house and parked it in the driveway. They put the rocket suits, helmets tools and other items they might need for later. They both run back in and grabbed food boxes from the kitchen. "I don't think the truck will hold the trailer and the craft together," Mom tells them "So you boys hurry up and switch it over now." "OK Mom" Alex replied. As the boys were finishing unhooking and re-hooking up the trailer, they reload the craft onto the truck.

After they finished, they loaded up blankets, medicine, and cases of soda too. "OK" Mom yells out "everything else stays. Boys, go back into the house, shut down everything, and turn off the power. I have already called the power, Phone Company, cable, and water. Everything will be turned off first thing in the morning. OK – is everything secured and locked up?" "Yes, and everything is turned off also" Alex tells her.

"OK" Mom replies, "You boys take the truck and please drive the speed limit! If a police officer follows you or gets close, I want you too slow down and whatever you don't panic!" "OK Mom" Peter says, "We will follow you." "All right" Mom tells them "But stay right behind me – you hear me? OK then, turn the house alarm on." "OK Mom – did it!" Alex replied. "Well put in your earpiece and plug in your phone so we can talk back and forth. Let us roll!" Mom pulls out and stops at the corner. She looks for her boys and sees them. She drives ahead about eight blocks down to the freeway entrance. They approach the freeway setting their blinkers on and motioning as they enter.

They look back in their rearview mirror, making sure they are not being followed. Mom calls her boys when the phone rings Peter answers "yeah Mom?" "Is your speaker on? OK well, just to let you know stay alert! We have another forty-five miles to go – OK. "We'll be alright" Peter replies. "Look we are all dead, you guys realize that?" she tells them "There is no way they are going to stop now, because you both found out the truth.

The little secret is out they were trying to keep hidden. You know guys– they must think that his sons knew what their father was working on." "No Mom!" Alex asks, "Why would they think that?" "Because" Mom replies "if they thought you two knew the truth, they would have already come after us."

"Well maybe not then, but now – yes" Mom replied "and this time – if they even think you boys really know the numbers, the same numbers your father knew . . . I'm telling you– we can't go back home for a while" she tells them. "Well, I have emergency cash that's around $10,000" Mom continued "but we'll have to close the bank accounts." "I think we're going to have to wait on that," Alex told her. "You can't be seen going back into town. You know our house, school, your work is all being watched."

"OK" Mom responds, "Well, I will get you settled then go back and try to take care of some business." "I don't think you should do that," Alex tells her. "Let us just wait and talk about this when we get to the cabin. Look Mom, it is all of us on the line now – not just you. Let us see if we can arrange someone else to close the bank accounts, manage the house and other things.

OK?" They arrived at the cabin and suddenly stopped. They waited for a minute for the electric fence to be turned off and the gate to open. They went around to the back of the cabin to the large brown garage in back. They got out, unloaded the craft into the garage, locked the door, unhooked the trailer, and stored it up against the wall on the backside of the garage.

The boys drove the truck around to the front of the cabin and parked the truck in the garage, right next to Mom's car. The boys unloaded the truck and brought everything into the cabin. "Hey boys" Mom tells them "This is Tom Winters. He is a friend of your father and knows. He collaborated with your dad too." Tom tells them "I helped your dad plan his escape which save his life and save your life and your mom as well.

If he stayed, they would have tracked your dad and used his family against him. He knew it – your dad was not going to allow his family to be hurt or used as pawns in this dangerous and twisted game. "Well, OK" Alex replies, "We have to get going – what's the plan?" "I have to take care of the bank and the house," Mom tells Tom. "You can't go back there" Tom replies "so I have a friend who works at the bank.

I will call him." Tom makes the call to his friend at the bank on his cell phone. "It's Tom, we have a 911 on Bower account. Shut it down now! Put the cash in an envelope and I will be there within an hour." "OK" his friend says to Tom "but you'll need to fax me a signature card and I will erase everything else." "Yeah good" Tom replied. "Leave no trace" his friend says, "Got it. "I already sold the house and got $100,000 in cash; it pays to have contacts" Tom smiles. "The bank will shut down my accounts and I faxed over my signature. He's a friend of mine, so I don't have to go in and he will meet me in a few minutes down the road at the cafe." "Tom and I will go to the cafe to pick the banking envelope and we'll be back in a few minutes," Susan tells her boys.

Tom and Susan get in the vehicle and head down to the café. Once they were in the car, Tom hands Susan a gun and asks her to put it in the glove box. "It's just in case," he says. "OK" answered Susan. They head to the café to manage the last-minute details. They get to the café; Susan meets with a friend who works at the bank and is closing her account.

The friend looks at Susan as she sits down. She hands him the signature card and title to the house. He gives her the large yellow envelope with the cash in it. "Thanks, so much Michael," she tells him. "You're welcome," he says. "Is there anything in the house you want or need Susan?" he asks her. "No" she tells him. "OK, well I better get going. Thanks again" he responds. Susan walks quickly to the car and shuts the door. Tom looks at Susan and asks, "Is everything OK?" "Yes" she says with a smile "now let us get the hell out of here and back to the cabin." As they drove back, Peter called and checks in on Mom. Her phone rings and she answer it. "Oh Peter," she says. "Is everything OK" Peter asks her. "Yes" she says "we are done and there, just a couple miles away now.

Be there in a moment." "OK" Peter replied, "See you in a minute – bye." Tom and Susan get back to the cabin and everyone goes inside. Tom says, "I am leaving you now." "Oh" Peter said, "where are you going?" "It's better that no one knows the location where I'll be, but I do have a radio. Your father and you boys will have the frequency, so you can reach me in case of anything should happen." "OK" Susan said. Peter and Alex say thanks. Tom tells them "Try not to worry.

I have a RV and I will be mostly traveling. I just want to say thank you for everything. Your friendship and Rob's friendship have meant the world to me." Susan looks at her friend and thanks him "we love you too and please take care of yourself – be safe." "Well," Tom tells them the three of you better be thinking of taking off yourself soon." Peter and Alex are outside in the garage. "I think that we need to talk" Alex says to his brother. "Yes OK," said Peter. "Are you aware of the fact that Mom is coming with us?" asked Peter. "Yeah" said Alex "but Dad got the invitation and so did the two of us, but Mom wasn't invited. Look, do not worry so much, nothing bad will happen if she comes with us. I believe that if Dad is there – and we both think he is then Mom has permission and do not worry.

It is out of our hands. If it is not meant to be then it will not happen. A force greater than us will send their own message to us. I just realized something standing here in the middle of the garage." Peter looks at Alex and asks, "What's that?" "The rocket fuels!" Alex says. "We never placed our order." "Well," Peter responds "we can't launch without fuel" "Well I think there must be fuel here, Dad was always prepared" Alex answers. "Let's start to look around" Peter responded. "OK" Alex answers.

The boys look in the garage for the fuel. Alex leaned against a long wooden table up against the wall. As he leaned in, suddenly the wall behind the table opens and – holey molly – there was the fuel. The boys loaded the fuel. "Hurry" said Peter "before something happens." "OK" Alex answers. They both took turns grabbing one tank at a time. They walk over to the craft with the tanks of fuel for the craft.

After the fueling was completed, Peter goes into the craft, puts the numbers, and directions into the on-board computer system. Alex goes back into the garage, gets the rocket suits, and helmets. They load them into the craft. The boys then load up all the freeze-dried food and secure it into the small wall freezer and lock everything down.

Peter and Alex grab their clothes to store in the craft. After running around and trying to get the craft ready to launch, they finally move the craft outside. The boys put the craft onto the launch pad signaling they were ready to launch. Peter stops and looks at his brother and asks, "Do you think Mom is going with us?" Alex looks at his genuinely concerned brother and says, "well already talked about this." "Yes" Peter said, "but really, what do you think?" "I don't know what the universe has in store" Alex replied "but Mom wasn't exactly invited to come along, and I hate to think what's going to happen next. You and I better hang on tight because something evil is coming this way."

As they were talking Peter's phone rings its Mike from the agency. "Oh" said Alex "just a second Mike, I will put you on speaker." Mike says, "I have something to tell you and it's not good. "OK" Alex replies "well, what's that?" The boys they knew NASA went through the computer their home office bugged, it is the only way they could have known the things we talked about.

Mike tells them "I think you both better blasts off now! They are or should be there with armed guards and guns. Look, they have orders to shoot you both and stop you at all costs from launching your craft. They will use your mother against you, or try too, if they get a hold of her. Please be careful and leave now." "OK, thanks for the heads-up" Alex responded, "OK no problem – bye." Peter and Alex run back into the house screaming "they are almost here we got to leave now! Come on get to the craft!" Mom is running outside, the boys board, putting their suits on and grabbing the extra one Dad must have had – they found it in the garage – for Mom. As Mom is one-step of the house running, she hears something. She suddenly stops, turns around, and sees gunmen all around the property. Mom screams out and the two boys run to the craft and board it.

They turn on the switches and engines. The gunmen grabbed Mom by her arm and took her down. As she fell on the ground, they point a gun to her head. Ordered the boys to turn off the engines. The boys looked at their mother – she gave them both a little wink and they knew – she must have had a plan. Therefore, the boys strapped themselves into their seats.

The engines fired one by one and the craft sways and shake back and forth. The boys knew this was the decisive moment for them both. Then, they see their mother suddenly throw dirt into one guard's eye. She then runs into the garage. She locks the door and takes a secret elevator down to a room her husband had built. There in the room stood a transporter – and her way out.

As she turns it on, she could hear the guards breaking down the door. She leapt into this magic mirror transporter – hoping it would take her to Rob. She remembered him saying, "Just turn it on and leap – see you soon." As she leaps into the wondrous invention he built, a giant explosion took place leaving nothing behind – not even a trace for anyone to find.

CHAPTER NINE

TO THE UNIVERSE AND BEYOND

"I know she ran into the garage for a reason, and she had it all planned out." Alex said to his brother. "OK, so what is that supposed to mean?" Peter replied. "Well," Alex responded, "I would say, if I was a betting . . ." "Don't say man," answered Peter, as he laughed. "OK – OK," said Alex. Peter asks, "but if I was a betting man you would say what?" Alex responds, "That she is with Dad – as we speak. They both planned it and now they are waiting for the two of us." "Well, it's a nice theory," said Peter.

"I guess we will just have to wait and see what happens. I mean, after all, let us just hope they send us a sign." "Well," Alex says, "Let us not forget the secrets the universe has given us." "Yes" Peter answers him "to the white door." "Yes" Alex responded, "and don't forget to press the button now, so that we can't be tracked." "Already done," said Peter. "We have an invitation to attend" Alex tells his brother. "Yes, we do" say Peter "and I'm going to say it!" "Alright brother" answers Alex "goes ahead on. "TO THE UNIVERSE and BEYOND!" As the twin brothers shoot off beyond the stars and the passed the Milky Way, they both wonder with excitement and curiosity.

With every mile reached brings them closer to the door in space. A world beyond their imagination lies wait for the two twin brothers that will soon knock on their door. As they turn the music on and it is blasting away, the boys sit back and listen to a little of (Train) fifty ways to say goodbye, the (the Doors) break on through and (Dire Straits) money for nothing. The darkness of the universe above contacts the stars that shine bright next to our small window.

 As we look out, it seems like we can just reach our hands out and bring them closer to our world. "I can recall," said Peter "and really . . . it reminds me of a song that Mom used to sing to us. Do you remember it? "I do" and so the song (CATCH

A FALLING STAR PUT IT IN YOUR POCKET SAVE IT FOR A RAINY DAY).

As the boys continue their journey into space and the unknown, they laugh and remember times of happiness and sorrow. As they wish themselves a happy 15th birthday. "Happy birthday brother and we couldn't have asked for a better birthday present than us being together on this magical wondrous adventure." "So how long did we figure it would take before we reach our own little place of happiness?" asked Peter.

"I don't think either one of us knew for sure" answered Alex. "We plotted the course and put the numbers into the computer, now we are on autopilot. The craft is on course to take us there – all we must do is enjoy the ride to the docking station. It looks like it's going to be awhile." "Right" asked Peter "you mean days?" "I think it will take us longer than that to get where we are going" answered Alex "but I do hope it will be worth it." "Yeah, hope so too" said Peter "well stop teasing – you know how long!" Sorry brother" answered Alex "just having a little fun."

"All we have now" Alex continued "is the certainty that the two of us we will face something new and different and the both of us will be welcomed in this place. We are risking everything for a future that is not clear to either of us. We're not even sure or clear what we will face when we dock, what will happen when knock on the door and who will wait for us on the other side of the white door."

"Well," answered Peter "we will be there soon enough, and our questions will be answered as soon as someone opens the door and welcome us in." "Well brother" Alex replied, "Look at the universe and the sky – have you ever seen anything so amazing? Look of those stars in the heavens above!" "Shoot," said Peter "I still can't believe that we're here now, looking out of the small window in our craft and seeing, right before our eyes, this absolutely amazing view."

"Yeah" said Alex "and how do two brothers say thank-you to someone we not only don't know but we haven't even met yet."

"I wish Mom and Dad were with us right now" Peter said. "To be able to see what is right in front of our eyes. I wish our parents didn't have to pay such a heavy price." "It's really not fair that they're not sitting with us and be able to reach out and to touch them both." As the boys get closer and closer to their destination, the sky above looks a little different in colors, more of a darker blue with hardly any stars out in the galaxy.

As the boys check, the onboard computer system to make sure that their heading is correct for this point in time. Rechecking their numbers and doing figuring to make sure everything is spot on. The course and directions they are heading now is where the boys must be. Alex and Peter realize that if they are off even a little bit, they will be stuck in space at a place in a peculiar spot that is incorrect.

As they continue traveling to the unknown destination in space, the boys realize an opportunity has been given to them to go somewhere no one knows about and is unheard of. Remarkably, by itself – they are both here for the long run – no matter what happens to them. They will deal with any danger that might come their way together by standing physically and mentally strong against whatever across their path. They realize they are not sure what will look and staring at them face to face.

The boys cannot wait to finally see the platform that will allow them to dock their craft right before their eyes. They will finally get to see the famous white hanging door that will drop down and allow them to finally knock on it and enter a world much different from their own world. "I'm sure we'll calm down and relax a little, and at least then we'll get to explore as well as find out what kind of place it's going to be because really – it might just be home" says Alex.

They kept themselves busy measuring fuel and running tests to make sure everything was running correctly. They sit back and enjoy the ride, discussing what will come and what will happen. They are hoping the rest of the ride will be rock free. "Well Peter" said Alex "it's time for us to go into the sleep chamber – it will keep us from aging in space.

We will awake when we get to the station pad and dock," said Alex. "OK brother" Peter responds "but if anything happens . . ." "Like what?" asked Alex. "You know – like a meteor shower or rocks hurling at us," "Look Peter" answered Alex "you know as well as I do in the event we are caught in danger – well please don't be nervous or scared – our locks won't open until we get there.

However, if the craft shaken and our sleep chamber are disturbed, the seal will be broken, and we will awake. The two of us will deal together whatever emergency has awakened us to begin with." Alex and Peter enter the sleep chamber, the seal locks and affix the oxygen masks to cover their face for breathing. The two are put into a deep sleep until they arrive at their destination. As the boys sleep away in their chambers, their course is plotted for an unknown place, they sleep and have no worries or concerns until the moment arises and they are in danger, or they have both arrived at a place they call the white door. Well to tell you the truth, the boys are not sure what the place is called. They mentioned the word Star Zone because of a dream they had. If you asked them, they would simply just say

"Well shoot – you must call it something, so we did and we're not quite sure if, in fact, our dreams came across the right way." Dreams can sometimes be difficult to figure out their true meaning. A story behind dreams like a name of a place, including a different world, which might be called the Star Zone. As the two brothers sleep, it seems like it was just yesterday. Five years have gone by already.

Their journey seems right on course. They both sleep and the craft adjust directions, staying right on course, while the boys sleep away in their chambers. It is the evening hours, and all is quiet when the craft makes a slight turn in direction toward their path to the docking platform, which will lead them both to the white door. The sky is looking clear when suddenly, giant rocks were heading right toward the craft. rocks were small, but as the craft kept going in the path of the boulders, were changing sizes, and looked medium size and much larger ones. The craft can maneuver but cannot turn away from the large boulders directly in their path.

As the rocks come closer and closer, the craft shakes as the meteors hit the craft on each side. The boulders were growing, the danger grew. Since there were too many, the craft could not maneuver its way out of danger. As the craft shook violently and spin, an alarm sounded signaling the sleep chamber, waking up the boys, causing the locks to unlatch and the doors opened.

The boys awoke to alarms ringing and the craft shaking. They awake and put on their suits, heading to the front seats, and buckling themselves in. "OK Peter" said Alex "let us see if we can get ourselves out of this mess. Let us see if we can go above the storm and take control." The boys try to move the craft away from the meteors moving straight toward them. They were trying to go up and away from the storm and it was working, but they were hitting still more boulders. Alex looks at Peter and says, "We've got to get away, or the storm and these boulders are going to rip the craft apart." As the two brothers were sitting up and looking ahead, they realize the storm was ending and the rocks disappeared.

Alex looks at Peter and says, "You'd better reset the course." "Yeah OK" answered Peter, who then asked, "hey, just how long was we asleep?" Peter gets up to look at the locks and the timer to see. Well," said Peter "it appears we were sleeping for five years!" "Oh really" said Alex "well the two of us didn't age!"

"No, we didn't" Peter said "but we are five years older and that makes us 20 years old now – wow! We still look like kids – weird huh?" "Yeah" Alex responds, "we might think like adults, but on the outside our bodies are the same – we haven't age at all! "Well, what now?" Peter asks. "I don't know," answered Alex "look at the computer, does it give any kind of status on how far away we are to the door?" "Well," Peter responds, "it looks like we're just days away." "Well said Peter" answers Alex "we better stay awake and wait for the platform to appear so we can dock the craft." "Well, OK" says Peter "but we won't know until it just appears right on top of us." "OK" answers Alex "look out and pay attention to anymore storms or anything else. We better check for damage to the craft." "OK" Peter said, "I'm on it, but first we need to get some water." "Alright" answers Alex "but remember, the water's going to float up when you open it. "Yeah, I know" Peter says. "OK then, hang on" Alex responds, "I need a candy bar. Got a major sweet tooth craving!" "Yeah, me too!" said Alex "grab me one too." "You bet" Alex tells him.

The boys float over to the storage closet to get candy bars and water. Peter grabs each as they take a break to drink and eat. After taking a break, the boys get up and damage control. They look over the craft after the storm and check to see if they suffered any major problems from the meteors smashing up against the craft.

After righting down and readjusting the craft, the boys feel they are ready. Everything on the craft is fine and no major problems occurred from the storm. The boys go over to their seats and buckle themselves in. They keep an eye out for any signs of trouble with any more storms approaching. As they look on, Alex is studying the universe.

Checking for any more signs of trouble heading their way. "Anymore candy bars?" Alex asks. "Yeah" said Peter "would you like Nutter Butter or Butterfinger?" "It doesn't matter; I like them both!" smiles Alex. As they sit and eat their candy bars, they look out the windows on both sides of the craft, keeping an eye out for any signs of trouble.

As Peter and Alex look out, Peter sees something ahead of the craft. Alex says, "Peter looks out your window." "I am!" answers Peter. "Well look to your right" responds Alex "what's that coming toward us?" "It looks like a craft," says Peter. "Yeah, it does" Alex answers "and it's huge – my God!" Alex looks at the size of that thing coming toward them. "OK there's something else," Peter sees.

"Yeah, what's that?" asked Alex. "It appears to be not moving and there's no light on it" Peter responds. "Yeah, I see that," said Alex "well keep looking, because it's dark and just orbiting in one spot." "Yeah, I see that" Peter says, "very strange indeed." "Well let's get closer to it and see if there's anything around the outside." "OK" answers Alex "and let us turn our overhead spotlight on.

Shine it slowly as we look around to see if can notice anything moving. Also, look for a name or a serial number on the side of the craft." As this mysterious spaceship comes closer and closer to Alex and Peter's craft, they slow down and aim their light on the dark craft floating right next to them. Peter puts on his helmet and hooks up the hose attached to the craft outside.

He then opens the airlock door behind him. As Peter gets close to the dark spaceship, he flashes his light to see if he can get a name or a serial number on the spaceship.

Peter flashes his light on the craft – he cannot see a name or any numbers. Nothing seems to be on the side of the ship.

As he grabs his rope, Peter pulls himself closer to the front of the spaceship and looks for a latch to open the door and go outside. Alex drops anchor next to the ship, puts on his helmet, and joins Peter outside near the top of the dark ship. Peter pulls his brother closer. They both see the ships hatch door, they open it up, walk inside and unhook their hoses then hooked them both up to the wall next to the door.

Peter finds the light switch on the wall by the door, which light a long corridor, and down a long hallway, but no one seems around. The boys yell out "HELLO is there anyone here? Anyone need help?" As they continue walking around, they went to the control room and the deck, As Alex pressed the button on the wall, the door opens to the control room.

They both entered the room looked at the computer system console. They could find no information. The brothers see a video player on the console. As they press the play button, the screen shows a man that might have been a captain or a leader. It said that he was a savage hunter, and he picks up alien's life forms and sells them at a nearby star post.

As the boys are watching this, they now think that it might be a trap. "OMG! Peter!" says Ales "let's get the hell out of here!"

As the boys take off running, they try to get back to the door hatch, hook up their hoses, and enter their own ship. They hear a voice as they were running toward the door. It came over the intercom. A voice saying, "Where you two aliens think you're going? Once you enter and board my ship, you are mine to keep or sell. This is the law of space.

I am Harry T. Bone, and you aren't going anywhere." The boys stop and raise their visor up and said "you can't keep us here . . . we're on a mission. We have invitation from the door." "Wait one damn minute" the voice says, "that is impossible – no one gets an invitation!" "Well, we did, and we have the course already in our computer. We are heading there to the door, and you will not stop us. We have come from a different galaxy. We have been in space for 5 years now and are getting closer to our destination."

Harry asks the boys what galaxy you are from. The boys answer back "Earth." "You are lying!" screamed Harry. "Well," Peter yells back "that is twice now that you have said the impossible! You were wrong the first time and guess what! You are wrong this time! It does not change that my brother and I are from Earth . . . and we received an invitation from the white door to come . . . so we are their guest."

The boys yelling back continued when Peter said, "now what part of this conversation are you lost in, Mr. Harry T. Bone?" There was a silence for a while and the boys were thinking they were out of the woods, so they continue walking to the door hatch.

They hooked up their hoses, opened the hatch, walked out the door, and closed it behind them. The boys reached their craft, unhooked their hoses, opened the door, and went inside. Alex and Peter were so shaken up by the experience as they sat down and belted themselves into their seats. They started to unattached themselves from the other spaceship, when, on the intercom, they heard from Harry T. Bone.

The captain of the craft saying to them. "To the brothers from a different galaxy called Earth. On a long journey from home to the white door in space, you may continue your journey with no further disruptions from me, Harry T. Bone savage hunter in space.

Good luck to you both in your journey to the door. You must be incredibly special guests to get an invitation from so far away from your home." "Thank-you" the boys said back and asked Harry "what is the white door? And what is behind this mysterious place." Harry laughed at the boys and said, "You mean you don't know about the door?" "No!" said the boys "we just got an invitation and we're looking for our parents who went ahead of us.

So here we are – together accepting the invitation from a world far, far away we have never heard of before. Can you tell us what is behind the door?" Harry answered them "it's like nothing you have seen before or will ever again. In your wildest imagination boys!

You cannot begin to imagine this world. Good luck to you and I hope your search and your journey ends with all your expectations and your dreams fulfilled. It is a world like no other – that is what I can say. stay forever and others only stay for a day. Hope it is everything to you both. Goodbye and good journey to you twin brothers. Goodbye from Harry T Bone and bye to you – Alex and Peter. We will see each other again when you need me the most."

Well, the craft pulled away and Harry T. Bone is still on his search for alien life forms to capture and make his money. He leaves meeting two brothers from a different galaxy called Earth, the boys venture on into space, and they can still hear him laughing as they disappeared out of sight. They are going to a different world much different from their own.

A place that will bring their imaginations, to a new level.

Well, every step closer they take to the door – excitement grows. Even more as the boys try to imagine what kind of a place it will be but still no matter how hard they try a part of them can still hear Harry T. Bone saying 'you can't imagine such a place. stay forever and others just for a day. Good wishes Earth boys, your journey will end, and the door will open.'

The boys travel on and after hours passed, Peter is looking ahead out of the window. Alex says, "well Peter, according to the numbers – we have reached our new place." They both looked out and saw nothing yet. Peter looks at his brother and says, "Should we be worried – there is nothing here."

"Well hang on" answered Alex "maybe we just need to be a little closer, so that the docking station can appear." As the boys and their craft grow closer and closer . . . suddenly, Peter says, "Alex – look! The docking station is right there! Oh, my GOD! It is real . . . it is real.

I knew it but I was not sure. But now it has appeared before our eyes." The boys have a total look of amazement. "OK" says Alex "let us park this craft."

As the boys get closer, they finally reach the docking station. When their craft gets close enough to dock, the station grabs the craft and pulls it in.

A loud breaking sound was heard and then they had stopped . . . the craft was dock. "Well Peter" said Alex "we are here . . . what do you say?" "Well," answered Peter "I say let us step onto this platform at this docking station and see the white door." "OK" answers Alex "remember, keep the helmets on – there is no air in space. "OK" Peter responds. As the brothers, open the hatch door, with their spacesuits and helmets still on.

The boys take their first step onto the docking station, and in doing so, the white door appeared right before their eyes. The brothers seem nervous, but they have waited so long for this moment in time and space. They look at each other and gave the thumps up and in doing so; they took one giant step forward and knocked on the door.

"Well, are you nervous?" asks Alex. "Yes, you are . . . aren't you?" "Yeah" answers Peter "but it's more curiosity than anything else. I wonder just how different things are, what it looks like and the people – if they are humans." "You know, we never talked about the fact that this place might not house humans, but something else," answers Alex. "Well, in any case, they want to know us" Peter responds.

CHAPTER 10

A LEAP OF FAITH

As the door opened, they realized they are not sure what would happen. The door opens wide and standing there in front of the two boys was a being that was half-human and half-canine. The boys just stood there and could not believe their eyes! They slowly lifted the visors on their helmets so they could get a better look at what was standing right in front.

The creature had a head of a lab dog; it was tall, stood straight up, and was looking at the two. It was black and had big floppy ears. The rest of the creature had human features. His neck had skin on it; his chest was big, puffy, and stuck out with ripples of muscles running through it. Our eyes moved downward to the rest of his body, which also had human form, as well his legs and his feet.

The creature knew how to dress – wearing a black suit with a red top hat and red tennis shoes.

"Hello Alex and Peter" he said to them both. "It sure did take you awhile to get here and we're all so happy the two of you finally made it. Welcome! Will not you please come in and stay forever or a day. Please hurry, he has been waiting for the two of you and we must not keep him waiting." The boys stepped through the white door, removed their helmets, looked at each other, and said "OMG! I didn't see that coming!" and started to laugh aloud.

The white door in time and space disappeared the moment they both stepped through and went down a spiral staircase into a new world. For a day or forever they can stay – so they say – won't you please come in? The boys followed this creature down a spiral staircase – their journey into a mysterious world is now getting remarkably interesting.

The boys are on their way to meet a mysterious stranger waiting for them. As the brothers find the underlying cause of the stairs, they can hear people walking and talking.

They walk through and tremendously . . . their eyes are seeing things they have never seen before. As they step on a sidewalk, it moves with their movements – every step they take. When they look around and over their heads, they are both in amazement.

There are double suns above during the day and the double moons in the evening hours. The building is bright in color – very tall and high upon the sky. Billboards are small or large. At the touch of a button, you can control their sizes. As they continue their path, the boys look above and see flying taxis in the sky – moving fast from one place to another.

There were no other cars in the sky only taxis that people are using. Everyone is walking or using a flying taxi. Peter whispers to Alex "you know there are no animals here and no pet shops. "Yeah, I noticed that too" Alex responded. "Kind of strange" Peter saw. "Yeah – just a little bit" Alex answers him. "What the hell was that?" Peter asks his brother. "That lady had on a leash?" "I don't know" says Alex "pet – you guess, but don't ask me!

I have seen nothing that looked like that ever."

"It looked blue," Peter, saw. "Yeah" agreed Alex "but it also had green on it, also wings, and feathers." "Yeah, bird - I guess," replied Peter "you saw it too?" "Yeah" Alex said, "but not in my lifetime!" "Did the bird look like that?" asked Peter. "Yeah" Alex says, "did you see those eyes – so big and round!" "Yeah" Peter replies "and . . . those eyelashes too! OMG – it was walking, standing upright, and talking!" "Let us keep moving" Alex said, "I'm sure there will be more to see – even more strange creatures and birds.

" As they walked on, Peter says "yes – look, check out those sidewalks – cool huh? When you step on them, they move. When you want to get off or stop, they just do." "Yeah, strange – but kind of cool at the same time" Alex seen.

The boys continued walking until they got to a large building made from glass and continued going up to a point where you cannot see it ends and there is no top. "OMG" Peter said looking at Alex "can you see that? He asked. "Yeah – now you know – that's a first!" "Sure is!" said Alex. The boys walked in the front entrance –

it was grand and spacious, filled with unusual looking people. As they continued walking, further into the lobby of this building, they saw a woman walking by and Peter said, "did you see that or am I crazy?" "No, you're not," replied Alex "because I saw it too!" Yes, she had three breasts and Peter try not to stare. "Oh, don't worry" Peter said to his brother "I won't be staring at her, because I will be looking at the man who has three eyeballs! He just walked by us brother." They walked to the elevators, waited for one to open its doors and take the two brothers to the top floor.

The doors opened, they got in and rode the elevator to the top floor. The elevator slowed down and finally stopped. Then the doors opened, they get off and walked down this long hallway.

They came to this tiny door with a doorbell next to it, which read, "For service – ring bell, then knock on door."

The boys looked puzzled – even if they rang the bell and knocked on the door – how were they going to fit in a door so tiny?

Peter and Alex looked at each other – confused. Peter said, "oh well, I guess we'll find out when we do what the sign says." "OK" said Alex "let us give it a try." He learned over and rang the bell then knocked on the door. Suddenly, the door grew large enough for both to walk in. As they walked in, a small Hobbit man greeted them both and said, "Please, come in – won't you stay for a while? Please have a seat."

The boys smiled and the thank-you. They sat down on two comfortable green chairs. "Thank-you for coming" the small Hobbit man spoke in a soft and gentle voice. "I am Alex, and this is my brother Peter. Are you the one that sent us the invitation to come?

Our father also sent us something saying he also might be here. Have you seen him?" "Well yes" the Hobbit man replies, "I sent you the invitation. My name is Thomas." "OK" replies Alex "why did you sent for us to come and what about our father.? "Well now" said Thomas "we have a problem here where everyone's lives are in danger.

I thought since the two of you are geniuses, you could help us. "Well," said Peter" how do you know the two of us are smart and what is the problem you would wait five years for us to come to help you?" "Well," said Thomas "I have been watching you two brothers grow up ever since you both were exceedingly small. Our special telescope allows us to see into other dimensions. I knew the two of you were special – so I guess we have always kept an eye on you.

We could see, as you were getting older, just how smart you were getting to be, how fast the two of you could catch onto things and how quickly you could solve almost any problem together. I must tell you something bad about your parents, your father. "Oh" said Alex and Peter "what about him? They asked. "He came here without an invitation" Thomas replied "and that's against the law – either punishable by life in the star zone space prison or death.

But since he was your father, we decided not to put him to death, but to imprison him instead."

"OK" Alex responded, "Am I to understand you stuck our father in prison for coming here!" "OMG – you can't do that. It's because of our father that my brother and I are here in the first place!" said Peter. Alex spoke up and said, "You don't understand, Mr. Thomas." "Yes Alex – I do and if you both think I don't know everything you would be wrong."

"I do know. OK – I know your father was the one who found our little world here and that other agencies on your planet tried to have your father killed for that information. Nevertheless, I will give it to your father – yes indeed – he is strong and determined. Not once did he give the location and directions to our little place here. However, boys, your father made the decision to fake his death and come here.

He entered our world through a portal he built and did so without permission." "OK" answered Alex "we get that. I understand you have rules here, but really! Maybe – just perhaps – our father did not know your rules and thought your world would treat him with kindness.

Welcome him since after all – you already knew of him and his family." "Yes brothers" Mr. Thomas replied, "I understand your concerns, but we here have rules, and your father was aware of these rules. He knew the consequences facing him and letting his wife come using the same portal. He is incredibly lucky to be alive and in prison and not sentenced to death. However, because of the two of you, we have spared the life of your father.

However, in exchange for us doing this for you, we will need aid with a problem facing our world. In return of your help and cooperation, we will release both your parents unharmed and let you live here among our people or within another portal of your choosing. However, please understand and make no mistake, if you refuse to help us with our problem, our planet will be in great harm and danger. I will have no choice but to sentence both your parents to death by releasing them out to the star zone prison portal chambers." "I don't understand" asks Peter "where the prison is."

"Its location is above our galaxy in space," Mr. Thomas tells them "It's a ship that can hold in the hundreds of thousands of prisoners at a time. It can't be detected or seen, so there is no escape from there." "OMG!" Peter says. "Look" Mr. Thomas tells them "We wanted the two of you to come and we had no idea your parents were going to do what they did and put everything in such jeopardy, including their own lives. The situation is serious now.

You boys must decide." "A decision – what decision?" asks Alex. "What need to be done?" Peter asked, "You have to make that made clear." "OK" Alex asks him "can you tell me and my brother the situation here and how you think we can help you and your people Mr. Thomas?"

As the boys sit and listen, they ask Mr. Thomas what the name is here. Mr. Thomas looked at Peter and said, "It's called Star Zone. "Oh, OK, thank you for that information" Peter replied. "Well, I need to show you the source of our problem" Mr. Thomas tells them we must hurry.

We must go all the way to the other side of town called 'Star Zone Twin Towers'." "And what is the twin towers?" asked Alex "Well the towers hold our energy and give us light and is an energy source to power the taxis. You might have noticed; they are our only source of transportation here.

No other vehicles are necessary. Without it, we would all be in the dark. We could not exist without it. It allows us to have our two solar suns." "Yes" Alex replies, "we saw them." So, the tower, when fully energized – powers up our solar suns" Mr. Thomas explains "making it warm/hot. It also has special abilities like the creatures that live here.

It allows them all to walk upright among us and have Special Forces to speak among us. It all works together, and one could not work without the other. OK – so do you both understand what I have explained to you?" asked Mr. Thomas. "Why yes, we do. But what is the tower that holds the energy made from and where does the source of energy come from?" asked the brothers. "Well," said Mr. Thomas "the towers have always been here –

if I can recall. The source was found centuries ago in a dark forest near to here. It has in a secret place called the Grim Light Caves.

An extremely dangerous journey. The Grim Light Caves are not safe. There are hidden dangers everywhere. Deep within the cave walls holds the source of energy to our homes and our life. Without it, we could go into complete darkness. Panic and mayhem would arise, and riots followed by animals reversing back and attacking the humans."

"Look" Mr. Thomas continued "you should know something. we have sent many men out to find the energy source so we could replace the one we have now which we believe is failing but no one has ever come back alive." "Well," Peter said, "take us to the towers so we can see the energy source, what it looks like and see how it works." "OK" said Mr. Thomas "but I can't take you myself –

the journey is too far and too hard on my body." "Peter and I want to ask you something before we go any further," says Alex.

"Oh yes," said Mr. Thomas "what is it?" "Well," Alex replies, "we want to know if it's possible to see our father in prison and make sure he's there. Also, we have not seen our father for the last four years on earth plus another five we took to get here – so yes, a long time." Mr. Thomas looked at the boys and said, "Well I'm not sure that is going to be possible. No visitors are allowed.

"Well," said Alex "we have a problem. My brother and I will need proof you have our father in custody – could you help us out?" "Well," Mr. Thomas replies, "We need your help. If you refuse to help us out – well boys – I can end your parents right now and neither of you should worry about seeing them. However, I will tell you this, they are here and housed in our prison.

If you help us – we will return them in one piece." "Yeah, you keep saying that" answers Alex "but I tell you what – my brother and I are not going to help! So, goodbye – kill our parents! If you will not let us, see them, then really, we have no choice but to leave.

Because we will always wonder if you have them or not. We are sorry but taking your word with no proof is not something we can live with." "OK" Mr. Thomas said to the boys "come with me where we are going – just hurry up." The boys follow him back to the office. They all sit down. Then Mr. Thomas disappears and just leaves the boys sitting there.

As the boys are waiting, they are not sure for what – suddenly, a monitor switches on and right in front on their eyes they can see both their parents on the monitor. They were being speaking to – as both boys just sat there and watched. As they talked, Peter said, "Is that really them?"

"Well, it looks like them," said Alex. "Yeah" said Peter "no tricks!" "I don't know – these people seem a little desperate if you ask me," responded Alex. "Yeah" answered Peter "let us just listen to what they have to say OK?"

As they both continued listening, Mom said "please boys, do whatever they say. In return, they will let us go because of your valuable service in saving their world. I am OK and so is your father.

We are together in the same confinement area, so please do not worry if the both of you are helping Mr. Thomas – we will be fine. They have agreed to release us. I love you and so does your father. Please remember that all our faith now rests in both your hands – please save us. I do not want to be here – but at least your father and I can be together. He told me to tell you – look for within the Grim Light Cave the energy source to save their world.

Don't open any portals within the Grim Light Cave – danger is all around."

CHAPTER 11

THE TWIN TOWERS

Mr. Thomas tells them "I will send with you two guides who know the area, the way to the towers and can answer any questions you may have. OK boys, your guides will meet you out front; you will leave right away and report back as soon as you have done an assessment on the twin towers.

Then we can make a decision on the best way to oversee this situation of ours." Peter and Alex got ready to leave and meet up with their two guides who would take them to the towers and answer questions.

The boys leave Mr. Thomas' office, the door shrinks back to a tiny door, and they walk back down the hall to the elevators. They wait to go back down and out the main entrance lobby of the large glass building they just went into.

They stepped outside and waited for their guides to show up. Finally, two men approached, they stood there staring at them, as they were talking Alex looks at Peter and says, "Wow, this place keeps getting stranger by the second." "Yeah, it sure does," says Peter "do you know what, I don't think we are in Kansas anymore."

"Hello there" said Peter and Alex. "Are you both ready to go?" asked Jay Bear. "Yes" Alex answered and asked them "do you think we could get a bite to eat?" "Oh, I'm sorry" Jay Bear responded, "no one has offered you anything yet." "OK, yes let's go and eat, then we can be off to the towers."

"Oh" Peter responded, "that would be fine thanks!" They went with Jay Bear and Lion to the local eatery. They walked in and saw long old-fashioned tables – the kind that might have been in a castle in the old days, like with Robin Hood. They gathered at one table, sat down, and ate together. No one experience loneliness here. People here are very friendly, especially when it comes time to eat.

Everyone usually just walks in and sits down wherever they would see a group of people gathered. It is customary to gather, sit, and talk. It is outlawed that you would sit alone to feel lonely or despaired. People always gather, around others to brighten their mood and make others feel warm and accepted. It is also a customary practice the boys seemed to enjoy. They found a table, gathered with others, sat down with Lion and Jay Bear.

People all around them at the table were excited to see the new strangers from Earth here to hopefully to save their little place called Star Zone.

They talked and the boys felt very welcomed. They ate vegetables, eggs, cheese, and fruit on their plates. The people around them seemed interested and friendly toward them. Alex and Peter even thought that though they were in a different environment, at least they could always get something to eat and enjoy friendly conversation with their meal at a long table with Lion and Jay Bear.

Peter looked at Jay Bear and Lion and said "thank you for being nice to us. We have been alone for a long time, it's nice to have met you both and have new friends to enjoy a satisfying meal with." Jay Bear looked into Peter's eyes, smiled, and said, "You and your brother have been through quiet an ordeal. We are all happy you are here safe and well."

As Lion and Jay Bear stood up, they gave a toast "Here's to Peter and Alex – our new friends! Here's hoping they will always want to be here with us." Everyone yelled saying "Yes – Yes!" aloud to both, gently looking at them and saying "we do hope you will stay in our humble little place here in the Star Zone, where one can stay a day, a year or indeed forever, my dears. At that moment, everyone in the eatery stood up cheered aloud to them.

Alex and Peter stood up and said "thank-you all very much. What can my brother, and I say nice of you to ask us to stay here for a day or a year or even forever. We will consider that!" Everyone screamed out "

Yes! Yes!" with laughs and cheers as they clicked their glasses to the boys. Everyone then sat back down and finished eating. Jay Bear and Lion told them it was time to leave and go to the towers. They all got up, headed for the door, and stopped a flying taxi. Everyone got in and headed off to the towers, so the boys could check out the energy source and see what was causing its failure.

The boys were going to the other side of Star Zone to check out the twin towers and the energy source. They arrived after time had passed, which was hours later. The taxi stopped, they all got out. The towers were later, and they must walk the rest of the way. Lion, Jay Bear, Alex, and Peter walked on a dirt path surrounded by trees on either side.

Jay Bear tells the boys "There are dangers out here, but nothing will happen if you stay on the dirt path. Do not wander off the dirt path – no matter what. I hope both of you understand." "Yes, we do," answered Alex. "OK" Jay Bear responded, "let us continues on then." The boys and their guides were walking later and saw a tree, which had fallen on path "Shit," said Lion. "What's wrong?" asked Peter.

"It's a trap" Lion responded. "What do you mean a trap?" asked Peter. "We see is a tree which has fallen on the path," replied Lion. "Yes" said Jay Bear "that is a problem, because you can't walk off the path. Remember?" "Yes, OK" says Alex "but let us see if all four of us can pick the tree up and throw it off the path." "Yeah, promising idea!" said Jay Bear. "OK" said Alex "1-2-3-Lift!" They lift the large and heavy tree up. "OK" Jay Bear says, "now on three – let us throw it!" They all let go of the tree simultaneously.

It flew up in the air and successfully landed on the left side of the path toward trees. They all smiled, saying "excellent job guys!" They then continued. Lion let the boys know the tower is just ahead now and is not far away.

The boys are walking behind Lion and Jay Bear; they can see the tower ahead of them. "Wow! Can you see those towers ahead?" exclaimed Peter Yeah" said Alex "my god – look how tall they are! "It is so amazing. I never seen anything like it in all my life," said Peter. They look like two dark towers with remarkable markings on the sides.

The towers had sixty steps, which led to the tower that held the energy source. They walk up close to the tower and enter a door off to the side of the tower. They started the long climb to the top where it is open, round and has a hole in the center on the ground. In the hole is a metal rod sticking straight up and as a round disk attached to the rod.

The disk is made of glass, which opens. In the center of the open glass lies a rectangle shaped impression that holds a solar bar. When charged, it powers their city Star Zone.

"The boys look closely at the solar bar, and noticed it was getting less bright with more dim light. Peter asked Lion "how long before it loses energy all together and needs to be replaced?"

Lion looks at them and says, "Well guys, we're not sure. Sometimes it flickers and we think it is going to go black now. However, it has been going from bright to dim for quite time now. We believe it could be fairly soon – no doubt that's for sure."

"After looking and studying the bar" Lion continued, "I think we might have less than three months before it stops working all together and goes totally black." "My God – are you sure?" asked Alex. "Lion and Jay Bear – what do you think?" asked Peter. "Well, I guess you don't have another bar to replace this one?" "No" said Jay Bear "we thought this one would last much longer. Well – it is not going to. We had better find a replacement in a hurry.

I do not even know if that is even possible. First, both of you don't even understand just how dangerous it is." "Well," said Peter "dangerous or not – we don't have a choice. We had better get back and talk to Thomas. He's going to want to discuss this matter to figure out the best solution for this horrible situation we're facing." "

OK" Jay Bear replies, "Let us get back and climb down the stairs and back outside." They walk back to the taxi, which was waiting for them. Back to Thomas went to have an emergency meeting about the solar bar and what they wanted to do.

Hours pass before they are back. in the city at the glass building. They enter and head straight to the elevators, back to the floor where Thomas' office is found. They got off the elevator, went down the hall, rang the doorbell, and knocked on the door once again.

The door grew tall, and everyone sat down to wait for Thomas. Thomas entered from another door off to the side. "Well gentleman" he says, "what do you think about the problem we're facing?" "Well Mr. Thomas" said Peter "I believe you have about three months left replace the solar bar that's losing its energy."

Are you sure?" Mr. Thomas asks, "Are you quite sure?" "Yes" said Alex "you can tell the center, inside of the solar bar, is really dim. Thomas, it would be a huge mistake to wait the entire three months to replace the solar bar; you must replace it right away. Oh, I was wondering," asked Peter "does the other tower have a solar bar?" Mr. Thomas looked around the room, and then said, "No, it doesn't, but the two are nevertheless connected."

"How?" asked Alex. "Well," Mr. Thomas responded, "We're not exactly sure, but we believe it has something to do with the markings which are on the side and all the way up the tower. When the other tower has the solar bar, it is put in the glass display on top and it works. I hope this gives you some understanding."

"Yes" said Peter "but what you are really saying is – the solar bar wouldn't work without the left tower and the markings on it." "Well yes," said Mr. Thomas. Peter asks "how long have those towers been there? I mean, have they always been where they are now?" "Yes said Mr. Thomas "for if we can remember, those towers been in the same spot for centuries."

"Well," responds Peter "I wouldn't mind figuring out what those markings mean and how they work together." "Well," said Thomas "as interesting as that may be, if the two of you decide to stay here, that might be something for you to do – research the markings. Anyway, right now have to discuss the failing solar bar."

"Well," said Jar Bear "we have no choice." We must go into the forest, back into the Grim Light Caves." "Oh, my!" Mr. Thomas said as he paced back and forth. "This is not good! Extremely dangerous! Oh, my!" "Yes, what a situation we are facing!" said Lion. "Yes, yes! Oh, my!" said Jay. Alex and Peter looked at the others in the room and wondered "OK" Alex said "it's a tough situation – yes, but we can find another solar bar.

I mean, it's not hopeless!" "It's not that simple," said Mr. Thomas. The forest is extremely dangerous – almost impossible to get through. Even if you were lucky enough, the Grim Light Caves! Oh, my! No one has made it out of there alive! We haven't been able to find another solar bar – extremely dangerous!" "Well, we don't have much of a choice, my friends," said Jay Bear. "OK" said Mr. Thomas "Lion, Jay Bear, Peter and Alex – you gather what instruments you'll need for your journey to the forest and into the Grim Light Cave."

Lion and Jay Bear are part of a special team unit to protect the citizens and are called upon when there is danger. They gathered the instruments they must protect themselves. Everything they have is handmade, except for the solar bar Ray made. The solar bar puts out small solar pulses powerful enough to knock someone down.

The Ray is his nickname – 'The Getaway Ray' because it allows you to emit small solar pulses that can affect you, giving you the ability to run away from your attacker, who is knocked out for seconds. They all left and gathered the tools for their journey to find the solar bar. They also gathered water pouches – because plastic does not exist here.

They also grab food to take with them. They all met with Mr. Thomas in the lobby of the glass building one more time before leaving. "Please," says Mr. Thomas "be incredibly careful – we have had others before you go on this journey to find the solar bar, but not one has ever come back alive. That fact should tell you just how dangerous this journey will be."

"Please watch out and watch each other also" Mr. Thomas says, "I want all of you to come back alive and safe, of course. I would be incredibly happy if you could come back with the long-lost solar bar. Because without this, our home here will be figment of our imagination and we would cease to exist. We are counting on the four of you to survive and come back safe so we can celebrate your success and have a feast in your honor.

Is there anything you must take or need to know before leaving?" "Yes" asked Peter "do Lion and Jay Bear know what types of danger that lay ahead?" Mr. Thomas replied, "Well yes, they have heard stories and have seen a lot of dangerous creatures. Therefore, we feel it is good for you two to have them in your company – OK. Any other questions or concerns." "Yes" said Alex "what type of dangers are we facing that has caused no one has come back alive?"

"Well," said Mr. Thomas "I can't tell you completely, just that when we had to send someone out there, they don't make it passed the forest.

Various creatures fly and have other dangerous qualities – big and small . . . and yes, are very smart, they watch you and copy your moves. This will not be easy you boys need not go. "Well," Alex responded, "Since you are holding our parents at the Star Zone Space Prison because they entered your world without your permission – which is illegal, then – we don't have a choice.

We want our parents set free. You have agreed to release them both if my brother and I help with this situation. "Well," said Mr. Thomas "still . . . Peter and Alex – you can refuse . . . even though you may feel there are consequences. But Lion and Jay Bear must go." "Well," answered Alex "we will go with them and try our best to work together to accomplish this challenge and bring hope and happiness to your home.

OK well, we will leave first thing in the morning."

"OK" answered Mr. Thomas "please eats something and gets a good night's sleep.

Dawn will come early."

"Yes "answered Peter "OK." "There is a room for you at the hotel across the street," Mr. Thomas tells them "Here is the key to your rooms, numbers 112 and 113. The four of you get rest.

"OK" they all said to Mr. Thomas. They walked to their rooms and put things away. "Let's go, eat, and have a drink," Alex said. "Yes, that's a clever idea" Peter replied. They walked down the street to enjoy a drink and a meal then head off to their hotel room to sleep. They ate fish, ice and had a drink, called Blue Ice. it appeared this is the only drink they serve with alcohol in it. Wow, after drinking one of these the boys realized it packs quite a punch. Therefore, after drinking one blue ice and eating, they walked back to their hotel rooms and Lion and Jay Bear went to theirs.

CHAPTER TWELVE

JOURNEY TO THE GREEN MOON FOREST

After a good night sleep the boys are up early and so are Jay Bear and Lion. "OK" says Jay Bear "let us grab something to eat, fill up our water pouches, and roll up our sacks." Peter burst out laughing. "What's so funny?" asked Alex. "Sacks – LOL, I actually understood what he meant!"

"Oh" said Alex "right – sacks are the code word for sleeping bags, did you catch that?" Lion and Jay Bear just looked at each other and scratched their heads. "Alright you two," Jay Bear says, "let us keep it moving!"

They all settled down, had something to eat, and talked about a plan. Trying to produce the best way to achieve their goal and still come out alive, since no one before them had been able to.

"Well," said Jay Bear "the forest has dangers on the ground as well as in the trees. We will be watched from the moment we step off the path." "Well," asked Peter "is there any way we can stay on the path and still get far enough without being targeted?" "Well," said Lion "it takes you in the wrong direction, but we might be able to go far enough on the path, then cut through the forest and that just might get us close enough to the entrance of the Grim Light Cave."

"OK" Peter responds, "That sounds good, just be careful and make sure we're watching each other's back." "The forest can be filled with a lot of dangers," Jay Bear tells them "You might not see at first. Things move fast, so just because we're on the path doesn't mean that we're not in trouble."

"OK" Alex says, "We understand. "So, stay close," Jay Bear reminds them. As they head out to the Green Moon Forest trail entrance, they all walk on the dirt path, leading them deeper into the Green Moon Forest. Huge trees bend sideways and twist together into other branches. Appearances can be very deceiving in the Green Moon Forest.

The Green Moon Forest has a way of twisting and bending shapes into other objects, it can amaze, but it is also, what makes it dangerous. As the pathways bend and wrap around, everyone keeps moving. The trails seem endless, and danger can lurk in every twist and turn on the path. A long way is still to the Grim Light Cave entrance.

They reach the towers and keep moving as the trail bends deeper into Green Moon Forest. Peter hears a loud noise in the trees ahead and asks everyone if they hear the same thing. "Yes" said Lion "whatever it is, they are going to want to attack. Our presence here is not helping matters – just keep moving. We must get to the other side of the Green Moon Forest. We will be much safer there and can camp for the night."

Everyone marches on to the other side of the Green Moon Forest. Peter is looking ahead and thinks he sees something tall in the trees above. It looks like it is covered up – so he keeps staring into the distance and feels a little freaked out. He yells out to the others "did you see that ahead?

Well, it looks like it is in the trees and covered up. You cannot quite make it out. Do you see it?" "Well," says Lion "look – we know we're being watched by creatures. Sometimes you cannot see them or make them out. Best thing to do is keep moving! Try not to do anything stupid to alarm the creatures. They are already uneasy cause of our presence here. "OK" said Peter. As they continue down the dirt path, Alex says, "Hey – it looks like something is covering the path right here!" "Oh my! Peter replied,

"What do you suppose it is? They walk closer and standing in front of the path was a golden gate. It appeared closed and completely covered with bushes. "OMG!" said Peter "what the hell is it doing in the middle of the path?" "Well, Lion and Jay Bear, do you have any ideas on the subject?" asked Alex.

"Well, no" Jay Bear responds "I have never seen it before. Really, this is the first time we have taken this short cut in the path. Remember – there are many other paths leading in different directions."

"I know this way will lead us to the Grim Light Caves" Jay Bear tells them "But for Lion and me – it's our first time seeing this gate on this path." "Well," Alex asks, "What do we do? Open it and continue on?" "Well," said Jay Bear "it's either that or we go back the way we came." "What do you think Alex and Peter, what do you say?" Jay Bear asks them. "We say, unlock and open the gate, let's continue on our path" Alex says.

"I mean, after all, time is not actually on our side." "Yes" Jay Bear speaks out "we need to continue on." "OK" Alex and Peter agree. As Lion opens the gate, the rest walk through. Alex closes the gate behind him because he was the last one through. The gate is gold with bars running across the entire length of the gate. Green bushes covered the gate.

"By the looks of it" said Peter "no one has been here in many years. "Yeah" replies Alex "makes you wonder, was it meant to keep something from coming in or the opposite." "I don't know" Peter replied, "but I hope it was meant to keep something out!" "Yeah" said Jay Bear "out works for me!"

Everyone smiled and agreed. They approached something called Dark Wood Lake. Peter asked, "did anyone else see that sign?" "Yeah" said Lion who asked, "ever heard of this lake before?" "Yes "answered Jay Bear "I am not sure, but I recall Thomas saying something long ago that people used to live here. Before where we live now but shoot! You are talking about when the Deming world was first created! "Oh" asked Alex did Thomas say what happened to this place?"

"Sorry, it really has been a while since I heard the story" Jay Bear said. "Well – keep your eyes open!" said Alex "if this place was active, and people lived here, they mustn't have had solar power to heat and power everything." "Well, that's true . . . but" said Lion "anything that worked then, is long gone and destroyed by now." "Yeah OK" replied Alex "but it doesn't hurt to just watch out." "Yeah, I agree," replied Peter "can't hurt!" "Yeah OK" Jay Bear said, "We get it! Just keep a look out and keep moving, we have a lot of grounds to cover still." They continued through Dark Woods Forest trail and passed through, what might call, the Golden Gate.

They all seemed a little nervous, like something long ago is still here and around them on the trail and in Dark Woods. "There's an old building just ahead yeah," said Jay Bear. "I see it" Lion replied. "Well, it's getting dark" Jay Bear tells them. "I think it just might be a promising idea to make camp and head out at first light – OK?" So, they all went inside the empty building and made a fire in the old fireplace.

They rolled out their sleeping bags, cooked up something to eat and looked around a little. They did a search before shutting down and calling it a night. As the night grows dark and during the darkest hour in Dark Wood, everyone is lying still in their sleeping bags – as the double moons brighten up the darkest of hours of the Dark Wood trails.

The morning rises with no incidents during the night. Peter and Alex pack up and get ready to head down the trail before realizing Jay Bear, Lion and all their gear is gone. They are nowhere in sight. Peter wakes first then Alex is up. "Hey" said Peter "any ideas where Jay Bear and Lion are?" "What do you mean?" asked Alex.

"They're both just gone" answered Peter. "Look around, they're nowhere in sight!" "Well now that's strange!" Alex replies. "They both were here last night." "Yeah" said Peter "you're right – they're not here now and by the looks of things, all their stuff is gone too." "Well, I don't know what to think," says Alex "they were both sitting around the fire last night. We both saw them when they turned in right before they went to sleep.

They were lying right beside us too." "Well one thing is for sure" Peter replies "I don't believe that either one of them would have left us without word. I mean they need our help find the solar bar. "Well," Alex responds, "They both said we have to be careful because we took a short cut into Dark Wood. They said neither of them had been this way before.

Therefore, either they left on their own, or someone took them in the middle of the night. The two of us had better keep our eyes open! No telling what is here in Dark Wood, and I don't want to find out." "Well," Peter says, "There are no blood on the ground and no sign anywhere either.

We better keep going to the Grim Light and pray nothing has happened. I hope we find both safe. However, until then, we had better keep moving quickly. Whatever happened to them could easily happen to us." The brothers continue down the Dark Wood Forest trail. Peter says, "neither one of us had mentioned the way Jay Bear and Lion looked physically." "I know" said Alex "and its kind strange – Jay Bear has a face of a bear and a body of a man. Lion the same thing his face is of a Lion with the body of a man.

You know, their bodies are so toned!" "Yeah" said Peter "and don't forget ripped . . . but you know what they say!" "Yeah, what's that?" asked Alex. "They have a face only a mother could love – now that's funny!" "Well let's get going and move on to the Grim Light Caves," Alex said to his brother. "You just want to leave them both?" asked Peter. "Well Peter" Alex replied, "Where do you suggest that we look for them? Remember there is no blood, no sign anywhere and really the best thing we can do for ourselves and for our parents is to keep try not to get killed ourselves.

"OK" Peter responds, "I guess you're right – let us go and keep moving." As the brothers continued down the Dark Wood Forest trail, they did not know what to expect and were a little nervous to continue their journey. However, what choice did either of them have? So many people were counting on them to save their world. They got up, rolled up their sleeping bags, and put on a brave face. The brothers walked out and got back on the path. The two-kept walking later, but still saw no sign of Lion or Jay Bear. Therefore, they just kept marching on in the daylight with two double suns bearing down upon them.

They both kept walking in silence, but for sure, both brothers were wondering the same thing – what happened? Did they leave on their own to check something out, or did someone or something take them in the middle of the night? Peter and Alex were wishing their friends were both OK and alive. They felt they had no choice but to march on and get back to the journey at hand – getting to the Grim Light Cave and finding the solar bar.

They continued down the mysterious path known by the name Dark Wood Trails. Peter and Alex were walking down the path Alex suddenly stopped walking, looks at his brother, and says, "I just remembered something Mr. Thomas said to us before we left. You had just left and were standing by Jay Bear and Lion. You were talking to them when Thomas looked at me and said, "just one thing" he said to me and I said, "what's that?" then he looked up said "listen, there's a story in those parts of the Dark Wood that says blue fairies live in Green Moon Forest, you have to be incredibly careful. If they approach you, they can be dangerous.

They hold magical powers also they say the blue fairies can magically shift their shape into anything they desire – at will!" "OMG" says Peter "and you just now are remembering this!" "Yes" Alex replied, "I mean, so much has happened, in light of Jay Bear and Lion are now missing – I just remembered. Mr. Thomas told me it was a myth, so I did not think it was true. But now, well Peter, what do you think?"

Peter says to his brother "well, I think we had simply better keep our eyes open, our feet walking and – brother maybe you should just move more and talk less. I mean really!" Peter says, "Shape shifting blue fairies – really Alex!" "Well," Alex replies "one thing is for sure what was that, well – Dorothy said it better 'we're not in Kansas anymore.'

Let us just find the damn solar bar and the Grim Light Cave that holds the key to our parent's safe return – to us both." "Well, here's to us" Peter says, "continuing on to find our friends safe." They got up, rolled up their sleeping bags, and put on a brave face. They both walked out and got back on the path. They kept walking down the path, but still saw no signs of Lion or Jay Bear.

They kept on marching in the daylight, with two double suns beating down upon them. They kept walking in silence, but for sure – both brothers were wondering the same thing – did the blue fairy have anything to do with both Lion and Jay Bear leaving and did they leave on their own? Peter and Alex are hoping for the best.

They are wishing their friends were safe and here with them to ensure their safe return from the journey they started together. "Well Alex . . ." "Yes Peter? "Here's to us finding the solar bar in the Grim Light Cave, getting our parents freed from prison and being a family again. "I'm thinking the same thing myself" Alex replied, "and here's to getting to the Grim Light Cave safely."

They continued walking down the path Jay Bear and Lion woke up at the entrance to the Grim Light Cave. They tried to recall what happened to them. "OK" Lion said to Jay Bear "what can you recall?" "Well, we were all sleeping in our sacks and were fast asleep, when I felt someone tapping us," said Jay Bear. "Yeah, that's right!" said Lion "trying to wake us up – after waking up, I looked up and couldn't believe my eyes! I saw this little blue fairy saying 'don't wake up the others – follow me! Your destiny lies ahead on the path you must take'" Jay Bear said. Lion and Jay Bear tried telling the blue fairy to go away "we are not leaving our friends, we're on a mission, and we can't be separated now."

Cave, getting our parents freed from prison and being a family again!" "I'm thinking the same thing myself" Alex replied, "and here's to getting to the Grim Light Cave safely." They continued walking down the path Jay Bear and Lion woke up at the entrance to the Grim Light Cave. They tried to recall what happened to them. "OK" Lion said to Jay Bear "what can you recall?"

"Well, we were all sleeping in our sacks and were fast asleep, when I felt someone tapping us," said Jay Bear. "Yeah, that's right!" said Lion "trying to wake us up – after waking up, I looked up and couldn't believe my eyes! I saw this little blue fairy saying 'don't wake up the others – follow me! Your destiny lies ahead on the path you must take'" Jay Bear said. Lion and Jay Bear tried telling the blue fairy to go away "we are not leaving our friends, we're on a mission, and we can't be separated now."

The fairy looks at them and says, 'you don't have a choice, you will both come, or you will both not live.' They looked at the fairy and said "NO! We are not coming with you!"

Just then, the blue fairy blew magical dust in the air. Suddenly, right before their eyes, the fairy changed herself into a giant blue monkey. Then the giant blue monkey grabbed them both and disappeared into the night. Within the Green Moon Forest, you could hear a slight scream of fear within the two friends.

The darkness of the night wrapped around them both – they were gone. They found themselves awake at the entrance to the Grim Light Cave and as they looked around, the blue fairy was there looking at them and said, "you will have to be punished for entering the Dark Wood Lake area. No one is allowed in this area – it is off limits. Since you brought the two Earth boys here – it is on the two of you to be punished. You must stay here and the two Earth boys must find their own way to the entrance.

Any interference by either of you will result in death." Then the fairy was gone. Jay Bear and Lion looked around; Lion screamed then Jay Bear screamed too. They both realized they had each eye.

Realizing they were wearing a patch over their lost eye. "Well," Jay Bear said, "I didn't see that coming!" Did you know?" asked Lion. "I didn't know of the myth or the story of the Dark Wood Lake, so now we know, and we've paid a heavy price for not knowing." "Yeah" said Lion. Then, before the fairy left, she gave them a clue to find the solar bar that would save the town. The fairy said, "What you seek, you must go down very deep within the bottomless bottom of the Grim Light Cave, find a nest hidden within the walls of the cave and remove it from the ugly belly of the beast – which has had it within the reach of his hands.

His nest you will see buried very deep." The fairy took Jay Bear and Lion to the entrance of the Grim Light Cave to wait for Alex and Peter. Right before leaving, the fairy said, "you must fight together or all of you will die in the Grim Light Caves. Also, you must cut off one of his hands to dig with within the nest." Then, as quickly as she came, the fairy was gone. Peter and Alex continued the path to the cave. Lion and Jay Bear were in a daze about what happened to them.

Jay Bear asked Lion "have you ever heard of the blue fairy and that she can change her own shape?" "No" said Lion "but she did more than that – that blue dust was really a game changer! Shoot! We must have imagined things! What a trip! Well, it was the dust which caused us to forget – we didn't remember her taking out our eyeballs!" "Well, anyway" Lion said, "she gave us a clue to the whereabouts of the solar bars." "We don't know what's in the Grim Light Cave," Jay Bear said, "until we all enter together when our paths cross. All four of us will then go down to the very depths of the bottomless part at the very core of the cave to find the solar bar.

To tell you the truth, none of us knows what lies ahead in the cave or just how far we should go down to save our world. We will first fight to remove the hand of the beast and dig with it to remove the nest buried within the hidden walls of the cave. This to save our world and the brother's parents also Jay Bear continued, "The last twenty-four hours seems like a dream.

I do not know if what happened to the two of us was real or not! Neither one of us can exactly explain how we got here! However, I can recall picking wild mushrooms for dinner, after that our wild imaginations took control over us. It was more like we hallucinated the entire journey and ended up at the entrance to the cave." "Now that's wild" Lion says "yes, but what the blue fiery said was true because the two of us are missing our eyes thanks to the damn blue monkey fairy and the damn dust! Now all we can do is waiting for the brothers to show up here at the entrance of the Grim Light Cave." As Peter and Alex walked the trail, the two-kept moving in the hope they would get to the Grim Light Cave soon and see their friends again.

Trying to watch each other's back, look out for the dangers ahead, trying to make up time and move quickly through Dark Wood, they try to get far before night falls. They must figure out the best place to make camp for the night. The double suns were bearing down them.

They kept moving on the dirt trail, still looking for clues and signs of their friend's whereabouts and other signs about the solar bars. Just a clue might appear, and both will be one-step closer in finding the solar bar. A clue to help them in time to search in the Grim Light Cave. Alex and Peter stay alert, as they are two men down. They just have each other to watch out for dangerous situations that might be ahead.

Feeling tired from walking all day, the boys look for somewhere to rest and camp for the night. "Keep your eyes alert" says Alex "look ahead and see if we find some kind of structure." They continued walking on the dirt path, looking for somewhere to rest their heads before evening falls. The double moons appear in Dark Wood trails where there lurks danger at every turn and could sweep them away with blue fairy dust or the wild mushrooms growing next to the trails. The boys were still walking down the path; evening hours were approaching, and they were desperately looking for a place to crash for the night.

As the dirt road continued further, they finally see a brick building in the path ahead. They walked over and opened the door. The place was empty and quiet. They look around and see nothing, so they both settled down for the night. They make a fire, which takes the chill out of the air, and warm the place a little. They sat down and talked. The boys relaxed and ate a little fruit and bread with jam. They were discussing their day and how far they both come. They wondered just how much further they must go before they saw the entrance to the Grim Light Cave. They settled down, crawled into their bags, and got sleep. Tomorrow will be here with another journey to start all over again.

CHAPTER 13

LOST IN THE GREEN MOON

The morning rose with the double suns shinning bright. Peter and Alex are up early and already on the trail once again. "Well do you think – are we almost there?" said Peter. "I wish I knew," said Alex. "Really, both of us have no way of knowing. We have to hope we are going in the right direction and that Jay Bear and Lion are there waiting for us brother."

"I hope you're right," replied Peter. They both continued down more trails, leaving behind the long way back to Star Zone. Days and days have gone by – walking during the day and making camp at night. The boys wondered if they would ever get to the Grim Light Cave and what will wait for them. It is still uncertain but move forward they must – they cannot move back and forward is the only direction they both know now and so they just kept moving.

Walking to the Grim Light Cave was further than they realized. Just how far the cave was and how days they would spend walking to get there they did not know. They only hoped nothing would happen to them in their long journey to the Grim Light Cave.

Peter looked down – then up as he was walking and finally asked Alex if everything was OK because he was so quiet and not talking. Peter asked his brother if he was deep in thought about anything in peculiar. "No" Alex said "not really, but it just makes you wonder why us? Why, of all the people in the entire universe including all dimensions, did they choose the two of us? I mean – he said they watched us for a long time. Just makes me wonder what are they hiding from us?

I believe something doesn't add up." You think so?" asked Peter. "Well – don't you?" answered Alex. "Well, it does make you wonder – why indeed the two of us among everyone else here? I also wonder how many others came before us."

"Yeah" said Peter "not only came before us, but was also asked to solve their problem with the solar bars in the towers?" "Well one thing for sure" answered Alex "we do not know how, but we do know not one solved the problem. Something is missing." "Like what?" Peter asked. "Well suppose they targeted others to help them with their problem?" Alex said. "OK" asked Peter "where you are going with this?"

"Well," said Alex "why do you think they asked others to help? Why did the others fail? What is it about the cave that others could not find the solar bar? What's in the cave?" "So, let me get this straight" Peter replies "you think others have come here before us to help them and failed?" "So, they keep reaching out to find that perfect someone, or in our case, two to fix the situation."

Alex responds, "Only I think we are missing something." "Like what?" Peter asks him. "Well," Alex says, "The cave – I'm worried because everyone has died. We do not know if people came before us.

I think we should figure this out by asking Jay Bear and Lion when we meet up with them at the cave – where both are waiting for us outside the entrance." "Do you really think they are at the cave?" Peter asked. "Yes, I do," said Alex. "I have no doubt no one and believe me. They will produce an excuse as to why they left.

We are walking alone in a place we have never been to. Curious, isn't it?" "Yeah brother" answers Peter "you, said it – we have a few questions to ask them before we go into that cave. But let us be fair, you and I both could bark up the wrong tree with this whole thing – and we could be wrong."

"OK" replied Alex "let us not allow our imaginations to run wild with all kinds of possibilities. Let us just wait and see what happens when we get there." Walking on and continuing later, they wondered if they are being set up on this journey. They were asked to come for an hour, day, or forever.

They wonder what kind of heroes we are supposed to be for everyone in the place – later in a town they call Star Zone.

They both walked on with questions lurking with every step they took. However, in their minds were just two brothers, marching to a place and they are just not sure if there even are solar bars in the cave or not. They were sent there, and they will continue searching until they come out with a solar bar in their hands.

They wanted to bring it back to Mr. Thomas and all the others in Star Zone – take it to the towers and Light up the town.

Peter and Alex had been walking all day. They were talking about if they were lied to. "You know what I've been thinking about Peter," Alex says.

"What's that?" Peter asks. The alien savage hunter on the spaceship. Remember what he said about Star Zone? What didn't he say about it – when the two of us tried to ask him? Yes, he laughed, right?" asked Peter.

"Yes "said Alex. "Harry T. Bone said – I recall that 'we must be very special guests' Do you remember Peter?" "Yeah, I do. I recall Harry T. Bone said, 'it's a world like nothing we have ever seen before or will ever again'.

"It's one big mystery" answers Alex "and everyone else seems to know the answers, but they won't give it to us straight or tell us exactly what we want to know. Eventually, we will find the answers to the questions we look for. I am sure everything will have no choice but to reveal it to us and show the answers we want to know. I just hope it won't be too late for us when we find out the truth."

"Well," said Peter "we are here now and there's nothing else we can do but march on down the road, get to the Grim Light and see if Jay Bear and Lion are there. Also, see what they must say." "Well," said Alex "we're not even sure if they know anything – for one thing. Second, if they know something – would they tell us? Just how honest will they be in protecting us? I mean, would they protect us if we were in danger?"

"Well," said Peter "I believe it's in their nature to protect. However, if they are put to the test, we must see just how much – if at all – they will come to our aide and lend us a hand in face in danger. Will they save our lives or leave us hanging nearly at death and leave us wondering why?" With all these thoughts going through their minds. Peter and Alex are wondering if they were set-up – right from the start when the bolt sent down from their world to earth – placed within their dreams, including the messages that followed, the numbers and the other clues, contacted them.

"I'm wondering if we really were set up and if so – why they want us so bad?" asked Alex. "I mean – why did they pick us! Why us – out of everyone else – and why do they have us on the hunt for something that may or may not be real. You know Peter?" "Yeah Alex" Peter replied, "We really have no back door. We need something if we are right. Something to protect us – like what I don't know – but it would be in our best interest to figure out something if we need it – and we'd better figure it out."

"OK" says Alex "let us get going. I want to see what's exactly in that damn Grim Light and see what's waiting for the two of us." "I don't know brother" Peter responds, "but I don't think it's a good sign that we're both feeling the same way." "Yeah" says Alex "that's what bothers me the most." They kept moving down the path, walking during the day and finding a place to camp at night when dusk approaches.

They got lucky in the evening hours and find shelter. The brothers would make a fire and talk about how they got to where they are now and wonder – are we here and are we really in danger? The brothers would say only time will tell. Thinking about this would cause them to become curious, but also nervous, about what awaits them later. The path to the Grim Light Cave is around the corner – soon they should deal with everything making them a little uncomfortable.

"Well, let's see," says Alex. "OK, Peter – let us go over everything. First, we need to know if Jay Bear and Lion are with us or against us. Second, the solar bars – did they really bring us here to find them and restore their energy source?

Third, is something extreme waiting for us – I mean something evil or something disturbing coming our way? I wish we knew the truth before we get to Grim Light Caves. "Well," said Peter "maybe Lion and Jay Bear will tell us what they know and be honest about it. If they know anything first and if they'll share it with us to protect and help us – our own lives might be at stake."

"Well," Alex reminded his brother "don't forget Mr. Thomas is extorting us into finding the solar bars, which may or may not lie in the bottomless bottom of the Grim Light Cave. So really, what choice do we have? You know Peter, do you think they will release our parents – if we find the bars?" "I don't know brother" Peter replied "but if I had to take a guess, I would say probably not – because of all of the lies how everything has come about.

I am sure there is much more the two of us do not know and it scares me to find out the whole truth. The bastards are lying – I cannot take all the thoughts running through our minds since we came here.

We are only trying to help their people live a happier and danger free lifestyle. Is it possible that we are in danger of losing our lives; we have been set up to lose and destroy ourselves? I don't know what to think brother, but we damn well better find out right now!" "What are you saying?" asked Alex. "I get the feeling maybe we should turn around and not go any further" Peter replies "but we can't do that!" "Yeah, well then" answers Alex "we just might be doomed if we continue on to the Grim Light Cave."

"What choice do we have?" asks Peter. "We'll continue on to Grim Light Cave and hope the only thing waiting for us is the solar bars – not anything else. "Well, I'm tired," Peter says. "Yeah, me too" Alex replies "but it looks like the path ends ahead." "Oh – really? Peter asks. "Yes, Peter – look!" Alex replied. "Oh yes!" says Peter "I see now - just a bit further, it looks like we're at the entrance area to the Grim Light Cave! "Finally – hurry up Peter!" Alex yells to his brother. "OK Alex – do you see Jay Bear and Lion?" Peter asks. "Not yet – we're not close enough yet" Alex responds.

"Well," says Peter "let us get walking – I can't wait to see if they're there waiting for us!" As Peter and Alex walk faster and faster to the entrance, they have on their minds. Talking to Jay Bear and Lion is first on the list and they are hoping the two can clear things up. I hope that Jay Bear and Lion will enlighten them on things they have had on their minds since they started on this journey together just days back.

"I was just wondering something brother" says Peter. "What's that Peter?" asks Alex. "Do you regret following the signs that led us both to where we are now?" "Well," Alex says, "It's an adventure I don't think either one of us regrets. One day, we will write about it." "Yeah" says Peter "whatever happens, it is all because we took a chance and came somewhere no one has been before – you and I are the first." "Well, we're getting closer, I guess. We can see the cave, but it still remains further away than we thought" Alex observes. "Well," Peter tells him "At least we know that today we'll be at the entrance. I hope Jay Bear and Lion will be there."

I hope that the danger ahead has something to do with the solar bars and both of us – dear brother – will not be in danger – will not be set up or killed. Time is almost up, and the Grim Light Cave is here." As the boys continue getting closer to the Grim Light Cave, they feel a little anxious – nervous. The unknown can surprise. Yet, the boys feel a little upbeat facing their search in the Grim Light Cave. A little more than they bargain for – but they are still looking forward to the danger – to hunt for the solar bars and find out the real story behind Star Zone and whether Star Zone has lured anyone else to their world.

If so, why, and what happened to those people. "Alex?" "Yes Peter." "I was thinking we need a weapon so we can protect ourselves." Peter says. "Good – I agree" answers Alex. "Well," Peter responds, "I'm going to tell you what it is. I brought the gun from the craft!" "You did!" responds Alex "that's great! Well, keep it hidden and we will not say a thing. "Yeah" says Peter "just in case our adventure turns into danger – we'll have the gun to protect ourselves.

"But look Peter" Alex reminds him "don't show the gun and don't pull it out. I do not want Lion and Jay Bear to find out about it. Not until we chat with them about what they know and see if the two will tell us if anything." "You know Alex, the two of them just might lie and not tell us a damn thing" Peter reminds him. "Well brother" Alex answers "we'll just have to figure it out together – just the two of us. Besides, we have incredibly good instincts and I'm sure we can get to the truth." "I hope so" responds Peter "we just have to stick together – and Alex – just one more thing . . .," says Peter.

"OK – what is that?" asks Alex. "When we get ready to enter the cave, we just have to stay together and make our choices as one – let us not to let anyone try to pull us apart or tear us apart. We have to stand united when we enter Grim Light Cave and stand strong – by standing together as one my brother."

CHAPTER FOURTEEN

ON THE OUTSIDE OF THE GRIM LIGHT

"Well brother, we'll defeat anything in our way that comes to harm either one of us." Peter states. "Well then" says Alex "I guess than we're as ready as we're ever going to be, brother. Let us march on – we're almost there." As they move closer to approaching the Grim Light Cave, they turn a corner on the path. There – just ahead – was a huge mountain.

The size of the mountain was amazing! Neither of them had never seen such a huge mountain. The height and size were just enormous. As they walk closer to the huge entrance of the Grim Light Cave, they see Jay Bear and Lion sitting on two rocks. It looks like they are waiting. "Hey" yells out Peter "what the hell happened to you both? Thanks for just leaving us like that!" "Good to see you both" yells back Jay Bear.

"Sorry for the confusion, but we're here and have been waiting for you both! What the hell happen to you?" As Peter asked the question, they walk closer, finally sit down, and drank water. They rested and listened as Lion and Jay Bear tell them what happened.

They explained they were sleeping when a blue fairy, tapping on them and saying 'don't wake up the others' and follow her, wakened them. The fairy was saying something like 'your destiny lies ahead on the path you must take.' We both tried telling the blue fairy we were not leaving our friends; we must stay together. However, you can see how the fairy felt about that, "Yes" said Peter 'your eyes!" "That's right!"

Jay Bear explained, "She removed one eye from me and one from Lion too. The fairy changed to a giant blue monkey, grabbed us both as we screamed and disappeared into the night. We woke up here, at the entrance to the cave. The fairy looked at us, said we must wait for you both here and do not move.

In addition, she said all of us must go deep within the bottomless bottom of the Grim Light Cave and find a nest hidden within the walls, fight the ugly beast and cut off his hand. We are to use it to dig, find the secret chamber behind the walls, find the nest, and discover the solar bars. The fairy left, we have been sitting here nursing our wounds and waiting for the two of you to show up.

Thank God, you both found your way here safely. "Well," said Peter "that's some story. We believe you! Besides, you look like you're in pain" Alex replied. "Yes "said Jay Bear. Just then, Lion and Jay Bear looked at each other, gave each other a little nod, and removed the patch covering up their eyes.

The boys got a good look at what this creature had done to them. "Well," Alex told them "You didn't have to remove it." "Yes – well we don't want any misunderstanding of what happen to us" Jay Bear explained. "We need to be able to trust each other." "OK Alex said, "We agree. The next part of this journey will be dangerous. Trusting and counting on each other will be the key."

After listening to the Jay Bear and Lion tell their story, the boys realized they were being honest and real with them. Really, the boys felt bad they both lost an eye and had to go through that experience. However, at least they were alive and safe at the Grim Light Cave entrance. They were ready to begin their journey together to find the solar bars buried and hidden somewhere within the bottomless bottom of the cavern – and the beast that lies within. They will fight to the death to protect the bars and find the secret hidden chamber.

"Well," said Alex looking at Jay Bear and Lion "Peter and I would like to ask you both something." "Oh" said Lion "what's that?" "Well," asked Peter "is my brother and I the only ones who have searched the Grim Light Cave for the solar bars?" "Yes" said Jay Bear "the solar bars never blacked out in the past." "Oh" said Peter "is you sure about that?" "Not one time in the history of your world?" "Well yes" Jay Bear replied, "I told you that already. The people used to live elsewhere, but then we found the solar bar and a new place to live. We have been here ever since."

"So, we are the first to search for new source of the solar bar for the tower?" asked Alex. "No one has come before us – is, that, right?" "Yes" said Jay Bear "we found the ones we have now. They have lasted for some time, but now our time is almost gone, and we must find another source." Alex looks at his brother and Peter shrugs his shoulders to Alex as if to say he does not know what to think. They cannot tell either if of them are telling the truth or if they are good at being very dishonest.

"Well, there is one other possibility," said Alex. "Oh, what is that?" said Peter. "Mr. Thomas has been keeping his little secret from the two of them also," Alex, answered. "They don't know what he's been up to or for how long – perhaps. I'm thinking it's kind of hard to hide other people coming in from all over everywhere to make exclusive deals with Thomas in finding their solar bars." "OK" replied Peter "so you think they know something?" "Well, Thomas knows for sure! He's hiding something," Alex said. "Yeah, I believe you are right about that" Peter responded.

"I mean look how they got us here and where they put our parents. Now, we're being forced to help find the solar bars." "Yeah" Alex agreed, "we've just got this feeling Thomas has been looking for someone to help. I am not just talking about finding the solar bars either. There is more going on here than we know about, brother. You and I are maybe just caught in the middle of something brewing and it's coming this way – I'm not just talking coffee either!" "Well let's just take it one step at a time right now" Peter responded. "I want to eat – let's see if Jay Bear got any fish for dinner." "Overhearing, Jay Bear spoke up and said, "Yes, I did – I put them in the stream below."

"OK" said Alex "let us build a fire and cook them up with rice and bread." "Sounds good" Jay Bear agreed. Everyone was running around, getting the rice out, and putting the fish into a pan to cook. They gathered around the fire, waiting patiently for the food to be done cooking, so they could enjoy the meal.

They gathered around the fire after dinner, relaxing. Peter asked about the cave "is there a mystery surrounding this cave Jay Bear?" Jay Bear looked at Peter and said, "Well, I heard stories growing up." "Yeah, what were they?" asked Alex. Lion spoke up and said, "We heard the stories – if you entered this cave and seek what you're looking for, some say, the Grim Light will show itself to you." "

What exactly is the Grim Light and how will it show itself?" Peter asked Jay Bear spoke and told of the history of their world. How it became Star Zone. "The story was handed down the generations, how our world was created, – some say by the Grim Light. People who have passed away now told it. However, like stories were told and they passed them on by telling the stories to their children.

Anyway, they say there was an explosion. It was massive. This was before life was here. There was a light they called it the Grim Light because everything was deep and dark. Out of nothing, the Grim Light made trees and plants. A massive cave was created, and other things started to grow.

The towers appeared, as well as the first solar bar along with it. From then on, it took off – people came by in ships out of the sky from different galaxies. Anyways, I guess that's how most of it was told and that's how the story has been passed on and told again."

"The Grim Light, they say, is in the deepest part of the cave. If you enter and go to the heart, the belly of the Grim Light, say, a light – a bright light – will appear and open up to the person who stands before it" Lion said. "What will happen if you stand before it?" asked Peter. "Look, I don't know," said Lion. "Well, what do you think Jay Bear?" Peter asked. "Well," Jay Bear responded, "You do realize that no one has entered or found it. However, it has been told, if you stand before the Grim Light, a part of the cave wall will open like a massive door.

What lies on the other side – they say – is something amazing and has never been seen.

It will let you enter and pass through the door at the opening of the entrance to the Grim Light." "Does anyone know what lies on the other side?" asked Alex. "Just stories really." Jay Bear replied. "Someone once said the real Star Zone is on the other side." "You mean your true wishes, not exactly like that, but a world like no other – like you have never seen before? You mean another Deming world?" asked Peter.

"I guess" said Jay Bear "who knows!" "Well," replied Alex "I would like to find out and see for myself." "Well do you realize there's a reason it's never been found?" Jay Bear reminded them "and as far as we know, no one has seen it."

Peter looked at his brother Alex and said, "You know what this remains me of?" "What's that?" Alex asked. "What Harry T. Bone, from the savage spaceship Peter says, "remembers what he said in describing the world?" "Yes, but Peter, he was describing Star Zone, wasn't he?" Alex asked.

"Or was he talking about somewhere else? Inquired Peter. This conversation and what Jay Bear said about it sounds a lot like what Harry T. Bone said, don't you think so?" Peter continued. "Well, now that you bring it up, it does sound familiar," answered Alex. "Yeah, what did he say?" asked Peter. "Oh yeah" responded Alex "it's nothing like you have ever seen or will – something like that." "You're right," answered Peter "Harry T. Bone wasn't describing Star Zone – he was referring to Grim Light, or what's behind the Grim Light wall.

"Yes" said Alex "I do believe your right brother. Tomorrow morning, we are in search of the solar bars, the Grim Light secret chamber, and what is behind the wall. What the universe will reveal and open up to show and amaze us both."

"Well, brother we should get some sleep" Alex reminds his brother. "Our journey will begin at first light, and we will see for ourselves." "We will find the solar bars, but once we do" Peter says "I'm – or rather we – will continue our search for the Grim Light Cave wall on our own."

"What are you saying brother?" asked Alex. "Look – if Lion and Jay Bear want to leave let them" Peter replies. "Well," Alex says, "They have to leave and get back to the towers to put the solar bars into place. There's something of a time issue, you understand?"

"Yes! Yes! I do!" responds Peter, "But I think, brother, it is in our best interests to find the solar bars as quickly as Peter tells Alex. "Why on Earth?" asks Alex. "Because maybe it's the reason we're here." Peter responds. "I don't think we're here to help and to live here. No, I do not think so. It is time for us to move on, beyond the wall, and find what lies behind it, brother. It is another world – not like where we are now and not like Earth. I think it's where the two of us are supposed to be." "You think what!" Alex exclaims. "The numbers match up to the world behind the wall."

Peter explains. "I think the numbers got us here to further guide us to where we are going – to live and see – like Harry T. Bone said . . .

'It is a place like no other, like nothing you have ever seen in your life' . . . remember?" "Yes brother,
I do recall what he said to us both on that day" Alex responds. "OK" answers Peter. "So, you really think that finding the solar bars is like a pit stop on the real journey to where we are supposed to be?" responded Alex. "Yes" said Peter "and just look where it took us! Look – we are about to enter the Grim Light Cave. This is no accident.

It is where we will begin our journey. The two of us will be surprised." "I really thought you knew," said Peter "when we first landed here and stepped off and down into Star Zone that this was not the place the two of us were supposed to be. I just got this feeling this was just a steppingstone to where it would take us both."

"So, what do you think is going to happen?" asked Alex "the wall opens up and then reveals another world?" "I don't know," said Peter. "What about our parents?" asked Alex? "To have them just stuck in prison. And our craft, do we just leave it and our parents also?"

"I just don't know yet" Peter responded. "I think we can help our parents by finding out all we can" Alex says to Peter. "We will discover another way into the prison, get them out, and disappear into another world. As far as our craft is concerned, I am not sure – we can find a portal that will allow us to move it. I do not have all the answers, but we must find out everything we can. Not only to help ourselves – but our parents as well. They are depending on us to keep them alive. We must find a way to save them and us too."

"Don't forget" Peter reminds him "if the blue fairy is right, we'll have to fight the beast in the cave somewhere and remove his hand to dig and locate the nest within the walls of the chamber. "I do get a sense" Alex says "that entering the Grim Light Cave is the way the two of us are going to be heading. There might be a surprise or two in store for us all."

"You know" Peter says "it is obvious, there's a good chance what lies ahead could be filled with danger and death.

Who knows what else will happen around every corner and every bend?

Once we enter the cave – and do you know what – it's extremely exciting in a way – even if death might be the result." "I don't know, brother" replies Alex "what to think, really. It is to take in and think about. Let us just take it one-step at a time. Let us see if we can stay alive, not kill ourselves, and find those damn solar bars for the replacement towers and save their world. It is also possible we will enter the cave and not find the solar bars. I mean, no one has been in there to look and where to look inside the cave is an issue.

It is huge inside – massive size – we could be in there for days or longer and still not find what we are looking for. It is very possible we could get lost and not find it. If so – how long do, we stay and look for it. Tell me Jay Bear – what do you think? "Well," Jay Bear says to the others sitting around the fire "it's not going to be easy. We have no map or any directions to help us, except for what the blue fairy told us – to look at the bottomless bottom of the cave and – well, you remember the rest."

"Yes, we have an idea of where to look" Alex replied, "at least it's a starting point." "We need to save and to help our people here and our world destroying itself," Jay Bear says. "We have to look – not give up and we really don't have much of a choice in the matter. Most important, in our situation, when we enter the cave – is to pay attention.

Look for clues everywhere and by doing so, hopefully, we will get lucky and find the right direction, which will take us to the bottomless bottom of the cave. The cave is so huge we are going to want to see signs that may point to the path or which way we need to travel – which way to turn. We also must stay together and not get lost. If we get separated, our chances of finding it or saving each other when danger happens will be slim."

As Lion was listening, he suddenly spoke up and told everyone "I know this part of the journey will not be easy, but I feel if we just follow some simple rules before we enter the Grim Light Cave our chances will be increased.

Not only to survive this part of the journey but standing together and being strong will help all of us. We might not know what direction we are going to take once we enter, but if the four of us can find the solar bars and save our people. But we must follow the clues in every aspect of the cave once we enter." "OK, look" Jay Bear responds "we don't know what kind of forces – if any – we're going to face here. We must – each of us – use our strengths and listen carefully to what we hear and see. The danger inside is real. Staying side by side is the only way we'll get through the Grim Light."

CHAPTER 15

ENTERING THE GRIM LIGHT CAVE

As the morning rises, Jay Bear, Lion, Peter, and Alex are up early fixing and slicing up apples with cinnamon sprinkled on top and heating water on the fire for loose tea. They all relax sitting by the fire, sipping tea, and gathering their thoughts while munching on apples. They all finished eating and drinking their tea. The fire was put out; the sleeping bags rolled up – stashed into their bags and tied together.

They carried everything on their backs. They all walked down to the creek close by. They filled their containers with water and caught more fish for something to eat later, as their journey was about to begin. They all wanted to make sure they had enough water and food to last.

They caught fish, wrapped them up, and walked to the other side of the cave – down a short distance to a small lake to catch more fish and to fill up their water bags. Soon they were ready and walked back to the cave entrance. "Well boys, are we ready for this! Alex said. They all looked at each other and smiled. Suddenly, they all took their first step into the Grim Light Cave. Jay Bear, Lion, Peter, and Alex took out their torches and lit four for each one of them.

They started to make their way inside the cave. As they started to go further inside, they noticed the ceiling was massive. It looked endless and had moisture dripping from the ceiling, down the walls on both sides. The walls seemed cold from the water that dripped down slowly, creating a massive – slightly frozen puddle that lay on the cold, wet floor – as their shoes walked over it with every step they took. Jay Bear yells out "if you see any kind of sign or direction that would point to a path which will lead us downward to the bottom of the cave, be sure, and take your time looking for the signs, or you just might miss it."

They moved on into a narrow passageway that curved around and around until it ended. Right in front was steps that led into darkness. Another unknown passageway awaits them. They marched on, not sure, where this passageway might lead them.

They took each step down to the final last step, taking them into an open room with a large column, which stood in the middle of this cold and empty cave. Everyone looked around for other passages or rooms, looking at the columns for signs or markings that would lead to the solar bars. They were also looking for any clue to show them which way would lead them to a downward spiral – into the bottomless bottom of the cave. There they would find the beast they must battle – remove his hand to dig and dig. Only this would enable them to find their way to a wall, which would open, show them a nest with buried solar bars and a mysterious secret chamber. say this will lead and show a way to what they call the Grim Light and a world beyond their imagination or worst nightmares.

Jay Bear, Lion, Peter, and Alex looked carefully for any signs to show them the way. Everyone splits up in this huge room. Peter walked over to a wall, took a rag, and wiped it off. He then saw an arrow – he called over the others to look at what he had found. Peter, with his rag in his hand, wiped more bizarre to see if anything else would appear on the wall next to the arrow. After wiping off the area, more writing came up under the arrow with pictures. By that time, everyone came over, trying to interpret what the writing and pictures were saying. The pictures looked like a story on the wall.

Everyone stood around to trying to read the writing and tell a story. I hope that the pictures would guide them in the direction, which would bring them closer to the Grim Light and the solar bars. Something else would surprise them all as they walked down inside the cave and read the walls that would guide them closer. They hoped – to what they came here looking for. According to the direction the arrow was pointing, they should go left – but all they can see there is a wall and nothing else.

"Well," said Peter "what do you think that means?" Alex spoke up and said, "It means go left." "Yeah" said Lion "I agree, just follow it exactly – one step at a time – besides it does say more with the writing and the pictures. But we're not sure what it means or how to read everything on the wall." All four agreed to read what they could understand and take it slowly. As they understood it, the rest of the writing on the wall said, so far, they know, to go left, stand in front of another wall, and see if they could find another clue.

They would look for a sign on the wall to see where it would take them and what would open and reveal itself. As they gathered by the wall, they stood in front of it, and they were all thinking the same thing – "what now! What do we do to take the next step and what are we looking at?" Peter and Alex were standing in front of the wall, took their hands, and went over the wall to feel for anything that was not smooth. They were looking for bumps or something else – they were not sure. Peter and Alex both felt something was there. They both continued as Jay Bear and Lion were looking around on their own to see if they could find or see something.

They both moved forward on their own searching for something anything that would develop and take them in a new direction. As they went off searching on their own, Peter and Alex were by the wall – still rubbing their hands over the cold surface to feel for anything that might trigger a clue. Suddenly, Peter's hand went into a hole. Alex went closer to his brother and they both investigated the hole to see if anything was inside it. It was dark and cold, Peter put his hand inside the hole, and he felt something sharp inside. As he went to grab it, Alex was asking him what it felt like. Peter was telling him it felt like kind of lever – like something you might pull down.

Alex asked Peter "can you reach it to pull down on the lever?" "I think so," said Peter. Peter grabbed it and pulled down hard – as he did, a part of the wall broke away and opened. They both stood there in shock and amazement – as the wall became a door and opened to stairs, heading downward in the darkness.

The stairs disappeared into the cold cavern below and the boys lit their torches. Alex looks at Peter and says, "Should we just go down or should we yell for Lion and Jay Bear to tell them what we found." "Well," Peter said, "I don't see either one of them – we should stay together. I don't think it's a clever idea to get separated, we might get into trouble and need their help."

"OK" says Alex "yell for them and see if they can hear us." Peter hollers for Jay Bear and Lion and again hollers – loud. "Hey, you, where you? Hello – Hello" but nothing. The two waits in silence for Jay Bear and Lion to answer them back, but still nothing – everything was quiet. "Well," said Alex "they must have wandered off to check something out, what do you want to do – wait here for them or make our way down the stairs without them.

 I mean, we must leave them some sign if they come back this way."

"OK" answered Peter "I'll make an arrow on the ground leading toward the door and an arrow by the hole in the wall just in case the door closes when we enter it." Peter and Alex take their lit torches and start the dark journey downward into the unknown, once again not knowing what is around the next corner or the bottom of the next step ahead.

Systematically they both take a deep breath inward, feeling anxious. Each step they take together, and they will soon see where these mystery stairs will lead them on the next part of their mysterious journey ahead. They are eager to see what lies in the next room, cold chills made of stone – a cold cavern of ice. The steps seem to never end as Peter and Alex make their way down to another door of ice. Looking for the doorknob, Alex takes his hands and pushes the door with Peter help, as hard as the two could.

The door burst open to a room, which was frozen – and they saw unlit torches on the wall. The brothers go over and light them up. The room brightens, to the boy's surprise, what they saw in front was a frozen wonderland lost in time.

The floor was frozen, and the rest of the room had icicles hanging off the walls. Peter and Alex could not believe just how strange the room looked to them. All around the room was this tiny path of powered ice you could walk on. Therefore, they walked around on the edges of the powered ice. Slowly they walked around the room and looked at the walls. They went around looking for signs of the next clue, which would take them one-step closer to the Grim Light.

Peter and Alex walk slowly around the room. They touched the ice-cold walls and looked to see what was different or smooth and rough about the surface and the texture of the walls and the room within itself to find a clue. Jay Bear and Lion were in a different part of the cave. They seemed to have wandered off into a room and could not figure out how to get out. Jay Bear and Lion went over to the other side of the room, where they were checking out different surfaces. They were checking the walls also, when Lion leaned up against hard button sticking out of the wall.

This caused it to open. They both looked around when the door closed securing them inside. They both panicked and then tried to figure out. Both Jay Bear and Lion kept moving around, looking for anything that would trigger something to open the door and release them. They wanted to find Alex and Peter and see what happened to them. Alex and Peter were still in this amazing frozen Arctic Room. Both brothers were still wandering around, checking everything their eyes could catch.

I hope they will find an interesting handle or button – something. A mysterious door or passageway eventually led them to the Grim Light. They were still walking around the room slowly so not to miss a thing and were halfway around this huge room, when Peter saw a large chain attached to a hook on the floor. Peter yells out "Alex come here and has a look at this! Can you see it on the floor?" "The chain that's right here?" Alex asks. "Yes," answered Peter.

Alex responds, "What the hell do you think something like that was used for?

Why is it attached to the floor?" Peter spoke up and said, "Well – looks to me like it was used to hold something here – to keep it from moving away – like humans – weird huh?" "But why would you say humans?" Peter asked. "Well, remember the conversation – how we both thought Thomas was recruiting other beings from different galaxies around the dimensional world to come here? We thought it was to get the solar bars, but now I am not sure anymore. Maybe it's something more sinister than we know about brother."

"Well, this makes you wonder, doesn't it?" said Alex. "Well, let us hope it isn't what we think. Let us continue our path and finish searching the room. Peter grabs the chain to see, or to make sure; it was attached to the hook on the floor and not to a hidden door to the floor below.

As Peter picked the chain up and grabbed it, he realizes the chain is attached to a hook, so Peter moves on and looks at another object.

One by one, he moves slowly within the room to find other hidden treasures, doors, and secret passageways they hope to find and continue their journey to find what they came here for and move on. They both continued walking around, looking for anything which would lead them out and to another clue. In their searching, Alex stops, looked down and around the room, and realized this room housed other humans from all parts of the dimensional world – more chains were discovered on the ground.

CHAPTER 16

THE FROZEN WONDERLAND

Alex looks at his brother and says, "Maybe this was a zoo of some kind. Well, if not a zoo, then someone chained up something else and it makes you wonder, doesn't it?" "Well, let's find the door or we'll have to back track and find another way out," Peter said. "Well," Alex replied, "I'm thinking it might be possible not every room will have a door or a passage leading to somewhere else."

"Well, you might be right" Peter responded "but, it does look like every room throughout in the cave is hidden. One must seek what you are looking for, whether it is a door or something else.

They are seeking answers – wondering what they are seeing in here, where it came from, and how it got here. Therefore, they both walk off to looked and touch and feel their way in the room, looking for anything that would take the two to another room – a passage to somewhere else.

Jay Bear and Lion are still trapped in a room away from Peter and Alex. Still trying to find their way out and meet up with the brothers, but poor Jay Bear and Lion are still struggling to find their way out. Walking all the way around the room, they are still looking for anything that would be an opening to a door. Jay Bear and Lion are figured out not to give up in their search to find a way out of this chilly and cold room.

Their search marches on in a cold room in which the two have been trapped for time now. Both want to get out. Looking in the corners – touching and feeling the wall for anything that does not seem to fit or feels out of place.

Lion and Jay Bear were both touching the walls on different sides of the room, when Lion went back to the door that shut them in. He felt his hand all over the door when a latch popped up and the door swung open. Jay Bear and Lion finally escaped and walked out of the room they were stuck in. They tried to get there by bearing straight – they both felt like they were turned around a little. They stood in the main room the two were in before they entered the room, they both were stuck in. As they stood there, they tried to figure out which way to go.

Lion spoke up and said, "Let us go to the other side of the room over in the corner. I believe that's where Peter and Alex were." When they walked to the other side of the room to the corner, they saw the note the brothers had left, with an arrow pointing which way to go. Jay Bear went over to the hole, stuck his hand in, and pulled on the lever. The door opened, Jay Bear and Lion followed the trail down to another room. When they yelled out, Alex and Peter hollered back at them "over here!"

Then the four were back together once again, trying to find the clues to the Grim Light. They all looked around while Peter and Alex told them the bolted chains hooked to the floor. Lion went over to the middle of the room to check out what type of chains they were. As he was picking them up, he looked at the others walking around him and said, "You know, these chains are very heavy." "Yeah" said Alex "we know." "We figured they must've held other humans in place." "Humans!" said Lion. "Yeah" Alex replied, "my brother and I kind of figured it out.

Thomas had other humans brought here from other dimensional worlds in and outside your galaxy." "Really, for what reason?" asked Jay Bear.

"We aren't sure just yet why. Nevertheless, it really does beg questions. One important being why on Earth would they be catching and storing humans of all types? At first, my brother and I thought it had something to do with finding the solar bars. Remember when we both asked if others had come before us and tried to find them? He said yes – but no others have ever found the bars.

In fact, they never came back." "Oh" Jay Bear said "right, I recall that myself." "Well," Alex replied, "We believe parts of the story. He told the truth – they came here. However, we believe he or someone else had other things in mind. We must know the truth and find out what's going on." "Well," Jay Bear says, "It must be something big if the two of you don't have a clue. I mean, you knew Thomas had all or the others who came here or was brought here under false pretenses. If you two know nothing well brother, I'm concerned." "Yeah" Peter said to them "it's either that – or the two of you know a lot more than what you're saying to Alex and myself. Time will tell and the truth will come out – you know it always does. Besides, we will not rest until it does."

"Well, let's move on and find another passage or door," Alex tells them. "Yeah, OK. I'm going over here and look," Peter says. As Peter walks, off, Alex moves to the other side of the room. All four search for a hidden room with a knob or button – something that will open and let them in.

As they were looking for a door, Peter picked up one chain on the floor and followed it to see where it would lead. He held the chain in his hand and walked with the chain to follow it to a wall, where the chain seemed to go under. Peter yells out "hey, over here! Look, the chain is frozen; it seems to go under the wall!" They all rushed over to where Peter was standing and looked. It appeared the chain was going under a wall. Everyone was checking it out when Peter spoke up and said, "There must be something to pull down – look carefully at this wall."

They were touching the wall, slowly trying to feel for the one thing that would open the wall. As Alex was touching the left side of the wall, he felt a button hidden on the wall. So gently, Alex pushes the button. The wall on the left side opened wide. It swung open to the right and half of the whole wall opened. You could hear the crack within the wall as the ice was breaking apart. A seam ran all the way down and yes, – all four were surprised.

The look on their faces, as the door broke away and opened to reveal a room full of frozen wonderland. Their eyes could not believe what they were seeing! Looking straight ahead then to the left and right – "Oh, my!" Everyone was silently whispering to themselves. They all stared straight ahead in disbelief - - "is that . . . you know. . ." looking at his brother, Peter asked Alex "is it what it is?" Alex stared quietly, then looked at his brother and said, "Well, it looks like a zoo. Only in this world – here and now – this one is not filled with animals, but humans, of all kinds from all over – it looks like and from different galaxies."

CHAPTER SEVENTEEN

THE HUMAN ZOO

As the brothers turned their attention to down below, Peter says, "Look at what it says. "Yeah" Alex replies, it looks like sort of number along with a name. I'm guessing it's maybe where they're from." Jay Bear and Lion stood alongside them in silence then they looked at each other and at the brothers too. "I can't believe it!" said Peter. "Hey, Jay Bear! Why do you think someone would collect and freeze humans? I mean they're frozen and chained on their ankles."

"Oh my!" said Alex. "Hey Peter, do you think Harry T. Bone from the savage ship – the one we ran into before we landed on the white door, had anything to do with this?" "Well," said Peter "Harry told us he was a savage man and collected species from all over the galaxy." "Yeah, that's right" said Alex "but why are they frozen and chained?"

"Hey Jay Bear" asked Peter "this is your world – have you seen anything like this – ever?" "Well," said Jay Bear "just stories really. "Do you think they're all still alive?" Peter asked. "Yes, they're being kept in a certain state of animation until whoever put them here comes back for them," replied Alex "only then will they be defrosted – one by one." "But why?" asked Peter. "I don't know," said Lion "but we've heard stories of long ago – people would come here to the Grim Light and put what they collected each time. Each time they made a deposit, I mean a human deposit – the human would be chained and frozen.

Then the person would then collect a fee for each one." "Well, we know it was Harry T. Bone – he goes all over the galaxy," replied Peter. "Yeah" said Alex "that is right, but there must be one hundred or more here. Harry T. Bone is not the only one collecting humans for a fee and taking them to the Grim Light."

"Yes" replies Peter "but we do not know who is behind this or why . . . any ideas, Lion?" "Well," Lion answers, "We were not only told the stories. neither Jay Bear nor I knew this was real . . . and that someone was doing this. "However, you know! Tell us what they do with the humans" Alex asked them. Jay Bear and Lion silently looked at each other, in their eyes, for a moment then looked away.

They said the stories were of long ago . . . yes, but they were also true and not just stories. "So" Alex said "why don't you just tell us what do they do with them? "Look" said Jay Bear "you both keep asking us, I don't know what to tell you. Lion and I are in shock; we can't believe our eyes!" "OK" said Peter "but you both grew up, knowing about this . . . all of this through stories being told to you. Now that Alex and I want to know . . . you both suddenly cannot and remember nothing! Well, that is bullshit! Alex and I both want to know right now! What is going on! Is your memory going to suddenly improve and you will tell us the whole story . . . or are we going to part ways?

Alex and I want to trust you! How can we if you don't share everything with us?" "OK, calm down Alex – and you too Peter. Everything will be fine, you'll see." Alex looks at his brother, moves a little closer, and says, "I'm getting a very bad feeling – you and I need to get out of here and away from Jay Bear and Lion right now brother – you understand me?" "Yeah, I do," replied Peter and I agree – something isn't right here." "We're being set up. I'm getting a bad feeling," Alex answered. "OK – you push Lion down and I'll run pass them.

OK are you ready?" "Yeah" answered Peter. "OK – on three" Alex instructed. They both made a move to save their lives, they knocked down Jay Bear and Lion and ran past them to the next room. Jay Bear and Lion yelled out – "come back, this won't help! Will not you stay with us for a day or forever – so they say. Won't you both come in and be with us forever frozen until time has run out? We need your body parts! Come back and stay! You said you would come and stay for a moment in time – for a day or forever.

I did tell you; you can't escape – there is nowhere to run in the Grim Light." Alex and Peter got away and into another room within the cave. Upset and shocked, they both realized they both were tricked and are both now in danger. They found a place to sit down and quietly gather their thoughts for a moment. They then realized they needed to produce a plan to survive. Alex and Peter sat down in another room, away from Jay Bear and Lion and talked about what happened.

"OK – what just happened?" Upset and shaking, Peter had his head hung down between his legs, his head in his hands and was shaking his head back and forth in disbelief. "We were lied to!" he finally said. "Yes – and we were used also" Alex answered. "Look, now we just need to get out of here – but how?" "But how?" Peter repeated. "Well, I think the zoo might be able to help us" Alex told him. "How?" asked Peter. "Well, I noticed all the humans were standing on these pedestals." Alex told him. "OK so said Peter. "Well," Alex continued "I think if we can take off the chains on their ankles – lift them off their pedestals, they will thaw.

After that, we will explain who we are, what happened and where. We are all in the same boat, so I think they will understand and be willing to help us. In doing so, they'll be able to help themselves in return." "OK" answered Peter "I'm not sure exactly how they can help us, but I do know that there's strength in numbers – that's always a good thing. We can make it work in our favor also, I think. "I was thinking about something," Peter said. "What's that? Alex asked.

"The Grim Light is a dimensional world within the cave somewhere, if we can find it, we can escape to it. It's got to be better than here!" Peter said. "Yeah" Alex responded, "what choice do we have? We must find kind of clue to locate the other world in here – otherwise we could all be stuck in here for the rest of our lives." "Well, the others in the zoo might know more than us and can help search for something that will save us all," Peter says. Meanwhile, back in the cavern room, Jay Bear and Lion were left lying on the ground where the brothers shoved them.

They both got themselves up and were screaming so loud in this high pitch squealing sound it echoed within the cave. They were so pissed off and were coming after their prey with such anger. They went in search of the two brothers to bring them back to the zoo and collect the biggest fee of all for the two twin brothers from Earth. "How could we get this far and then let this happen, now the two of them got away!" said Lion. "Get the two of them back into this room and then to the zoo or we're going to be in seriously deep trouble!"

Jay Bear told Lion. "If we don't get the twins back here and into the zoo – the two of us will be taking their place," Lion responded. Lion and Jay Bear left the room they were in and went in of search of Peter and Alex. They back tracked into another room and started their search for the two brothers. Peter and Alex were trying to go back to the room with the zoo, which was behind the wall, pull the switch to the door, open it up, and enter back where they were. They opened the wall up by pulling down on the button recessed in the wall.

As it opened, they entered the frozen wonderland and removed the chains off all the human's ankles, one by one, until the chains were off them all. Then they, one at a time, moved them off their pedestals. After standing them up, they were now waiting for them to thaw.

CHAPTER 18

THE EXPERIMENT

The brothers kept looking over their shoulders to make sure that Jay Bear and Lion were not anywhere around. They needed to hurry and thaw all other humans and out of here. They could then look for the Grim Light dimensional world, with help from the others. They felt that their success would be improved with a hundred-people looking. As the humans thawed, they are standing there asking 'where are we?' and 'who are you?' Then, one man said, "My name is Colin.

I was brought here several months ago; I believe from my home planet Tzar." "This is my brother Peter – I am Alex, we were lied to and tricked into coming here. Now we are in danger and need your help. We're from Earth and where are you from?" Alex asked. "I am from a galaxy, not too far away, called No-Mar. It is within this galaxy system.

They came, tracked us down, caged us, and took us away from our families." "OK" explained Alex "we need to know if of you have heard of a world within this cave. It's hidden behind a secret wall." "What is its name?" someone asked. "Grim Light – anyone know of it? Peter asked. "Yes – most of us do. It is like your planet Earth, but different in ways. For instance, there is no meat – they outlawed it, they consider it dangerous now" Colin said. "Oh – yes, too many diseases" someone else answered. "Well," Alex replied, "It's like Earth in some ways – so we have heard – but we've not been there.

All our lives depend on finding this place. In addition, two two-half animals are tracking us now and we must not be caught – this could be extremely dangerous for all of us. Did they ever tell you why they captured you? And what were they planning to do with you?" "Well," Colin spoke up and said, "Because their planet is made up of a lot of animals, they were able to experiment and turn out half humans, alongside of their animal parts.

So, they capture distinct species and use their body parts to turn animals into part humans – do you understand?" "Yeah, I guess so" Peter replied. "They took the brains to make them smart, the voice so they could speak. They have been able to collect species from all over the universe so they could turn out their species – making them strong and very, very smart.

Whatever you do, do not underestimate them – ever . . . and do not turn your back on them. They will and can rip you to shreds in a heartbeat . . . a Nano second. Do not ever forget they are part animal, but have the brains, intelligence, and ability to track down anyone . . . and game over for you and all of us if that happens! Listen – there is no reasoning with them. One cannot beg or make your case. They all have their mission to achieve. Nothing will get in their way until they have succeeded in their mission. If caught – you are screwed, because you cannot outrun them, and they will tear you to shreds. The only chance one has is to stare them down and try to distract them – you know – catch them off guard."

"Yes, we know! We managed to do that – this is how we got away," Alex said to Colin. Where is everyone else?" Colin asked. "I know," said Peter "but to tell you the truth, not everyone got thawed. Perhaps the pedestals or platforms malfunctioned." "Anyway, there's only a few here with us" Alex said. "OK, well stop complaining," said Peter. "It's better this way, a larger group would cause problems and it would be much harder to get around without being seen."

"OK, that makes sense" Colin replied. "What about the others, are we going to leave them here?" Alex asked. "Look" said Peter "let us just try to take this one step at a time. We have help now. We have here with us. When we find the Grim Light world, we can come and save some of the others." "Yes" said Colin "look – the others here in the zoo have been here for quite some time – I'm not sure they can recover at all. Look I am glad I am free and here to help you find a way out to the other world, but we must save ourselves now! If we do not, we all stand a particularly good chance of going back into the zoo."

Colin continued to say, "Look, Alex and Peter, you don't realize – I think – what happens to you and what they'll do to you!" "OK, calm down Colin," said Alex. "No!" Colin replied to them "look, if we get sent back there, they'll send us to the doctor – and really – its game over! I would rather kill myself before I let him remove my body parts one by one – its torture and death. How did you think the animals in this world could think, have intelligence, walk, and talk – and much more than you can imagine! Trust me, you don't want to go back and get captured." "Yes, we understand – or rather my brother and I are getting a very alarming picture – painted in detail!" Alex replied.

"Anyway, let us get moving! Colin – you and the other three guys lead the way in the direction you think is the way to the place we're trying to find." "OK" said Colin "let us go back. I think if we go back by the zoo, there is another room hidden." "OK" Alex replies "led the way." As Colin and the others head off, the brothers are right behind them, hoping to find the secret world that is a little like home.

They enter the zoo and head to the back of the room, passed the platforms, pedestals and all the frozen bodies. They move toward the back wall, looking for a secret lever or button to press to find another room that will bring them one-step closer to where they all want to be. Looking and touching the back wall to feel their way around, to find anything that would suddenly crack the wall door and slowly open it.

With them all standing there – waiting to enter another room. As everyone works on the back wall, trying to figure away in, Lion and Jay Bear were using their sense of smell and hearing to get closer to where the brothers were found. Lion has a deep sense of hearing – it is sharp and can hear a pin drop or a baby's cry from a mile away. Jay Bear has a deep sense of smell and can smell human flesh and blood even further away than Lion. Together, the two know they have amazing senses. Soon their senses will bring them face to face with the brothers. They intend to take them both back to the zoo and to the man they call Doctor.

They know that the brothers have amazing brains and other features that would make this special animal the smartest half human and leader of their world. Especially with the brother's amazing twin power abilities with the effect of a double whammy feature that would enable this special animal, who has fought and killed others to gain the right to become leader of Star Zone.

He will become the smartest of his kind, the new leader of their world, and will stop at nothing to get these two brothers in the zoo – on the doctors table to begin a journey that has been years in the making. "Lion?" Jay Bear asked. "Yes, Jay Bear?" Lion responded. "We need to call him," Jay Bear says. "Oh, Mr. Hobbit!" Lion says. "Yes" Jay Bear answered, "Let him know what has happened so far, to keep him up to speed. If we don't – we could be his next two victims – buried six under!" "Yeah" says Lion ". . . after he shreds us both to pieces."

CHAPTER NINETEEN

THE RULES OF THE HOBBIT

Searching for the grim light

Mr. Hobbit is the leader here and follows his own rules. The people that live here fear and fear him. However, Hobbit is a small man with features that would scare anyone away, but he wants to look a certain way – taller, sharper, and more intelligent. To him, he wants to look more like a human man, with certain features he feels would gain him respect with the people around him.

He also wishes the citizens of Star Zone to recognize he is their leader. A leader should also be feared, to allow the citizens to know he makes the rules and judgments alone and decisions fall on the doorsteps of their leader. Everyone must respect and follow the rules of the Hobbit. His teeth are razors sharp and can shred you in seconds.

His hands are large and soft, with fingernails like sharp claws that can open you up, throw you across the room, jump on you within seconds, and rip you apart until nothing is left but the skin hanging on your bones.

His people, who live here, know they would not be who they are without his leadership and the goodness he brings them all. He gives the animals the ability to walk, talk, and live a life much richer and freer.

To think, understand and can decide. None of this would be possible without Hobbit and the doctor – who has brought medicine to a new level – the greatest for all animals of Star Zone. Peter, Alex, and the others who escaped from the zoo are still at the back of the room looking at the wall for a switch to open the door hidden within the wall. As Colin, the brothers and a few others are touching the wall – Alex is yelling out "hurry up – find that switch! Jay Bear and Lion will come back this way!" Just then, Colin spoke up and said, "Count on it – they both have special senses. One has hearing and the other has smell."

"Oh – crap!" said Peter "find that switch – come on!" Right at that moment, Alex heard a noise, looked in the back of the room over by the entrance, and saw Jay Bear and Lion coming their way. Peter ran back to the wall and said "Jay Bear and Lion are coming! They are by the entrance! Look – it is now – or we are all doomed! Oh, my GOD!" They all shouted out 'hurry finds the switch!' Just then, Colin leans over, touches a button, the wall opened, and an entrance appeared into another area.

They all go in and the wall closes behind them. Jay Bear and Lion enter the zoo. Jay Bear speaks to Lion and says, "I can smell them." "Well," Lion says "I heard them, so now, where are they? Let us look around; they could hide behind something or someone." As the two searches for the brothers, Alex, and Peter both suddenly realize that Colin is missing. The others are gone. "Oh my!" said Lion "if the brothers released Colin and several others, then that means they know the truth of the Grim Light world and are all on their way to find the entrance and leave forever.

"We've got to stop them from finding the entrance to the world" Jay Bear replied. Jay Bear and Lion continue their search for the brothers and others in the zoo. Jay Bear stops and takes out a signaling stone called Lobar – this is their way to send messages. It works like this: there is a light inside the Zobar, when you want to send a message, you hold it in your hands – one light will blink inside the stone, meaning everything is fine – two blinks of light mean trouble – and three blinks of light means trouble and send help.

You touch the stone you are holding in your hand either once, twice, or a third time. The other person holding another stone will see their stone either blink once, twice, or three times to let them know which message you are sending.

Mr. Hobbit has his stone sitting on the table – he looks over and sees it blink three times. Mr. Hobbit knows that Jay Bear and Lion are in trouble now.

The brothers have figured something out about the world in which, for now they all live; including what they are doing to humans all over the galaxy – even as far away.

As Earth, where the brothers are from Mr. Hobbit leaves his office, goes out of the building to the security room, and tells the guard to get the best animal guilds together and send them to the cave where Jay Bear and Lion are waiting for them at the zoo. He instructs them to help get and capture the brothers and anyone else who has helped them, or is with them, put them in the zoo and chain them up.

The doctor will be here soon. We must get everyone round up and in the zoo before the doctor comes. They need the brother's body parts.

Mr. Hobbit has gone to great lengths to get them both for his personal needs. Jay Bear and Lion still search the zoo for the brothers, trying to figure out where they have gone now. Lion and Jay Bear know Mr. Hobbit will send guards here to help them capture of the brothers.

Meanwhile, the search goes on for the brothers and the others with them who have aided them and given their help. Lion and Jay Bear realize now that Peter and Alex have the help of the ones that were held in the zoo and kept frozen. are missing and re not. They are not sure how they have with them to help them find Grim Light. Peter and Alex are now in another room on the other side of the zoo wall. They – with Colin and others have made it through to a different room and are hopefully one-step closer to a world that will welcome them all. As they enter, they wander around to see exactly where they are now.

Peter, Alex, and the others step into the room well lit – not cold or freezing either. However, it did not take them long to figure out the room they entered was the Doctor's laboratory. "OH, MY GOD!" said Colin. We must find a way out of here – right now! Hurry – everyone! Looks for another door now!" Screaming – Colin and Peter run to the wall and look for a door.

They find the switch right away, pull the lever. Another door pulled away and opened. The wall gave way and the door revealed itself. They all scrambled to enter another room – hopefully, they are safe for a moment. "OK – everyone inside" says Alex. They enter, one by one, until once again the wall and door behind them close. They are in a room that seems empty, but often – the brothers realize things are not always, what they appear to be, especially if one thinks they are alone – often you are not. Just like if you think the room might be empty – there might be a clue in this room, which would lead them a step closer to where they all might want to be.

"OK Colin, you take a few people and look for clues. Peter and I will look for the door so we can find the way out of here," Alex said. Jay Bear and Lion are still in the zoo looking for signs to find the brothers and the others who went with them. They realize they must have found a hidden door and went through it. "So" Jay Bear says, "we need to find the door and follow their trail exactly, so it will lead us to the brothers, Alex and Peter."

So, Lion asked Jay Bear "do we search and look on our own – or do we wait for the guards come join us in our search for them." "No" said Jay Bear "I think we should look on our own, so we don't lose the trail or their scent. We can leave a note for the guards to follow our trail. We'll continue on until they find us and help us out in the search." "OK" said Lion "that sounds good. Continue on." "OK" Jay Bear responds, "Then look for the hidden door on the wall." They both move to the wall behind the zoo and look for the hidden door. It did not take Jay Bear, Lion long, when they found the switch, pressed the button, and once again, the wall gives way.

The door opens and the two enter the Doctor's laboratory, which shows no signs of the boys and everyone else. However, Jay Bear and Lion walk around to look for them and make sure they were not hiding somewhere in the lab. Neither of them could hear or smell them, so they figured they must have moved on to a different room and passed another secret hidden door. Within the walls of the lab, they had once again disappeared, leaving them behind to track them down.

CHAPTER 20

FINDING A WAY OUT

As Peter and Alex dashed to find another door, they realized that Jay Bear and Lion are just behind them and one step away from crashing through another door and finding them all. They fear that capturing them might just happen. They hurry to escape to increase their lead. Colin finds a clue to the Grim Light and calls the brothers over to look. As the boys go over to where Colin is standing, they see a written message on the wall. "What does it say?" asked Peter "do you know?" "Yeah" answers Colin "it says something like 'look around and in this room, you will find an entrance where your journey will begin. Enter the wrong door and what you look for will be gone forever and your wishes will not be granted.

"OK" Peter says, "So look in this room – there is more than one door to choose from. If we choose the wrong door and enter it – we can't go back and choose the right door and our dream of finding this world will disappear forever!" Alex asks Colin, "OK, but how do we know the right door to choose?" "I think," says Colin "it's sort of a trick to keep the undesirables away, kind of. I think if we find the right door, it will open for us – because it will feel our hearts are pure and good. If we have bad intentions when we try to enter, something bad will happen."

"I see" Alex replies "OK, let us find a door. What do you people think sounds good – we have real evil behind us, so time is the key? Here - let us look over here . . . can you see? Wipe this area of the wall off." As everyone wipes a different dust that has gathered bizarre, they all realize, after cleaning it off, three doors appeared to them.

"I can see this," Colin says to the others "can everyone else see this too?"

"Yes, we do, it looks like there's dust that doesn't let you see these doors right away, to the naked eye, now we have to do what it says" replied Peter. "Well," says Colin "why don't you and Alex try, since you are both twins – they say that twins have power – so stand in front of each door and let us see if anything happens." Therefore, the brothers stand in front of the doors. One by one, they stand in front of each door. The second time, the middle door had a glow to it. They opened it and when they all went, they entered an ambush. "Oh shit, I guess we choose the wrong door!" said Peter. "Yeah" replied Alex "well, we know that now!

"Look, I'm sorry" Colin says to the brothers. Guess I should not have the two of you stand by the doors. I just thought that you two had kinds of twin's magic that would have help us determine the right door. Well, shit next time well just do Eeny, Meeny, Miny, Moe'!"

The guards had their weapons pointed right at them. They led everyone back to the zoo, where they were put back on platforms and frozen – except for Colin, Alex, and Peter.

They were taken to the doctor's lab and tied down in a chair. All three were waiting nervously for the man everyone called the Doctor. After they were tied up, the guards took their posts outside the door. They had orders not to leave their posts or go back in – especially when the doctor got there – just guard the room. Their fate awaits – certain death, they were about to undergo something so horrible, not even the boys realized just how bad life would change for them.

All three were facing death with removal their limbs and other body parts – something the doctor would tell the brothers as he performed this horrible operation – their certain fate awaited.

As they lay tied down and were forced to remain awake, the doctor would remove their precious body limbs and brains from each brother's body. He would reattach most to Mr. Hobbit and all-important figures that have paid for this service.

He waited years for the right brothers to come to the lab, which hid in a cave here in the realm of this dimensional world. Mr. Hobbit came down from his high-rise towers in the sky to the hidden lab in the cave. The Doctor and Mr. Hobbit are discussing his upcoming operation, how it will improve the way he looks, how all the citizens here will look at him and be more fearful. Mr. Hobbit thinks if everyone feared him then he could control Star Zone and the people in it.

The conversation grew intense between the Doctor and Mr. Hobbit. They were talking in the lab, with a huge window – the brothers could watch their conversation and – could hear what they were saying. The brothers were glued to their discussion and were fearful they would not get away or figure out a plan in time. The conversation continued – Hobbit was saying to the doctor "remember how it used to be in the beginning of Star Zone?" "Yes" said the Doctor "I can recall, in the past – so long ago – we were all animals in every sense of the word. Then, when the solar lightning storm struck, us could speak. Well – the ones who survived anyway.

When we got our voices, I remember the others also wanted so much more. More would cost us –our own citizen animals their lives! It would cost them to have our new abilities and can run our own world, without humans taking over and destroying it. They tried once; we tore them apart and dragged their sorry bodies – until nothing was left. That was the last time anyone came to our world and tried to kill us off.

Now we are much stronger, thanks to human abilities – because humans landed here and gave us their body parts to make us half-human. We are now one of the most fearless and strongest dimension worlds out there." As the brothers looked on and watched they whispered to each other – "Peter – can you get your hands free?" asked Colin. "Almost there, still working on it . . . what about you two?" Peter whispered back.

Alex and Colin both said "yeah – not quite, but it's getting closer almost – just need a few minutes more." "OK, let me know" Peter answered them. "Yeah – OK."

Then they all kept their hands to escaping this 'mad scientist' doctor and his plan to remove their body parts. As the brothers still themselves, the Doctor and Mr. Hobbit are still recalling days when they were trapped and could not walk or talk or do anything but be killed and hammered by others.

"The humans came here so long ago, but because we were all dangerous animals – most of us could defend ourselves by using our unusually sharp teeth, which looked like razors and could rip any human apart within seconds. the other animals had unbelievable claws on the end of their hands, other animals had different abilities like strength and speed to defend themselves or run away extremely fast and not are caught. The ones who had strength –

the animal could catch you once – once caught, they could use their strength to squeeze you until screamed your last breath. The ones who had speed were so fast; they were all gone very quickly. Yes, I recall those days when we had to fight for our lives and our world.

When we were just animals, and now – thanks to the solar storm, which helped, turned the animals here in our world to something much, much more. The storm. when it struck . . . I can remember when it hit us. We fell asleep and when the animals woke up, we suddenly had the ability to speak! We were in shock . . . but the voice in us grew, we became stronger in our abilities and wanted more than just, what we had. As time went by and days turned into months . . . we were still in danger of other humans from different galaxies and dimensions coming here and trying to steal – and take our world away from us.

CHAPTER TWENTY-ONE

HISTORY 101

The fight for our planet went on until one day a small half human, half-animal called the Hobbit came. He gathered all the animals together and had one largest meeting ever seen in this galaxy. He told everyone to believe in him. "I am Hobbit. I will lead you into a new future to become half human." The animals rose and accepted the new future and Hobbit as their leader of Star Zone.

The years went by, Hobbit and the new citizens were still defending their world from others who wanted all their solar bars, which supplied energy, their world had. Their world also has amazing hidden powers within the forest. Certain animals live within, and lead dangers lives within the forest. Therefore, a path was formed to keep the citizens safe, the forest green and strong and their powers safe also.

It grows stronger every year, in which certain animals live in the forest, making their magical energy forces strong and hidden from others. This keeps the little creatures safe from harm. The Star Zone animals were speaking for the first time and their world is turning into a city. A world of buildings, high rises, restaurants, medicine, and everything was turning into a world the animals wanted. Except, the creatures still here living in this changing world wanted more and desired more.

They wanted the ability to have brainpower to decide, to think more human. To walk and eat like humans – to love and have others far away respect them – to have visitors want to come to their home to visit for a day or awhile or live here, not go home and become one. Therefore, as Star Zone was evolving and growing, there was, deep inside, a hated of humans. They had no respect for any. Humans throughout the years had invaded their world, started wars, tried to destroy their planet and home – the humans hated the animals! They had no place for any in their world and in their own world – they were not welcome.

They were just ugly little creatures whom the humans wanted dead – all dead. They would not stop at nothing to achieve this. However, as their world was growing, with every year that went by – their planet was now becoming a city . . . for the first time. The citizens were realizing they needed to become human if they would fight and protect their world and their city, and their home. They now needed to change into strong humans so they could stand up for their own justice, kick serious ass, and destroy others that wanted their home for themselves.

However, the animals knew they needed something or someone to help them all achieve their goal to become more human-like, to fight and capture humans to use in experiments and can attached human's limbs to the creatures. They wanted to walk and can reason, think and be intelligent.

They needed to have legs to stand strong and have arms with hands. The experiments and the capturing of humans were not going well.

The citizens were growing angry and restless because of their failure. However, one day, Hobbit brought someone to Star Zone who changed everything for the animals and for the first time they were seeing real hope and change. They saw a bluebird become the first half human – tall, unbelievably beautiful with human thin legs, feet, and human flat stomach with large and soft breasts. Her face was round with features all around the outside of her face and she had big, wide round eyes with long eyelashes, a beak for her nose and a human mouth and lips. Everyone was so excited they could not believe their eyes.

They loved it and they knew now everyone wanted this experiment to be performed on them. For this to be done, the collection and capturing of humans was essential. Everyone agreed to do whatever was necessary so the experiments could continue for every citizen here in Star Zone. Now, the citizens wanted to know who would run and perform these experiments, they wanted to meet this person.

"Well," Hobbit said "look, I checked into who would be willing to help us achieve our goals here in Star Zone. I asked myself who would help us, and our city become strong and able to resist anyone trying to start a war with us and take away our planet. The answer – well Hobbit said, I searched and searched the world over, from every dimensional world and the galaxies nearby. The only person I could find with the background needed and with done experiments with new age cutting and bodies, was a person everyone called the DOCTOR.

Now, he is here with us, and we owe him thanks for coming here, with us achieve our goals and desires of becoming half human with our half-animal side. The Doctor has experimented on thousands to perfect his talents. He has captured, sewed together, figured out their body, blood, and brains to join us. This match is pure magic. Now, because of his talents, we here at Star Zone can use these brilliant skills of his to help the citizens stand strong, walk freely, and take charge – so others will not invade us here, try to start a war and take over our world.

The doctor has given the half-human animals a unique way to live, love and fight. Never again will they have to die to save a world once terrorized with war from the humans who came here, hunted them down, and killed them on their own bloodied land. The half-animal, half-humans gave thanks to the Doctor. Now, they can rise above and stand tall. Together, with their weapons in hand, they can fight off anyone from now on who would try to disable and disarm them – no more war! No more humans coming here to take something away from them.

Now, they can build their city together, work together and have a life – which in the past, would never have happened. They would have died if other humans, so far away, had come here. However, thank God for all those humans, who gave up their lives so we, the animals, could rise and walk to make our world. Strong – so we could capture and kill humans – so we could be more than just animals. No more will humans look down upon us. We will never live our lives in the past again – so be warned humans!

CHAPTER TWENTY-TWO

THE PLAN

The brothers are still trying to break free, with Colin there beside them, trying to help and free him too. The Doctor and Hobbit can still be seen through the giant window in the next room. Their conversation together seemed lasting a long time, for which the brothers are grateful. It has given them the continue trying to break the ties that bound their hands behind the backs of all three. Now, with the conversation looking like it is slowing down, the brothers are very worried. They are worried about what the doctor has planned for them next, and their screams will be heard and felt from around the dimensional world and beyond.

The rumors are flying – buzzing around the galaxy that Hobbit has caught the two twin brothers from Earth for their next experiment. Humans from all over the galaxy are hearing the news these two poor, innocent boys were lured and drawn into Hobbit's world, not knowing what would happen to them next. The news is traveling fast and now, humans from all over know now, they must send in someone to save the boys and bring them to the hidden world of the Grim Light. It would be the one place they would be safe from harm and not hunted.

However, who could get in the animal world – they know of only one man. The animals trust and let in Harry T. Bone – the savage hunter man. Yes, Harry T. Bone would be the perfect choice to save the boys, but would he risk his own life just to save two humans. They knew they must produce something to lure Harry in save those two brothers.

The Council of the Grim Light rarely gets involved in other galaxies' disputes, but the world of the Grim Light will often get involved in saving another's life.

If it is determined to be an especially heinous situation and considered necessary to act right away. The Council has sent for information on the status of the brothers, awhile later a man goes before the Council and says the brothers has been captured and are being held in the Hobbit cave. One other thing, "yes what is the other news?" someone in the Council asked. The Doctor has arrived. "Oh, My God!" said each member of the Council "we don't have much time get Harry T. Bone right away! The brothers were supposed to come here – how did they end up in Star Zone? someone in the Council asked. "We are looking into that matter as we speak" was the answer.

"Where are the brothers now?" a Councilman asked. "Our inside person there has told us the boys are being held in the lab and are tied down in a chair for the moment. Hobbit and the Doctor are also in the lab in another room talking. We have contacted Harry T. Bone and he will be here within the hour" was the answer. "OK, now I think The Council should discuss sending a message to Hobbit to put a scare in him and the Doctor and put them both on notice.

Let them both know we know what they're about to do and we're not going to allow it in any stretch of the imagination" one Councilman said. "OK but let us talk to Harry first and let us send him to see if he can get the brothers out. If he fails, then right at that moment, we will send the message to Hobbit." "OK" was the vote as all members of the Council agreed to the plan set forth? Now we wait for Harry T. Bone to land at the Grim Light Board of Council. hours went by, Harry and his ship finally arrives at the Grim Light docking station. Harry is not happy to be here, summoned by the Council – simultaneously Harry is a little curious.

He wonders what the Council would want with him, Harry could not imagine. Harry leaves his ship and walks into the City of Grim Light. Normally, Grim Light is one of Harry's favorite places to visit, to eat and see old friends and hook up with the ladies – every now and then, when a little luck was on his side. Harry stood medium height and in shape, the ladies would smile when Harry came to town. 'Oh – those abs of his!' they were thinking to themselves.

Those brown eyes and brown hair, which he kept short in front and a ponytail in back and his trimmed beard – that looked scruffy. Harry was in his forties and a good-looking man, and the ladies thought so. The downtown city area has little tiny lights with bulbs that light up and are strung all over the beautiful trees they have all over the downtown area. The trees are set in Concrete Square with the beautiful twinkling lights that shine bright in the evening hours all the way down Main Street.

They have businesses to choose from to keep you entertained and nightlife to feel alive. When you wrap yourself around the beat of the music, you take away to the magic and heart of their city. They have protection here for the citizens and visitors. Their protection forces manage the rules enforced and governed by the Grim Light City Council of Men.

The buildings and homes here in the town of Grim Light have solar panels. The sun creates the energy, which powers up the solar panels. Everything has solar panels on the roofs and on all the sides of the buildings. Everything is run off and powered up by the sun, even the businesses.

Law that all buildings have solar panels needs it. Nothing may be built without solar panels; it is required by the Council and enforced by the protection forces. As Harry T. Bone walks through the city, he is going to the city's planning building and will stand before the Council, as he was summoned to do. He opens the door, walks through the main lobby and straight toward the elevators to the top floor.

Once there, he gets off and enters the Council Chambers to wait for the other members to come in. They will let him know why they have summoned him here and what they want from old Harry T. Bone. As the Council members enter the room, they sit down behind the long, wraparound desk that is big enough for everyone on the board.

They all started by saying thank-you for coming. "Harry, we have an urgent matter to discuss with you and time is of the essence."

"Well," Harry replies, "What is it? What is wrong and how can I help. One member stands to explain to Harry the reason he is here. "Well Harry, you see it's about two twin brothers who were supposed to come here and live with us.

We sent them an invitation and . . . well something has happened to them along the way and the two have ended up in Star Zone. We are not sure how this happened, but they are in there. The Hobbit and the Doctor have them both in the cave in a lab. They're tied to a chair and are waiting to be ripped apart by the terrible Doctor." "Oh, my!" said Harry.

I met these two brothers before they got to Star Zone. They told me that is where they were supposed to be and the two had received an invitation to come. "Well, they must've put in the directions wrong" one of the Councilman said. "Well," said Harry "I don't think so – what happened was the Hobbit somehow changed their directions so they would end up docking at Star Zone. Look, I can tell you the brothers didn't know they were supposed to be here in Grim Light."

"Well nevertheless, the boys are supposed to be our guests, now they are in danger of being torn apart by the crazy Doctor. He is planning to remove the boys' brains – both – and replanting them into Hobbit's brain. He is very evil – but needs the bothers' brains to be able to produce more ways to lure others into his world. We believe the boys' brains can solve the problems on which they are working. If they continue this path and succeed, all of us will be in danger and we can't allow this."

The Council continued, "we want you to go over to Star Zone, get the brothers out and bring them back here to Grim Light.

We'll explain more once they're safe and here with us."

"Well," said Harry "I can probably get in, this is true, but I'm not sure if I can manage this all by myself." "Well, you could take someone with you" the Council answered him "if you thought it would help Harry . . . but please hurry!

If you can get these two boys over here and safe, there will be a reward in it for you. So, what do you say . . . will you help us get the two boys back?" "What if I fail?" Harry asked them. "Well then Harry – we go to war," one Councilman said. "We cannot let them kill these two brothers – too much is at stake for all of us." "When do you want me to go" Harry asked. "Right now,

Harry! Go now see what you can do" they answered him. "OK" Harry replied. "Oh, and there is one more thing, there is a man with the brothers. His name is Colin bring him back too" the Council instructed.

CHAPTER TWENTY-THREE

THE RESCUE

After Harry got finished speaking to the Council, he prepares to leave, trying to figure out the best plan to break the brothers out and bring them all to Grim Light. So . . . on the way down in the elevator, Harry started thinking – since Hobbit likes to collect well let us say human parts . . . Harry thought he might bring something that would distract him long enough to see the whereabouts of the brothers and see their condition.

OK Harry thought, this could work! I will tell Hobbit I have a prime specimen for him to have a look at. I will bring him to the lab and if evil Hobbit, he will be interested in checking this out. There are two things I must do: 1-Send a message to Hobbit and 2-Find a species even Hobbit could not resist having all for him.

I must send a message to the Council first telling them I need a decoy to take with me. It must be someone of value to Hobbit, someone I can distract Hobbit with. I will be there to pick up the person right away and hope you have someone in mind. Then I can send a message to Hobbit. Harry heads back, hopefully to pick up his specimen to bring to Star Zone. He knows he has little time . . . and time for Harry is running out. The Grim Light Council received Harry's news and request for a warm body for Hobbit to get excited over – even if only for minutes – to take his evil plans off the brothers and onto someone else.

Harry goes through a portal, which allows a person to travel to one dimensional world from another. It is faster and allows Harry to pick up his cargo, and then meet with Hobbit at the lab. Harry picked up his valuable cargo to bring to the lab. I hope it will take Hobbits mind off the brothers long enough for Harry to help them. Out of the portal, here comes Harry and a man in his custody. He makes his way to the cave and into the lab.

Hobbit comes out of the lab and sees Harry standing there with someone. Hobbit looks at Harry with an evil look in his eye and asked him "what are you doing here Harry? Why did you send me that message?" "Well," Harry said, "I have a gift for you, since you helped me out a while ago and sent some business my way. I just wanted to repay the favor. I hope you don't mine Hobbit." "No Harry, thank-you. So – what did you bring me? Hobbit asked. "Well, look to my right Hobbit" Harry replied.

"Oh my! Harry! Well, thank-you!" Hobbit exclaimed. "Let's take him to the lab for safe keeping," Harry suggested. "Yes OK," said Hobbit. As they entered the room, Harry sees Alex and Peter tied down in two separate chairs. "I will be right back," said Hobbit "let me put him away." "OK, I'll be right here" Harry answers him. "OK" said Hobbit. As Hobbit walks away, Harry knew he had but seconds . . . so he unties the boys. Hurry – let us go!" he tells them. They make their way out of the cave and get to the portal. Colin goes through first.

Harry goes to turn around and Hobbit was standing there! He says to Harry "I'm sorry it has come down to this, if the brothers make one more move toward the portal Harry – I'll kill you and the brothers! Harry – you know I can make this happen. I am lightning fast! I can get to you and the brothers before you go through the portal and think you are safe.

Harry just stands there, looks over at the brothers, and says, "I'm sorry, I just can't risk it." Then suddenly – Harry turns his head around and tells the boys, mouthing the words, "go into the portal now! Don't worry about me – you understand?" The brothers put their fingers up to give Harry a sign they understood. Harry turned his body slowly back around, looked at Hobbit, and said, "Go on – give it your best shot! You are not getting these brothers! Not now – not ever, Hobbit! Even if I have to die to prevent you from laying your firsthand them." Hobbit open his mouth, exposing his sharp jagged teeth and let out this scream – so piercing – Harry was convinced everyone could hear Hobbit . . . even in the next dimensional world.

Then, with his head tilted back, a scream came out of Hobbit's mouth. Harry runs to the portal, the brother's step onto the portal platform and reached with their hands out to the other side. Harry sees their hands extended outwards, grabs them and the boys pulled him safely through the other side – before Hobbit could get to him. In Grim Light, Harry turned their side of the portal off.

The Council came over and said, "Welcome to both Alex and Peter, you are in Grim Light. We are the ones who sent you the invitation in the first place. We wanted you two to come here. I am so sorry - - you have had quite an ordeal . . . and quite a mix up, but we are glad you are here now Alex, and you too Peter. Welcome to Grim Light."

CHAPTER TWENTY-FOUR

GRIM LIGHT CITY

"It was you who sent us the message?" Alex asked. "Yes, we did" a member of the Council told them and asked, "but how did you both wind up in Star Zone?" "Well," said Peter "we're not really sure . . . we followed our directions. The next thing we knew, we were docking our craft at their station and going through this white door and staircase.

Well, it was a trap set up by – well, we know now it was the evil Doctor and Hobbit – but my brother and I don't understand why?" "Well from what we gathered, their world has a long history," the Councilman told them. "Why do not we go, eat something, and have a seat. I'll try to do my best to explain it to you both." Peter and Alex agreed. They walked blocks to the downtown area, sat down in the local eatery. People all around them in the restaurant were coming around to say how happy they were we both made it and congrats.

You boys are local celebrates here – you are the only ones from a world that is a long way away in a different galaxy. People are happy you are here on one hand and surprised you were both able to find us. "Why are people so surprised?" asked Peter. "Because Peter, no one else ever made it as far as you and your brother have. The two of you have really been through. Everyone here is happy you are safe and here with us now." "Well, Peter and I have to go back" Alex told them. "What do you mean?" asked Harry. One of the Council members was sitting with him, his name was Weathers.

They looked puzzled and everyone just stared at the two brothers and asked them why. The boys explained that Hobbit imprisoned both their parents in Star Zone, level one prison. He told us our father came here through a portal he invented himself, used the same portal to send his wife through – as they were in the middle of a shootout with another agency from their world. They found out about the white door in space and would kill them all for the directions, but they escaped and ended up in Star Zone.

When our parents went through, the two according to Hobbit, were caught and sent to Star Zone level one prison. He said it was against the law to come here without permission or an invitation. So now you know . . ." "Wow," said Harry "if they are both in Star Zone level one prison, you have real problems! There is no escape from there. This prison is massive it is like three giant spaceships in one. It holds all criminals from all dimensional worlds that have broken the law. It is also invisible and cannot be detected by other craft or radar.

Look, even if your parents wanted to break out, there would be nowhere to run to except space – and that is impossible. When they put a prisoner to death – they tie them down in a pod chair and shoot out them out in space with a limited amount of air they have tubed in through a device which they wear on their head. So" Alex asked them "any ideas how to get them out? We must go back and get them out! There just has to be a way."

"Well, first we need to find one of our contacts and see if they're still alive and in the prison at Star Zone. Let us wait and see what we find out and go from there before we even begin to draw up plans to try and bust them both out." "OK" said the boys "but we need to know as soon as possible – what is going on and what has happened." "We understand," said Weathers "we will do everything within our powers to help your parents." We understand there is a time issue, especially now – since the two of you have escaped from Hobbit and ruined his plans to kill you both.

He might go after your parents for revenge and try to use them to get the two of you to return to Star Zone." "Well," said Peter "if we can get Hobbit to get them out of prison and bring them to Star Zone for us – we can try to convince him we will trade our lives for our parents." "Well," said Harry "that will be very tricky because there's no way Hobbit will keep his end of the bargain." "Well," said Alex "we already know that – just maybe we can use that in our favor." "But look" Harry told Alex "Hobbit is very smart.

He will try to trick us, and we must be incredibly careful. "We'll find out through our contacts if, first, in fact they are in the prison," Weathers said. "I recall when Hobbit wanted both of us to go on the hunt for the solar bars in the Grim Light cave and well, Peter and I – just for a moment had this feeling come over us, not to do this . . . something was wrong. Hobbit felt this too. Therefore, at the time, he had a window that lit up and before we knew it, my brother, and I were, staring at what we were led to believe was our mother saying she and Dad were in fact in prison. He told us then if we did not help them, they were going to kill them both, because they broke the law.

But he told us if we were to help them find what they're looking for they would in fact let both go." "So" Harry asked, "that is why you both went on this journey in the first place?" "Yes" said Peter "what choice did we have?" "OK, so while we work on that – can you tell us about Star Zone?" Weathers asked.

"Because the Council here is launching an investigation regarding how they changed your coordinates and altered your directions when you got closer. We are not sure exactly, but we have our suspicions, and we will just leave it at that for now. But please tell us about Star Zone."

"Well," Alex told them "It's a world that, at one time, only had animals roaming around. These animals were unique in every sense of the word – nothing is like these animals. They are beautiful, but with beauty come danger. As beautiful as they are, the animals had unique features about them, which made them deadly. They took over Star Zone, until one year someone came to Star Zone named Hobbit. He told the animals he could change their lives and give them something no one else in the galaxy could.

He told them he would take one animal and give that animal human features, with special abilities that would allow it to, not only think like humans, but also have their brains. Intelligence is worth killing thousands of humans to achieve their goals.

Hobbit came here one day and turned a once quiet dimensional world, overrun with only animals, and turned it into what you see today. He is a sick and twisted person. He has captured, tortured, and killed thousands upon thousands of humans from all galaxies. The thing he has done to humans for animals to achieve their goals and become what they are today is unthinkable."

"One can't imagine – let me tell you, the two of you were right in the thick of things." Stan told them. "They had a plan in effect for you two boys that took them years to put into action and now, we came along, destroyed that, and took you away. This is not going to end well for nobody, and do not think for one moment that Star Zone is going to drop this. They will be coming for you both and we now just started a war between the two of us.

It is going to end very badly for . . . but in the end, we will come out ahead. We are humans not animals! They still think like their animal's side. They are only half-human – we believe we can have the element of surprise in an attack.

Finally, we will take down Star Zone, stop them from luring humans in, capturing them, dismembering their bodies for their own personal gain and use. It just makes me sick. It must stop. Grim Light is going to battle Star Zone. Our mission is to capture them and put The Doctor and Hobbit in Star Zone Level one prison, where they will remain for the rest of their lives. As far as the rest of Star Zone animals living there, we must destroy those animals the evil doctor turned into half humans. They are dangerous, and I can tell you – not one of them will go back to what they were before all this began."

The brothers listened to everything Stan had to say. He sat on the Council and made the rules. "Our protection force is our police here. They enforce the rules here," Stan said to them. "I see," said Peter and Alex. "We want to ask you about our craft," said the boys. "Oh yes," said Stan. "The craft, we had it moved – so it's safe – please don't worry." "If you could please show my brother and I where it is.

I'd like to check a few things" Alex asked them. "OK, sure no problem. I'll have one of our protection force members go with you and we'll show you our docking station." Stan replies. "Thank you so much," said Peter. "Oh, Peter – when you and Alex get through, we are calling an emergency Council meeting." Stan commanded the leader of the protection force "Now! Sound the alarm! Let everyone know we are at war. Marshall Law is now in effect as of this moment. Get the guards, the protection forces, and all our troops.

Get ready to invade Star Zone! Have everyone meet at the portal to storm the gate! Listen up!" The leader of the protection force was giving orders right before they went through the portal. He told the rest of the force to kill all the animals and capture the Doctor and Hobbit. They were to bring them back to stand trial for killing and torturing thousands upon thousands of humans across the galaxy. They are charged with crimes against humanity. The two will spend the rest of their lives in prison until they die. Life in prison without parole for both.

Peter and Alex go to their craft to check on things and make sure everything is OK. The rest of Grim Light got ready – took their battle stations for what might be the bloodiest battle in the dimensional world. To save two brothers who hold secrets within their brains, secrets that will unlock a new world. Unaware of the secrets they hold within themselves, Alex and Peter move forward and stand with the people of Grim Light to fight for freedom, for the safety for himself, his brother and for all citizens in danger of being captured and killed by Hobbit and the Doctor. The brothers are unaware their purpose. With time, a new light will shine and give the brothers clues to a secret.

CHAPTER TWENTY-FIVE

HOBBITS PLAN

The Council receives a message from Hobbit demanding the two brothers be brought back to the portal within one hour or the Star Zone Animal Force Guards will act upon the Grim Light and destroy you all. If we leave the portal turned off, they will come by ships and attack us all. Leave it off – let them think we are not attacking, just refusing their demands for now. OK – wait awhile, turn it back on, then peek into the portal and report what is happening right away to the Council.

The guard leaves and gets ready to turn on the portal – as he is doing so, he quietly sticks his head into the portal and see no animals waiting on the other side, and no traps as far as the guard could see. The guard goes back to Stan in the Council room and reports his findings to the other members.

Their orders were to lay a trap on the other side of the portal. The plan is to create a circle effect sweep.

The lead guard, Vic, explains his plan to the others. They all listen with intensity – they know they all play a key role to take down the animals. In part one, the stage plan – laying down the plan so all guards know what to do is vital to the second part – stage two Protection Police Guard's plan, which allows for the capture of the Doctor and Hobbit and will imprison them both for the rest of their lives. "

They will have a plan of their own, I mean sir . . ." as one guard has a conversation with the lead guard, Vic. "Yes, Hobbit and the Doctor will have a plan, we don't know what the plan is or how they are planning to attack us here. All we can do is stick to our plan and, when necessary, our own plan and execute it. I feel we will still have the upper hand in taking down Star Zone – take over their world as our own.

The Protection Force Police shipped in other guards from neighboring worlds to Grim Light.

They were asked to help, and everyone wanted to do whatever they could to take down, not only their world, but to rid we from the Doctor – who was evil and Hobbit – who enjoyed putting his evil plans into action.

The Doctor enjoyed hacking and carving the bloodiest victims into his own personal master book – in which he kept his darkest secrets, leaving out nothing and revealing every detail. He kept his journal private and most hidden.

The neighboring worlds close by were contacted by the Council members about their situation, including being given one hour's notice to bring the brothers back to Star Zone. They also let them know, not only Hobbit was involved but also the evil Doctor had surfaced again and was practicing his work alongside Hobbit.

The other dimensional world leaders aided Grim Light in their request for aide to defeat these two – if and only if Grim Light could not defeat these two.

Well after reading this, the Council members were delighted in knowing where they been defeated –

or in any other trouble, they could count on their other dimensional world leaders to aide and aid them in taking down the Doctor, Hobbit and restoring order in Star Zone. As Grim Light got ready to battle, Hobbit is making his own plans, not only to get the brothers back, but Hobbit and his science department are working on a solar panel invisible force field which would circle their entire world outside of Star Zone and not allow anyone in or near unless they have permission.

Here, the field would be lowered long enough to allow the visitor to enter Star Zone. This would be perfect, thought Hobbit – we have been working on this for time now. We are about to put it into action and give everyone out there in our dimensional world a little surprise. A guard from Grim Light, who went into Grim Light to find out information, overheard what Hobbit was saying.

The guard left – rushing back to Grim Light and to the Council to let them know what he overheard.

The guard jumped into the portal, walked into the Chamber, and says, "Council members, I have information pertaining to Star Zone and their plans." The Council spoke up and asked, "Yes, what is the news?" The guard told them "I overheard one of his scientists' say they have invented a solar panel invisible force field which will cover the entire outside of Star Zone in space and will wrap itself like a blanket. No one will be able to get into their world unless they lower the force field and allow the person entry into Star Zone

.

We also believe they are coming after the brothers. We think the force field will probably take effect after the brothers are captured and brought back into their custody." The Council grew concerned as they ask the guard to get the brothers. "I believe" one of the Council members says, "They are at the craft. Let them know the news this very minute, both are in protective custody. Take them both now for their own protection. Put two guards on both 24 hours until further notice."

"Yes, sir – right away Sir!" the guard replied. "Go now!" the Council instructed. The Grim Light guards head to the other side of the docking station to get Peter and Alex and let them know about the situation and what is going on. They must be told their lives are in danger. As the guard reaches the craft, they call out their names "Alex! Peter! We need to speak to you both" and waited, but no answer.

As the guards got closer to the craft, there was another worker cleaning – he says to the guards, "you looking for the brothers? They left just a few moments ago; and went into town to get something to eat." "OK" the guards said as they ran off in that direction.

The troops were standing in a line, getting the force field ready to launch. Hobbit and the Doctor knew it was an innovative idea to have a surprise plan of attack, to catch the Grim Light off-guard. They would start a killing spree and while that was going on – and most were caught off-guard, Hobbit would send in two guards to get the brothers and bring them back to the lab.

The lab would be locked down with a no entry. The Grim Light guards were still heading to the restaurant to bring the brothers back. The guards entered the eatery and looked around for them. Once again, the guards could not find the boys. The guards walked up to the server to ask if the brothers are still here – she points out a table in the rear. The guard walks over and sees the boys sitting there eating and talking. The guard goes over to the table says, "excuse me boys, I'm with the police." "Yes"-said Peter.

"The Council has determined Hobbit has designed a plot to capture you both," the guard tells them. "I need the two of you to come with me now!" "No" the boys said to the lead guard "we can take care of ourselves." "No, I'm sorry – the Council has determined your lives are in extreme danger. The Hobbit and the Doctor are planning something deadly and will stop at nothing to regain custody of you both. Please get up now! I am not asking you – you are both ordered to come with me for your own protection.

We are placing you under protective custody for your own safety. We are under a war order, and we expect the attack any time." "Why is that?" asked Alex. "Because they have put a one-hour timetable on your head, and we are out of time."

The boys got up from the table and followed the guards to a protective house. As they entered the safe house, the guards let them know this place is stocked with everything that they will need. There will also be two guards posted outside your door. If there are any problems, just let the guards know. "One more thing" the lead guard told them "There is an intercom on the wall for you to contact the guards outside – for any reason.

If the guards should be killed, there is a hidden door behind the fridge. OK – you both understand?" he asked them. "Yes, we do, just one thing, where does the hidden door take us?" "To a room within the Council Chamber" the guard answered, "whatever you do – stay there. I must go now and rejoin my troop."

"Thanks" said Alex and Peter. "You're welcome – both of you" the guard replies and adds "please take care of yourselves and are safe." As the lead guard leaves the brothers, they look through a window on the door. They see two guards posted right outside for their protection.

The boys had to admit – they felt a little better knowing they were outside to protect them. The boys felt a little better in this battle of life, death, and war than over the two twin brothers' body, brains, and soul from Earth.

CHAPTER TWENTY-SIX

THE WAR BEGINS

The battle lines were drawn between the Star Zone and Grim Light. As the evening hours approached, the guards with the Grim Light are waiting to take their orders to march on the soil of the Star Zone world, take down those evil animals – clean, sweep this entire area for the good of all, and capture their leaders.

Star Zone guards were standing by the portal waiting for their orders to charge into Grim Light world and destroy them one by one.

 As their bodies fall to the ground, with blood spilling from the weapons they carry, they pierce their hearts. As they scream with horror on their faces – as their eyes sink within their skulls – as each reaches out with their own weapons.

In their hands – stabbing each animal to death before stumbling to the cold hard ground – dying in honor not in vain – they will charge on.

The troops on both sides are getting ready to attack and make noise. Everyone was on edge and standing still. The orders were about to be given by the lead guard, who screamed, "Get ready! Move your feet and have your weapons in hand." They were aiming straight out to attack what is in front. The portal was about to be activated by the large red button on the side of the portal.

The troops were getting ready and awaited the sign – to turn from red to green, giving the sign that all systems are Go" and move forward. Star Zone guards stood in front – were ready to take aim and pass through the portal gate. The Grim Light also is waiting on the other side to attack them when the Star Zone guards try to pass through.

The Grim Light guards are waiting to take their miserable lives and push them back to the graveyard, where these terrible animals now half human will burn, their ashes in the graveyard forever and will be no more burden on humans anymore.

Both sides wait to hear the command. The hate they feel, with the fear, makes them stronger. Each wait to hear the footsteps beating on the cold hard ground coming toward and through the portal screaming, yelling, and shouting. As they each fall, they take another with them. As lives live and die on this day – they will never forget just how animals, with humans, must suffer and die – laying alongside of each other bleeding – today and tomorrow.

Another day will rise and fall, and the battle will continue to march on. More blood will spill, but when the killing finally stops, the air will finally give way from the smell of burning, death, and flesh. One leader will rise to lead their citizens to a new world. Two young heroes will be revealed, and the citizens will follow them to a new world. The heroes will discover their new future to come. Yes, the battle lines were drawn.

The Grim Light now and forever are trying to protect what they have and save their citizens and their world from a life of capture, death, and unspeakable acts thrown upon them. The leaders of Star Zone – their people have a reason to fear. The man – the butcher himself – the Doctor. Time stands still for one moment – you can hear the hearts beat near us in frozen silence. You could hear a pin drop on the quiet front.

A battle will begin, and blood will spill – the fight to the death is upon us now. Death all around – how long it will go on? Only time will tell. The silence is growing, and death is near. This battle they fight in honor of the rights of citizens. We will not fall to the sides of the wasteland and be cast away. The night will fall upon us now and we can see the fire shimmering bright, as their eyes glow in the distance. They are ready to take their stand – they want to draw their blades and strike first blood.

CHAPTER TWENTY-SEVEN

TIME IS UP – THE BOYS RETURN

The hour has passed, and time is up. The Hobbit reached his boiling point. The brothers had not been returned to him. The portal opened and the Star Zone guards sent in their troops to attack the Grim Light protective guards for refusing to return the brothers to them. The half-animal half human's guards of Star Zone stood tall with their swords gripped tight in their hands. They held onto them tight in their right hands, and upon their heads, they were wearing helmets with a tiny star symbol on top to let Grim Light know who was coming to kill them. In their left hands, they gripped a shield, holding on tight to protect them while they fought.

As the battle began, each solider slowly entered the portal systematically, until they disappeared through and came out on the Grim Light side.

They walked through the portal on the other side. The Grim Light protective guards were waiting for the Star Zone guards, those half-animal half-human creatures, to take them down. As they entered and stepped off the portal, they looked around – everything was quiet, no one was around, and they could not see a thing. The half-animal half-human guards from Star Zone split up and searched the landing area of the portal; they soon realized nobody was around.

The doors to the city had been shut down. The entrance was locked electronically and could not be opened. "What was going on?" the guards asked. They could not figure it out. "Why wasn't there anyone around?"

The guards figured they just did not want them in the city, so they locked it down, but where were the Grim Light protective guards?

The half-animal, half-human guards were sure they would be here setting up a trap for them and the battle would start at the Grim Light portal, but that was not the case. The guards had no choice to go back through the portal to Star Zone and report the news to Hobbit. What they did not know, the trap was set all right – the Grim Light protective guards already went through the portal earlier and surrounded the Star Zone portal after they went in before and they surrounded the cave.

As the half-animal, half human guards went back through – the Grim Light guards were waiting for them. Each Grim Light guard stepped through the portal and stabbed each Star Zone guard through the heart, killing them all who originally went through the portal to begin with. Hobbit got the news that the Grim Light guards plotted and conducted a deadly plan, which killed their guards. Upon hearing this bloody news, Hobbit was upset and set out a deadly plan of his own. To kill as Grim Light guards in return for the killing spree they caused.

As Hobbit got news that another trap was being set up by the Grim Light guards – they were waiting for them at the cave – hiding and ready to kill. Hobbit had known their plan. He sent out troops to find and surround them, to kill the Grim Light guards and then suddenly he says "No! Wait – capture as you can and bring them to the cave. It is about time the Grim Light guards find out what it is like to be half-animal, half human. Now they will know what it is like to be a Star Zone creature guard. This is perfect! They will kill their own Grim Light guards and of their own citizens too.

"Let the word out – the doctor is in and will be preforming several new operations on the Grim Light guards they have captured and are now in custody. OK – go now and spread the word. Make sure that one of the Grim Light guards gets away and knows what the doctor is about to do to the rest of the guards, who will be in our cells in the cave lab. Oh, just make sure you capture all of them but one and make sure that one gets away and knows exactly what the doctor is about to do." "Yes sir, Hobbit – right away!" the guards replied.

Hobbit plans to turn the other guards into his own army troops and set out to destroy. The Grim Light is turning into a reality, and he is hell bent on getting his way and making them all pay dearly for taking the brothers away. The Grim Light Council finds out what is happening to their guards. The Hobbit has already captured them all except for one and is now getting ready for the Doctor to take over and work his magic on those guards, with a great deal of pleasure. As Grim Light Council discussed their plan, they also talked about the ships heading to Star Zone "as we speak" and start their own blood bath.

"The Star Zone guards have not been seen, yet the ships are filled with hundreds of Grim Light soldiers. They will destroy the town and the animals they have ruined. The ships will not be detected because they are flying under radar, so they will not be seen or even come close to finding out until it is too late. The Grim Light protective guards will be in their town marching on a bloody bath and killing every animal. We will catch them off guard and by the time they figure out what's happening, it will be too late."

"A lot of dangerous animals will be deceased and lying face down on their cold concrete sidewalks. The sidewalks will not be the only thing that will be shut down. I have also ordered guards to capture the solar panels off the twin towers. Without that running, no power will be available and everything within their own city will be dark. It will take them back all right, to a place they forget. The Grim Light is going to remind them they are animals, not humans! In addition, their life here, on their world, is about to expire. The Grim Light be the ones to take their world and send them all back to the graveyard, where they belong."

CHAPTER TWENTY-EIGHT

GRIM LIGHT SURPRISE ATTACK

The Grim Light guards travel by ship to Star Zone, their arrival is to the docking station, a surprise attack is forthcoming and just to see the look on the faces of those half-animals will be priceless. One of the Hobbit guards was hiding in Grim Light City and overhears one of the Grim Light guards talking about the surprise attack. He runs back through the city to the Grim Light portal and back to Star Zone yelling "Oh my! I've got to tell Hobbit right away."

The guard is running as if his life depends on it, and he is running out of time. The town where the portal cave is found is back in the city, where he will find Hobbit, the man in charge of the town and everyone in it. Finally, exhausted, and tired, the guard arrives in town yelling and looking around trying to see if Hobbit is in town.

The guard finds him next to the outside building where his is office found. The guard arrives and stands in front of him, so tired he can barely speak. He is so tired and exhausted; he looks at Hobbit – trying to speak but cannot. Hobbit looks at him and says, "What's wrong with you – you're barely able to speak!" He has been running from the portal to the cave. He gasps, "Please water!" Hobbit goes to the restaurant and gets the guard water. Finally calming down, he says, "I overheard a guard from the Grim Light city talking about the surprise attack!" Hobbit grabs the guard by his shirt collar and says, "What attack!" "

A surprise attack by ships, any moment through the white door at the docking station! The Grim Light Council sent their ships here in a surprise attack to wipe out the town and take the solar panel from the twin towers!" Hobbit screams! "Shut down the town! Close the white door! "Sound the alarm, get every guard available, and send them to the white door and docking station.

Kill anyone who docks at the station and send guards to the towers to protect the solar panels.

No! Send enough to protect the towers do it now!" The alarm went off sending a piercing sound throughout the city, letting all citizens of Star Zone know we are at war. The citizens came out and gathered in the middle of town, running with fear in their eyes. Hobbit tells them "Listen to me – we are at war with Grim Light! Pack up whatever you might need and get to the cave." The citizens running to safety fear Grim Light will kill them themselves, before the guards get to shut down the white door and the docking station.

The ship carrying thousands of Grim Light guard's lands and they were surrounded. They land at the docking station and take over the entrance of the white door. They hear the Star Zone animal guards coming up the stairs just as they turned the knob to open the door. The Grim Light protective guards opened the door in a flash and surprised the Star Zone guards, picking them off one by one by using their electrified sword – one touch to the heart drop them like a stack of dominoes. The Grim Light guards now had control of the docking station and the white door.

They were one-step closer to taking back the city that long ago belong to them – but that was in the distant past. However, they remember what it was like before the animals grew dangerous and took control. Everyone had to leave then, because the animals took overtook over their world, what they now call Star Zone. Grim Light wants nothing more than to run them into the ground and take control back.

CHAPTER TWENTY-NINE

READY AIM FIRE

Hobbit has ordered more troops to stand guard within the city, to kill any Grim Light guards as they enter the city limits. More Star Zone guards surround the cave and the entrance. They are ready to battle the Grim Light guards as they approach the cave entrance, try to enter it, and take control over the Star Zone guards and everyone inside.

"What now?" one guard says to another while standing watch and waiting in town. "We wait for how long? Until all hell breaks loose, that should be anytime now, so man your weapon and get ready for the Grim Light guards to come down those stairs and through the door. At that moment, you will see the whites of their eyes and tips of their swords aiming straight at your heart, the other guards will be aiming straight at your head and slice it clean off your shoulders.

So, look alive or you just might be headless, lying bloody face up and detached from yourself, the rest of your body will be lying right next to your head – shaking and dripping slowly with warm blood spilling out of your neck. "You look scared solider!" one guard said to the other. "Well, I wasn't until you said all that!" he replied. "Man, your station" he says to him "and look out – the door is opening up!" The Star Zone guards run over to the door and just as they were near the door, the Grim Light guards swung it open.

The battle between the two came crashing in. Grim Light protective guards came blazing with their electrified swords in their hands, swung high in the air and then down. The Star Zone guards fell – one by one onto city streets where they were battling each other for their lives and for takeover of Star Zone world. The Star Zone people were fighting for the right to live and for the right to stay in Star Zone.

As the battle continues in town, the Grim Light guards were taking down the Star Zone animals guards, their bodies were piling up all over town and in the streets. However, as their swords were rising high and taking aim once more, the Grim Light guards are making their way to the end of town where guards that are more animal were waiting for them, and they are not going down without a fight.

They are lined up at the end of the street like an old western movie. They are standing tall, legs apart and their swords were raised over their heads. They are ready and taking aim at the Grim Light guards. They walk slowly over to the Star Zone animal's guards, with their swords held out straight in front. They both clash – their swords against the sound of metal. Again, they take steps back, raising their swords high and then down low against the sound of flesh. The screams could be heard from every animal near and far. They looked worried and scared – the possibility that animal guards were being taking apart one by one, gradually – with each breath.

They walk closer and closer to the twin towers and the cave, destroying everything in their path and one-step closer to claiming victory. The Grim Light guards are feeling confident in the battle of wills and takeover of the Star Zone guards. To find the evil Doctor and Hobbit and lock them away, so they cannot hurt or force anyone else to do their bidding against their will. The Grim Light guards look around, the rest of the town has gone into the cave, the guards in town are now dead, – so they move on to another challenge.

CHAPTER 30

THE EVIL DOCTORS' LABORATORY

At the lab inside the cave, the Grim Light guards were taken captive and were being held in a secure room, waiting on the evil Doctor to use on them and turn them into one of their own half animal half-humans. The guards knew what would happen to them. In this quiet room, they wait in terror for the Doctor to come, enter, and take them away one by one – to turn them into one of species that live here in their Star Zone world.

The poor guards were terrified and shaking with every fiber of their being. They knew it was up to them to find a way out of where they were being held. The only way out was through the only door in the room.

A plan was needed right away, one guard figured the next time the door opened – they would overpower the person and knock them out. If that worked, they would then run like a lunatic and try to escape. They would then stand together to fight their way out of the evil Doctor's mad lab, where he turned humans into these half animal combo creatures. They were waiting to set their plan in action. Sitting down and staring at the door, waiting for somebody to open it, so they could try to bust their way out of that room.

The evil Doctor entered the lab and passed by the room where they held the Grim Light guards. As the doctor walked by the outside of the room, the guards could see him for the first time through the large glass window they were all peering out of. The look of shock on their faces grew more alarming with every gasping breath they took, with their mouths wide open. They all watched the evil Doctor walk by their room and for the first time – in amazement. The guards turned around, looked at each other, and then finally closed their mouths. One guard spoke up about the evil Doctor's appearance "you thought what?"

One guard asked another "well what did you think, based on all the stories we've heard over the years about this man they call the evil Doctor? I mean, did you think he would have looked more disturbing and weirder or grotesque?" asked one of the other guards. "Well, maybe not so normal. It was strange, you know, to look at this – because he looked very normal and has an amazing presence when he entered the room." Here and in the lab, everyone is kept terribly busy.

The fighting and blood spilling outside has everyone on alert, nervous people are wondering if the fighting will enter the world inside the cave. So far, Star Zone guards have been able to keep all its secrets and hidden worlds no one knows of and has been kept hidden for time. The battle for control and the war between the two continued. Grim Light guards are still on their way to the twin towers to remove the solar panel bars, causing light out for Star Zone. One guard will then take it to the Grim Light Council, where it will be under lock and key – they can never get their it.

The guards are making their way to the twin towers, while back at the lab – Grim Light guards are being held and getting ready to make their escape, go back to the portal and back to Grim Light City and to the Council, to let them know exactly what is give an update regarding the battle and conflict between the evil Doctor and Hobbit. The battle is still under way, the death toll is high, and there are bodies all over in the city. The captured Grim Light guards sit, wait, and pray someone will open the door and their plan will work. They all stare out of the window and watch people walk by the door. They are all thinking the same thing, 'how much longer will we have to wait?' and the answer will come soon.

CHAPTER THIRTY-ONE

ESCAPE OF THE GUARDS

One of the doctor's assistants is walking straight to the door to bring one guard to operating room to begin the changeover to half-animal and a new life as a Star Zone guard. "OK – here comes someone, everyone gets ready – we'll only get one shot at this!" The guards look at each other . . . then suddenly, the assistant opens the door. He walks in to tell the guards to move away from the door.

It looks like he is holding shocking device and it is pointed at us. The guards move slowly away from the assistant, just a split second for the assistant to look away is all it took. One of the Grim Light guards grabbed the assistant and puts his hand over the assistant's mouth so he could not scream.

The other guard took his device from him and shocked him with it. He then fell to the ground, the rest grabbed his keys, opened the door, and snuck out – trying to stay low and hunched over so as not to draw attention to themselves. They are looking around the corner to see if the coast is clear.

The guards make their way around the long stretch of hallway that leads them all to the back exit of the cave and the way out. The guards could not believe it, but they knew they had to hurry – time was not on their side, and they did not intend to get catch; not now – never. They were exiting the cave; the portal was close by. The guards ran hard, them all made it to the portal and finally – they could relax.

The guards jumped into the portal and back to Grim Light City and to the Grim Light City Council to report. "WOW!" one guard said, "can you say Bow Wow! Damn – that was way too close!"

"You got that right!" one said, "but at least we made it home." A smile came across all their faces "yeah, at least none of us had to turn into a dog either!" and they all laughed. They made their way into the Grim Light Council room to make their report and give the Council an update on the latest activities in Star Zone, including what is going on within the city and around the outside of the cave.

After letting the Council know the plans of the Star Zone, one of the Council members asked, "What's next? Is there anything else you can recall or are aware of? One guard said, "Yes, they said they're turning on a force field that will wrap an invisible field around the outside of their docking station. This would cover the entire outside world." He continued to say how they would lower the field to let certain individuals in and others would not be allowed entry to Star Zone. "We also have most of the town in our control, the Star Zone Animal Guards were killed, – and the others were pushed back to the outskirts of town, making their way to the cave. The Doctor and Hobbit are there now.

We also learned Hobbit was talking and we overheard him saying he was sending in more of his kind. Hobbit is not the only one of his kind – there is more like him – not here but somewhere else. Anyway, they are planning to send in reinforcements, they are scary, and they do not look like – but they are extremely fast and have sharp claws and teeth. Their feet also have sharp claws on the ends on their toes."

"They have large round faces and large round eyes which look right into your soul. They are also short – short and fast.

Most do not see them coming before it is too late, and they are right on top of you. So, you didn't overhear where these other Hobbits are at did you?" the Council asked. "No, just that he's sending for them now. What about the twin towers – what are the stats on that?" The guard continued his report as he talked about the twin towers.

"Well, we know it does take time to get over there, but the guards should be there by tomorrow sometime. We should have the solar bars in our hands at that time."

The guard said to the Council "once the guards pull the solar bars from the twin towers sir, do you realize it will be lights out in Star Zone. Problems will arise because of the darkness." The Council replied, "Yes, we're aware of that. We are doing something about it as we speak. We have a beam that will shine down upon the city and light things up.

The guards will then be able to move around easier and get to where they need to be." "Well," the guard answered, "I am done here and need to get back to my post." Yes" the Council says, "you may go." The guard left the Council room. The other Council members reviewed all the current information they just received.

The Council continued thinking of latest ideas and what action they will take next. The members discuss everything behind closed doors, and then talk to the guards – giving the next orders for the fight of Star Zone. The takeover of their world and downfall of the animals, finally.

Meanwhile, back at Star Zone, Hobbit has raised the force field around the outside of their world and is not allowing anyone to land or come into the city.

CHAPTER THIRTY-TWO

REACHING THE GRIM-LIGHT CAVE

The battle has continued, past the city now and nearly approaching the Grim Light cave. This cave is on the boundaries to both worlds. The Star Zone has said for decades that the cave and the secrets of the Grim Light within the cave belong to them. They will fight and kill anyone who tries to take the cave away from him and the people who live there.

The Grim Light guards have reached the twin towers and now are hoping to have the solar bar within their hands in moments, take them back through the portal, and give them to the Grim Light Council, where they will keep them safely under lock and key until Star Zone is under the control of the Grim Light City Council.

The guards open the door to the long spiral staircase that leads to the top, where the glass case is found which holds the solar bars.

The only source of light and energy comes from the solar bars, but Star Zone knows of the Grim Light's plan to remove them. They have set up their own plan to stop the Grim Light guards and beat them at their own game. The Star Zone guards sent one of their scouts to keep an eye out for Grim Light guards, get to the towers, and set a trap for the Grim Light guards before they get there. The Star Zone guards thought their plan would work, lying and waiting for the guards to enter the twin towers.

The Star Zone guards simply forgot one thing; Grim Light guards made it to the twin towers before them. Well, the Grim Light guards were already on top the tower wall where the solar bars, inside the giant glass case were kept. They already removed it and were on their way down the spiral staircase. The Grim Light guards got to the bottom step, opened the door to go back outside –

when suddenly, one of the Star Zone guards swung the door open. One of the Star Zone guards said, "put down the solar bar and back up." The Grim Light guard looked at the Star Zone guards and shook their finger back and forth at them. They were letting them know it simply would not happen. The Grim Light guards raised their swords, in their attack with swords behind their necks – with all the strength and might the guards could muster they brought it down as hard as they could – they swiped off their heads with one hard blow. One by one their bodies gave way to them weaken knees – and down their bodies fell to the ground.

CHAPTER THIRTY-THREE

THE BLACKOUT

The dead bodies were lying next to their heads, which rolled down and gently stopped against the dirty soil. The battle ended, Grim Light picked up the solar bar they had stowed away right, before the battle, so they would not break and put them in their pocket. The guards head back to the portal area to give the solar bar to the Grim Light Council and to keep under lock and key.

The guards made their way through the forest and within minutes of leaving, one guard asks, "does everyone have their torches ready?" "Yes" said the rest of the guards. "OK then – light them up! Now!" said the guards. "Yes" the rest of the guards replied. "Hurry up – we are only moments away from being in total darkness." The guards took the torches out of the long inside pocket of their coats and lit them up.

The twin towers blinked often, there was a flash of blinking lights, which lit up the skies, then darkness drew in with a flash of light from above, then there was only complete blackness throughout Star Zone. One guard told the others, "If you listen, you can hear the sounds of screaming and crying very near, listen and we'll be able to follow the sounds home again – just keep the torches lit and stay on the path."

The guard kept the torch fire burning bright to guide them back to Grim Light cave, to the portal and once more back to Grim Light. Everyone fears the darkness brought down upon them. Meanwhile, back inside the cave, the Doctor and the evil Hobbit have realized their world is now in the darkness, thanks to the Grim Light protective guards in their battle and determination to get the solar bar. Hobbit's world is now in darkness and their citizens are scared and hiding inside the cave. "We must act now!" said the Doctor. "Yes, I know," said Hobbit. "Well," said the Doctor "what are you thinking about?" "I was thinking we should do something big!"

the Hobbit replied. "Like what?" the Doctor says, "what were you thinking of doing?" "Well, I know there are Grim Light guards making their way here, so I'm going to send our guards out to kill every one of them and tell them not to come back until they are all dead" Hobbit replied. "OK, that is good," said the Doctor "that is nothing . . . then I'm going to send two guards through the portal and set off two really big explosive devices on the other side of the docking station in Grim Light.

Also, we're blowing up the portal!" "OMG!" exclaimed Hobbit "that is great! You'll injure and kill a lot of Grim Light and they'll have no way of coming back to us here." "The portal will be gone and the secrets within the Grim Light cave will remain with us" the Doctor replies. "Oh, my!" one guard said to another "did you hear what he said! There is no time!" Both Grim Light guards ran and jumped through the portal and exclaimed, "There's been a bomb planted! Clear the docking station of any ships!

Take them to Station 2 now! Clear the station – get everyone out and seal off this room! Find that bomb now! Notify the Council as well." As the guards look for the bomb, the brothers Alex and Peter were being held under house protection, in a room with guards posted at their door.

The brothers realized something was wrong when both the guards left their post outside in a hurry... they were gone.

CHAPTER THIRTY-FOUR
THE EXPLOSION

The brothers looked around and could not figure out what was going on, until they heard one guard yell the word bomb. Locked in the room, the brothers used the secret escape door hidden behind the fridge. As the brothers gently pushed, a little of the top back corner of the fridge gave away to show a door. A passageway led out to the portal stand.

"Look," asked Peter look where we are!" "Yes"-said Alex. "What now? Asked Peter "go through and put us in harm's way again, with Hobbit and the Doctor? Or stay here and we could be destroyed in seconds if they don't find the bomb!" As the brothers decide, which for them was already made . . . when a guard suddenly yelled, "I found it! Oh, my God! Brace yourself it's going to blow in ten seconds – clear the room!" "We can't, it's been sealed" another guard replied.

The brothers and the rest of the guards were left in the room. With only seconds left, they all jumped through the portal, which put them at the back of the Grim Light cave . . . just then, the bomb went off. It shook everything so hard – both worlds could feel it for miles. The docking station within Grim Light itself was destroyed. The Council has guards and a cleanup crew there at once to start the cleanup and rebuild the docking station one. As for the guards on their way to the cave, they met up with the Star Zone guards.

The Star Zone guards took out every single Grim Light protective guard, who were on their way to the cave, and killed them. The surprise attack left Grim Light wounded and lying on the ground when the half-human half animals mauled them to death and left their dead stays on the ground for the animals to enjoy as a treat. Grim Light City tries to repair the damage from the explosion. The portal was damaged too in the explosion, but the docking station was gone.

The Chief Science Engineer, Dr. Sam Foster gathered other engineers from his department to help move the portal to docking station two and make the repairs, they figured that it would not be long until the portal was up and running once more. The Grim Light City Council closed docking station one while repairs were being made. One of the Council members asked, "What happened to the guards who were in here before the bomb went off. Has anyone seen Alex and Peter?"

"Yeah, the brothers left their room through the passageway behind the fridge when they overheard one of the guards who were standing guard outside their door mention something about a bomb. Therefore, the brothers took the passageway to the docking station right before the bomb went off. The brothers and the guards jumped through the portal right before the explosion," a guard reported. "

Oh, my God! They didn't!" the Councilmember replied. "Yeah . . . and don't forget its dark in Star Zone now – pitch black" the guard reminded him.

"Well, the engineers are repairing the portal and hopefully we can get the brothers back as soon as possible" the Councilman said. The Star Zone citizens met quietly about the docking station and Hobbit. "We're sick, tired and fed up!"

They all got together in a part of the cave in the back. They realized no one is around, they will not be disturbed, and they can talk without fear of being killed. Meanwhile, after all the citizens gathered around, the discussion began. "Well," said one shop owner "what do we want? Look at us – we're no longer animals because of the Doctor's experiments on us."

CHAPTER THIRTY-FIVE

THE DEAL

"We're freaks now! Where can we live in peace without fear of either being worked on or killed? Because we now have two who are trying to control us. I am sick of it! Sick of it all I said we leave!" one Star Zone citizen says. And go where?" asks another. Most citizens are yelling and raising their voices. "Well, I have an idea," says one lonely soft voice in the background. citizens had to turn around to see where the voice was coming from.

Way in the back, when they all turned around, they saw this tiny little girl standing only four feet tall, with long blonde hair and big beautiful blue eyes. She was saying with a big voice "I might be tiny, but I do have an idea that just might help us all." "Well, what is it?" asked the shop owner.

"Well, don't you think Grim Light City Council would do almost anything if they have both the Doctor and Hobbit in their custody? I did hear that they are looking to imprison them both on charges of crimes against humanity. If we could trap them, we could arrange a set up for Grim Light to come and pick them both up." The little girl continued, "We could tell them all we want in exchange for our part in helping to capture them is a quiet and safe place for us to live out our lives."

"I love it!" the shop owner said. "Yes, me too! Says another. "I think this just might work" the shop owner says. "Well, OK! Let us put this plan to a vote. All in favor of this plan say yes. Everyone opposed say nay. "OK, the yeas' have it, let us get busy. We need to get a message to the Council and set up a meeting – Jay you go and take one other person with you." "OK" Jay replied, "How will we set it up?" "We have to tell the Council something to see if they'll go along with It." the shop owner tells. The brothers are behind the back entrance to the cave and in one hour's time.

We will go and tell Hobbit where they are at and that the brothers want a meeting with him. We'll tell him that he and the Doctor must come together . . . and to sweeten the trap we'll say the brothers want to reveal a secret about the cave and they will only tell the two of them." "OK" Jay says, "That's perfect! He'll definitively be interested and want to know what it is, and they won't be able to resist." "The two of them will show up, they'll be talking to the boys and bingo. The Council will have them both in custody," the shop owner says. "OK, everyone – got it?" "Yeah, it's perfect" Jay replies. "The plan now is Jay you go through the portal.

The other side should be online by now – OK. We will need a two- person team to go and meet with the Doctor and Hobbit – any volunteers. OK – Katie, you own the restaurant" the shop owner said. "Yes, I do" Katie replied. "You go and take Jay, the bar owner, with you" the shop owner instructs. "Let's start people – let's get moving on this." The plan takes effect – all the pieces are put together and are lined up perfectly.

"We now just have to wait and see if everything falls into place," the shop owner says to everyone. Meanwhile, the bar owner Jay takes the portal to go to Grim Light City Council. As Jay walked into the Council room, they asked right away "what are you doing here?" As the guards entered the room and stood behind them with weapons pointing at their backs. "Wait," says Jay "we don't have much time and we have a deal we want to make with you." "OK, you have five minutes to explain yourself" a Councilman told him.

"It's like this – we're sick and tired of being under the control of Hobbit and the Doctor," Jay explains. "The citizens just want to live a safe, peaceful life free of threats, death, and experiments. Do you understand what we're saying?"

The Council looked at the two "Yes, we do and we're sorry your lives are under such distress. What would you like us to do?" Jay continued, "The citizens of Star Zone want a safe place to live out our lives.

In exchange for you supplying us this, we have set a trap for Hobbit and the Doctor as we are talking – within the next ten minutes, the Doctor and Hobbit will go behind the back entrance of the cave, where Alex and Peter are at right now. We've told them the brothers want to speak to them regarding a secret the brothers know of about the cave and want to reveal to them only, in exchange for their freedom."   Jay also tells them "You should also be aware the boys do not know about this plan and will be caught off-guard any moment. We will cooperate, if you agree to provide the citizens of Star Zone with a safe place to live."

CHAPTER THIRTY-SIX

THE TRAP

"The Council can go, spring a trap behind the cave, and capture the two evilest beings in the dimensional world. Oh – and yes – you only have just minutes to decide" Jay told the Council. "Yes, go back, send the citizens of Star Zone through the portal, and wait here in the Council room. When we have the two in custody, we will discuss where all of you want to live. OK, we agree, but to capture these two – timing is everything" the Council told Jay. "Yes, that's true" Jay replied. The Council yelled loudly for the guards to come to the conference room, and said, "Go – capture the Doctor and Hobbit and bring them back in custody. Make sure the two of them are in irons on both arms and legs." "Yes sir!" the guards replied.

"Go now, hurry" the Council instructed. As the guards ran off, Jay leads them to straight to Hobbit and the Doctor – trying to end this madness finally. To live a life free of worry. Free of the stress of being worked on, torn apart, and pieced back together by the evil madness of the Doctor. The citizens agree, so Jay and the guards went back to the docking station two and jumped through the portal a foot away from the set up. Jay went back to the cave to gather everyone else up.

The citizens of Star Zone walked back behind the cave, went through the portal, and walked into the Council room. There they are waiting anxiously for the second part of the plan – to capture Hobbit and the Doctor. The guards snuck quietly and slowly upon the meeting with Alex, Peter, Hobbit, and the Doctor. The Grim Light protective guards walked behind the two with their weapons drawn, aimed at their heads, and told them not to move. The guards told the brothers to back up and move to where they were standing behind the guards.

After Peter and Alex moved, – they watched in amazement – they did not understand this would happen. One guard went over, put iron chains on both their ankles and then on their wrists. Once the chains were attached to them, the guards took them, with the boys, back through the portal. They let the Council know Hobbit and the Doctor had been captured and were in a holding cell, waiting for the transport to take them to their final stop – Space Station Prison Level Two.

The Council put them there and not in Space Station Prison Level One, which was a much harder prison, only holding prisoners who were the most dangerous and were against the world. There is no escape – no death – only misery for the rest of their lives. This prison was designed for the most dangerous people. DO NOT STOP! DO NOT COLLECT! In addition, NO PASS! NO PAROLE! For these monsters with the capture of Hobbit and the Doctor, who are now in custody – everyone is celebrating and on a high. The word is out throughout the dimensional world. The two evilest beings are now on their way to prison.

The Council, back in chambers, let the citizens know that their freedom is now secure, and they should feel happy the threat of these two men does not hang over them anymore.

CHAPTER THIRTY-SEVEN

THE CLEAN UP

The Council told the citizens of Star Zone "the choice is yours to make now, you can stay here among the Grim Light citizens, or you can choose another dimensional world in which to live. Or go back to Star Zone – with the threat gone you can live in peace." It was Jay who spoke to the Council, "we don't feel safe at Star Zone now, even with them gone, – and someday they could come back here.

I do not think your humans here would fully accept us, so I speak for everyone when I say we choose another dimensional world that is already fully set up and ready for us to live in what we all desire. We give you our world – Star Zone and the Grim Light cave – and all its secrets yet to be discovered, is now yours to find the gateway into the world the two boys seek.

The answers that lie within them both are yet to be discovered." The Council looks at them and says, "Wait, what you mean?" "We can't tell you anything else" Jay replies "this is all we know – now we've shared this with you." The Council replies, "we have places for you to rest, and eat. Please relax now and get rest. We will have travel arrangements for all of you within a week's time." "Thank you very much" Jay responds, "If you ever need anything, or if we ever can help you again – for any reason, please feel free to contact us. Until our paths across again . . . we honor you."

The citizens left to enjoy quiet time, as they all wait for their travel papers to come through. They can finally go and live with purpose and happiness with no threats in sight. "Get ahold of Harry T. Bone, he will transport the two prisoners" a council member told the guard.

"Yes sir, right away" the guard answered. "I want you to send troops out to the Grim Light cave. Someone else to the twin towers – restore the solar bar and clear out the cave.

If there is anyone left there who was collaborating with the Doctor or Hobbit, put them in iron chains and deliver them here to the holding cell," the Council instructed. "Right away sir" the guard answered.

The guards left to go back to Star Zone, to check out the cave and restore the energy in the twin towers. The Council is feeling pleased because of what they have been done today. But what Jay from Star Zone had to say about what Alex and Peter were about to discover at the gateway and what their telling lies within the cave somewhere – only the boys will seek the answers that will open a new world.

CHAPTER THIRTY-EIGHT

SEARCHING FOR THE SECRET

"The answers will open up a new world," one Councilman said. "Well, they could be lying." "No, I don't think so," said another. "We all thought the boys were supposed to end up here, but I believe now, we are just a steppingstone to where they are going to go." "Well, we will see – in the meantime, just keep an eye out and watch the two of them carefully," the Council concluded.

"Welcome Harry T. Bone back to Grim Light City. Harry pulls into docking station two, comes out, and walks into Grim Light City. He goes to get something to eat but remembers something he needs to tell the manager at the station. He walks back and tells him the vessel needs to be fully stocked and fueled. "OK" he says, "won't be ready until tomorrow." "OK" says Harry "see you then."

"OK" the station manager tells Harry "Go, relax, and get some sleep." "Yeah" replies Harry "OK, see you tomorrow." Harry leaves the station again and heads to the restaurant to eat, have drinks and talk to the sexy ladies in the bar. After sitting in the bar, drinking, and talking to ladies Harry looks over and is happy to see Alex and Peter walk into the restaurant, locate a table and sit down. The brother's orders eggs, potatoes, and fruit.

They sit back to relax when they see Harry at the bar. The boys speak up "hey Harry" and gives a little wave to him. Harry gets up, walks over, and sits down at their table. "Hey boys – what's shaken?" he asks them. "Not much, what's going on with you?" "Just here on a pick-up – two passengers headed to the far side of Sector Four." "Oh, what's over there?" asked Peter. "Well, somewhere you never want to go." Then Harry smiled at the brothers and said, "the prison, but for this level prison you've got to be a very bad criminal to go there." "Oh really?" said Alex. "Yeah" said Harry "they check-in, but don't check out – unless you're dead –

or found the impossible way of escaping." "Well," Alex replies, "you must be talking about the Doctor and Hobbit." "Yes" Harry agreed, "These two are dangerous – watch your back with these two. "Harry – seriously, be careful with these two guys, OK?" Alex reminds him. "I got it" Harry responds, "No worries here . . . these two are going straight to prison, with no chance of ever getting out. Well, have you discovered anything interesting in the cave yet?" "Why you ask?" inquires Peter. "Well, because I know there's a secret world within the cave. I overheard the Doctor talking once – a while back. Just wondering if it is there and what it is like.

I know the two of them have not been able to find it just yet. Your journey here is not exactly finished by any means. Now, it's up to two very smart – and may I say – very good-looking twin brothers to unlock the mystery of the secret world in the Grim Light cave." I want to ask you something Harry," asked Peter. "Yeah, what is it?" Harry asked. "Do you think my brother and I can get into the holding cell tonight?" "You mean to talk to Hobbit?" asked Harry.

"Yes, exactly" Peter responds. "I think so," Harry tells them. "I should be able to arrange a meeting . . . maybe Hobbit will give some kind of detail to you guys." "OK – good," said Alex. After everyone ate, Alex, Peter, and Harry head off to the holding cell to talk to Hobbit before Harry takes him and the Doctor to prison. As Peter and Alex open the cell, Hobbit is sitting in a chair with his arms and legs chained down.

His ankles have iron chains around them with the chain fastened to an iron ring attached to the bottom of the floor. Peter and Alex stare at the chains, but then move their eyes quickly upward to his face. His round and full face has fur that goes all the way round on the outside of his face like a beard. His large beetle-like eyes stare back at you and make you feel uncomfortable.

His human arms are strange with large puffy hands and claw-like fingernails. It always looks like he is ready to rip you apart. He always lets you know that he is more animal than human, and you get a very strange feeling with Hobbit you should always watch your step.

Peter looks at Hobbit and asks, "Do you have a first name? Or is Hobbit your first name?" He looks at the boys and says, "Hobbit is my last name. People have always just called me by my last name. It happened one day and for some reason it just stuck." "Oh, OK," says Peter. "So, what's your first name?" He smiles and simply says "Charlie."

"Peter and I want to ask you about the secret world that's hidden within the cave," Alex tells Charlie. "Will you tell us about it and what you know Charlie? We heard about it and wanted to know how we can get there." Charlie looked surprised. The look on his face and the fact the brothers knew something was alarming to Charlie.

How can he throw the brothers off the mysterious world in the Grim Light cave without them knowing what he was doing? Charlie had to think about it for a second before he answered them. "Well," said Charlie "what makes you so sure I know something . . . I mean really!" "Look," said Alex "let us just skip this whole tap dance – OK? We already know you know.

My brother and I want to know, so Charlie what do you say? Can you tell us what you know about this world not discovered?" "Well," answered Charlie "I can tell you it's a story that goes back in time as far as I can remember and even further back than that. It has always been there. The story – I mean." "What is the story?" asked Alex. "Look" answered Charlie "why don't you two ask someone else about this. I am not so sure I want to help you discover the mysterious world.

I mean really Alex and Peter! I have been searching for this fable my whole life – why should I just give you both the information that might help you two bring you closer to finding it. It's what you both desire it isn't?" "Yes" Peter said "but for us, Charlie, it feels like something Alex and I are supposed to locate. If that is true – only we can open the gateway to this world – no one ever has done until now. So – are you going to sit there and stew about it or are you going to share what you might know to help us locate this supposedly fabled mysterious world in the Grim Light cave?"

"Well," Charlie replies "I could just take what I know with me to prison, then the two of you will never know." Just then, an evil little smile came across Charlie's face. "OK Charlie, you just do that – OK, Alex and I will discover this place and when we open the door to this undiscovered uncharted world – I will be the first of two persons that will walk through.

You will be sitting in your prison cell and just should live with the fact that you could have had your name written down in history helping the two twins from Earth find this uncharted world. However, hey, you do not worry about it OK. My brother and I will find another source, someone else who has information and is willing to share and get credit for the discovery of this world. I am sure opportunity will come his or her way. They won't mind a bit . . . so take care."

As the brothers get up from their chairs and get ready to leave, Charlie looks up at them and says, "OK you make a particularly good point, Alex and Peter.

I will tell you what I have learned. It might or might not help you – you must decide that for yourself. I've discovered mysterious writing on a column located inside the cave."

"Where exactly is the writing?" asked Alex. "I believe you will find the column past the lab and through the double doors, in another room, where it's cold inside – the room is empty and bare." Peter looked at his brother and says, "We've been in the room, haven't we?" "Yes" said Peter "it sounds familiar. Anything else?" Alex asks him. "Yes," Charles said, "the column is the key to unlocking the gateway, and you have to solve the writing and perhaps those numbers on it to get the location and open the gateway."

CHAPTER THIRTY-NINE

THE CLUES

"I've not been able to solve this, Peter and Alex, you should also be aware that no one here has been able to either" Charlie told the boys. "The scientists – not even the engineers and not anyone else. So, do not be surprised if you two are not able to solve this mystery either. Every now and then, someone tries, but it always comes out the same – failure." "Interesting" said Alex.

"Well," said Peter, "maybe not just anyone can solve this." What do you mean? Said Charlie. "Just that" answered Peter "if in all this time – and all these years, this hasn't been solved . . . maybe it's waiting for the right person or persons to come along on a mysterious adventure.

Enter a world that will be granted to them – and only them, if they can solve the mysterious writing on the column.

It will lead them to a location where a gateway will be opened and shown to them."

"This is an old world, which has been around longer than any other world, but closed off until now," Peter said to Charlie. "Soon perhaps, my brother and I will be the two-granted permission. You forget, we were asked to come, but until recently, we thought it was Star Zone who asked us, but NO.

I am sure Grim Light City did not send for my brother or me or send us the secret numbers to guide us from Earth to where we are now. I believe, Charles, this is not where we are supposed to end up. If it is the last thing my brother and I do, we will find whoever sent us the message in the first place. We will find our place, our home, and our adventure.

Oh, just one more thing about our parents – are they really in Star Zone Level Prison Charles?" Well, when Hobbit looked into their eyes – something must have happened, if only for just a split second. Charles looked up and said to the brothers "I haven't seen your parents, if they came here –

we wouldn't have known, because no one else has seen them either." "Well," Alex asked him "what do you think happened to them?" "I think" said Charles "they ended up somewhere else, if they were around and close by, I would have known about it."

Peter looks at Alex and asked, "What in the world do you think happened to them?" "Well," Alex replied, "I think they must've ended up in another portal and in another place somewhere. There is really, nothing we can do but finish the mission we are on – and oh Hobbit – my brother and I have the numbers . . . we just needed to know exactly where to look. So, thanks for the information. I am sure it will guide us both to the adventure we are searching for.

I hope you enjoy your stay in prison – forever." The boys got up – they had the smiles on their faces. "Peter! Alex!" yelled and screamed Hobbit – you tricked me! I will get you two if it is the last thing I do! You understand me! You are dead! Both of you! There will be no place the two of you can hide from me – get back here!"

Hobbit is handcuffed, chained, and carted off to Harry T. Bone's craft to face the rest of his life in a place where – for sure – he will wish he were dead.

As the brothers walked off, they were laughing and smiling. They looked at each other, and then Peter finally said, "Did he really think he was going to trick the two of us? Doesn't he know just how smart we are? They laughed aloud and walked away.

The boys went to get rest and seek tomorrow's treasures and mysterious new worlds to find. "Goodnight, brother dear," said Peter. "Goodnight to you too" replied Alex. After a good night's sleep, the brothers got up early, dressed and went over to the restaurant to get breakfast and do more research about the columns.

After breakfast, the boys went to the cave to look and see if they can figure this out. First, the boys want to talk to the Council and see what they know about the columns and the strange writing on them. They also want to find out if the Council knows about the fable.

Of this mysterious world handed down for years upon years upon years and then. It goes – so they say – all the way back to being one first planet, other than Earth, to be developed and has life – air, water, The people say, well – rumor has it – that it is not in the Earth's solar system. It is in the outside dimensional world system. My brother and I went into the Council and asked them to explain where exactly it is?

"Well," the Councilman told him "Legend has it – it's just outside our world. That would make it, really, a brand-new meaning – which would make it new to us. However, it has been around longer than even we have. Anyway, it is a discovery of a world that has been around first – and much longer than any other dimensional world, and supposedly just outside our solar system."

Peter asked, "Are you saying it's in a brand-new solar system, different than your own?"

"We believe so, yes – and you can't use the portal to get there.

No, we would have to have a series of numbers, which would line up with the portal. That would take you straight there and put you somewhere on their land – so to speak. The Council members talked to the brothers about the mysterious new world. The boys told the Council they think the new world were the actual ones who sent them the original message they received when they lived on Earth.

The brother's claims surprised the Councilmembers and they looked puzzled. One member spoke up and asked, "Why you think it was them and not someone else?" Alex answered, "My brother and I aren't sure, but we're extremely – highly intelligent young men." "Yes" the Council said, "we're aware of you and your brothers IQ, so that's why we can say to you 'we believe something to be true' without proof."

"We believe we're right," Alex told them. My brother and I can assure you, with time, we will have findings to show we were right all along. My brother and I were blessed with a gift.

I guess you can say we have no reason or the time to misuse our brains. The abilities we have were given to us." A Council member said "looking at the two of you – we believe that you are correct. We will grant you full access to anything you might need in your pursuit of finding the truth, the answers along with all the questions you may have."

"One more thing" Alex told the Council "The numbers that were sent to us . . . ." "Yes" one of the Councilmember said. "Well, those numbers were interrupted, and we were sent to Star Zone? "Yes, that is correct," the council member said. "Well then, we think it just might be those original numbers that will line up with the portal and open the doorway to this new world. If so, we would like to run experiments, with you beside us.

We want to study the column then send something through the portal . . . a note or something else. A message and see what happens." "OK" the Council agreed, "you have our permission to go forward with this idea. Take two chief science officers and two engineers with you.

I think it might be a promising idea to have Doctor Alan Green along – he is our chief historian and knows everything about our world and the other surrounding worlds. He also knows about legends, like the one you are trying to discover. A warning to you both, these worlds and others have rules about entering them – you must be invited.

The two of you should be OK. The brothers already are legends in themselves you know – the two of you are the only ones from Earth who has ever received an invitation. So, that should grant you access to most worlds."

"I caution you both – there are dangers you two can't imagine in your worst nightmares or your most vivid imaginations. Trend carefully." "OK, we'll stay very close and watch to see if anything does or will occur" the boys said to them. "OK thank you" the Council told them. Alex and Peter left the Council chamber and walked to the Chief Science Officer's office. Even before they got there, he knew the situation and recent developments that just occurred in the Council chamber's room.

The brothers got to his office door and knock. The Chief Science Officer, Dr. William Meyers opened the door and says "hello Alex and Peter. I have the best Engineers, and others that will aid us in our journey. They will be happy to meet with both of you over by the portal in five minutes to start the research on the column in the cave. So, we'll see you both in a few minutes at the docking station."

"OK" as the boys smiled and thanked Dr. Meyers for his time and using his department. The brothers left and went to the docking station to meet the others they walked with a sense of excitement and a little extra spring in their step, and they are thrilled to be a part of something new. "It is amazing! Isn't it?" Peter exclaimed. "Yes" said Alex "who would've thought or dreamed this was going to happen to us! Not just that but look at what we are a part of now! It is truly something else – hard to even put in words. To think we are at discovering a world like home but so far away.

CHAPTER FORTY

THE COLUMNS

"Yeah" Peter answered, "Who knew they would call on the two of us, in this amazing adventure? We're lucky, for sure brother, we wouldn't trade this for anything!" They get to the docking station to meet the others. They are going back to Star Zone and to the Grim Light cave. Everyone shows up and is ready to go forward. Peter, Alex, and the team step into the portal and once again is brought back to the cave.

The brothers and the rest of the team walk into front entrance and head back to the lab, through the double doors and into another room where it is empty and cold. The room is white in appearance and the column is off to the side of the room. As the brothers walk up to the white column, they right away could see the writing – under the writing it looks like empty holes and spaces are there.

The boys study the column closely. Then, Peter asked Alex "what do you think?" "Well," Alex answers, "they want the numbers to go inside the holes." "Do you see anything we could carve something out of and would fit inside the holes?" asked Peter. "No" said Alex "but keep looking! I don't think we can use just anything to fit inside there." Peter takes a closer inspection – he touches one of the spaces next to the holes – to his surprise it opens. Inside is a tiny square ceramic tile, it looks like it was used to carve the numbers onto the tiles and then put them back onto the column.

After sharing the news with his brother, the team opens the spaces, one at a time. Then they carved the first number Alex and Peter wrote down in their dreams. They would take it one day at a time carving each number into the tiles as they thought in their dreams. After working on this all day and through the night, Alex and Peter took a break from working and gave the team time off to go eat something.

After they have rested and finished eating, they came back and shut things down. They locked up the lab and the double doors leading into the room. The brothers have decided it would be a clever idea to post a guard in front of the doors, in front of the lab and to the entrance of the cave. He asked the team to send back six guards with weapons to guard the surrounding area of the cave.

They also protected the secrecy of all work about the secret room within the cave and the column. As the brothers wait for the guards to show up, they sat and wondered. They thought back to a time when they were small. They never realized when they used to stare at the sky above and said 'TO THE STARS and BEYOND' it would happen to them. "Yeah" said Alex "I'm looking forward to seeing a world that's calling our names."

They both smiled – every now and then, they would drift away in thought. You could see in their eyes they were wondering what would happen next. What would the two to see when the universe opens?

Once again, to these two amazing twin brothers – what was the universe going to reveal to them this time? To the smart young men from a place called Earth who received an invitation to come to a place far, far away called Star Zone and Grim Light City, now it is here. Soon, they will see a path designed for two young boys to come. Designed such a long time ago to enter a world calling their names – telling them to come home, begging them to stay an hour or a day and asking will not you please come in.

After the guards finally show up, the boys show them the post there. The two brothers take off to get rest and a bite to eat. They will come back fresh in the morning. They exit the cave and walk around to where the portal stands are found. The two brothers – once again, walk through the portal and come out at the docking station. They walk to the door and down the stairs to get to the Grim Light City.

They can finally sit, relax, and get something to eat. Then head to their hotel room afterwards. Tomorrow brings them one step closer to solving the mystery of the Grim Light Cave and a new world, which has not been discovered and is calling the two young brothers. The morning rises – Peter and Alex wake up and are eager to eat and get back to the cave to finish working on the column. They know the numbers were sent both while living on Earth – through their dreams.

This is the key to opening the portal and lining up the column to release the gateway to the other new world. The brothers are extremely excited, for the first time they feel this unbelievable pull to something they are both sure it is there and not but deep down inside –

more than a mere unspoken word between these two brothers. The boys feel something powerful inside themselves. They are seeking answers from the universe, for the first time in history –universe will answer these two young brothers. Give them the answers their minds have been yearning for.

walking back from the restaurant, head off to the guard station check if the team came yesterday is ready to work.

Within moments, they all arrived at the station and are ready to continue.

Therefore, off they went together to the portal, back to the Grim Light Cave, the mysterious column and the new world that awaits them both. They all enter the cave and walk through the white double doors in the back of the lab. Once there, Peter and Alex go to the worktable they had put in the room yesterday.

Peter goes to open the spaces, to remove the tiny tile pieces and hands them to Alex. Once Alex carves the first number into the tile and hands it back to Peter. He puts the tile back into the hole, it simply snaps into place – making a clicking sound. The sound you have waited to hear. your whole life

. Peter goes to the next space and repeats the same process and giving it back to his brother. Alex carves the second number into the tiny piece and Peter puts that back into the empty space. They figured the tile pieces were fitting the way should. Everything was going according to plan and working out the way they had both hoped.

After going back and forth, with Peter removing the tile pieces and Alex carving the numbers into the tile, hours went by. The brothers were trying to finish it, so they could see where the next step would bring them. After Peter hands Alex, the last tile to be carved and put back into place, they both wait expectantly – to see if the numbers they received all those years ago; were the correct numbers to give them the directions to the gateway – the portal that will open and smile down upon these two special young men. Giving to them what they secretly wanted for all these years.

As the last tile goes into the column – the boys move back and wait to see. The writing was above the spaces. The numbers moved around and around fast. Then suddenly, just stopped and slowly lined up with the numbers the brothers put into the spaces. Holy cow! The boys could not believe what was happened next – right before their eyes. The room broke away the whole column was spinning around and around.

The floor broke and flies off, giving way to reveal the glass underneath. A solid glass floors! They were stunned and could not believe what they were seeing under the glass floor . . . a working motor with gadgets and little parts working everywhere. turning and turning.

.

CHAPTER FORTY-ONE

SEARCHING FOR THE GATEWAY

The boys go outside to the portal – it was running behind the cave. Suddenly they walked up where the portal was and stared at the ring around the portal. It was moving in a circular pattern. "Look" said Peter "it's looking up the directions, lining up the numbers within the column – the ones we put in." "Yes" said Alex "they're working together and, in a search, to find the gateway and open up the portal to a whole new world."

"Well," asked Peter "how long do you think it's going to take?" "I don't know" said Alex "but we're not moving a muscle until this portal stops, the gateway is located, and it opens up to show us what we've been waiting for . . . for so long. "Well, you know what," said Peter looking at Alex. "What's that?" Alex asked, with a big smile on his face.

Peter looks at his brother and says, "Boy, oh boy, I could sure use a Pepsi right now!"

"Yeah" said Alex "over ice me too!" Peter and Alex are waiting for the gateway to line up with the portal and open. Alex asks Peter "didn't we bring any food like a chocolate peanut butter cups and soda and stuff?" "We sure did" Peter answered, "it's in the craft, but maybe later we can get it."

"Wow that sounds so delicious!" Alex says, "Too bad we can't get it now!" "Oh well" Peter replied, "good things come to us later." "Yeah, that's right!" answered Alex. They both smiled at each other. Meanwhile the Grim Light City Council is meeting privately to discuss just how far the boys have come. "Yes," as one member of the Council said "and now they're waiting for the portal to line up – just think if it does what they'll see. We are concerned the brothers will look for and find the hidden truth about who sent for them and why.

.

The Council wants the boys to stay and live in Grim Light City, to help them maintain their world and to be to discover new worlds – no one has done so much in such little time." The Councilmembers are wondering what happened to their parents. "We've looked into the matter, and this is we found. The father was here in Grim Light City for a brief time.

We were then told he went to the portal in the Gateway Sector 5." The Council looked puzzled, Sector 5 is an area – first and not a place – why would he go to Sector 5. "Well, we believe he found another portal linked to the gateway portal and the new world the boys are working on."

"Are you telling us there is a second portal that not even we knew about?" one Councilmember asked. "How can that be possible?" "Well," another Councilmember replied, "we think this is the portal once used many centuries ago, but back then Sector 5 – as you might remember, was a city."

"Yes, I recall that . . . but it was destroyed right after it was built. No one really lived there." "Well, in fact, the city was built and there were people living there – but only for a very short time" the Council responded. "OK, what's happening here? I want to know – OK?" "Well, there's a rumor . . . well – sort of a myth and the tale goes on" was the response.

"Yes sir" one of the Council members said, "so they say that these giant robotic things came into the city and took the engineers and people that were of value. The rest is not clear and well, like I said, everyone else was killed and no one has lived or stepped foot in the Sector 5 for all these years . . . until now."

"Yes" a Councilman continues, "the father we believe he found out about the portal. We don't know how, but we think he must've fixed and restored the first portal in Sector 5, we believe he must've used the gateway to launch it too somewhere else."

"Tell us about the mother," someone asked. "Well, she escaped Earth through a portal the father made himself in the bottom of a basement" a Councilman explained. "We believe they're together . . . but we don't know for sure." "No sir not for sure" a Councilman says, "but we do know the father is very smart, in fact he's probably the smartest man on Earth." "Oh really?" a Councilman asked.

"Well sir, just look at his two sons, if inception is any proof" another answer. "Yes, yes we understand just how smart this family is" the Council replied. "So, you believe he went to and fixed the Sector 5 portal then used it to launch himself to where?" one Councilman asked. "We're monitoring that now" another responds "we should have that answer for you shortly. The father is in search of something.

We now believe he's not sure, but more of a hunch on his part – we think he believes this place no one has ever seen or been to." "Well, if that's true, then how does he know about it?" someone on the Council asks. "He found it by mistake" another answer "we think . . . on Earth years ago;"

"Oh, – yes sir" someone on the Council replies "we believe he found the white door first - - - from that point on, he actually found another door and through the years, he unlocked this code that unlocked this portal . . . and other portals throughout our solar system. This man has been on a mission – he has risked his family life and his own. Even agencies from his own planet wanted this information and would stop him at all costs. He has proven smarter than them all, not only getting away but even his family is all alive."

"The brothers!" a Councilman says. "Yes, very interesting" someone else in the Council said "They received a message, from what we now know was another new world inviting them to come. This new world sent them both directions in their dreams, so they could plot their course and plan their escape. The rest, as they say on Earth, is history."
"Well, keep us updated on this situation" the head of the Council says. "I want to know where the parents went too."
"Yes, right away!"

Well as the Council members continued talking, one member said, "The two young brothers have something in their brains than most do not have. Really, they are not fully aware of it just yet. It has not been fully developed and they are still immature, their brains I mean" "The two brothers, we believe, will an unstoppable thirst for knowledge and understanding when it comes to different universes, the galaxies, and worlds. People from all around – everyone will want to hire the boys to seek information. I mean for them . . . it will never end!" a Councilman exclaims.

"Well," someone responded, "They will have many respected friends throughout this world and many others." The board members move on to discuss Charlie Hobbit and the Doctor, recently being sent to the far side of Sector 4 Prison, "where, I guess, we sent for Harry T. Bone to deliver these two to their new home." "Yes, I want an update" the head of the Council replied "and let Harry be aware the Council wants to be notified right away when he makes the drop to the prison, OK? Send him a message ASAP.

let him know these two must be watched every second – they are dangerous and will escape if given the right chance."

"Well, Harry is the best in the business" a council member observed, "believe me, he will get these two guys where they need to be – these two don't stand a chance against Harry.

I believe if they will try and escape – it won't be while Harry's around." "Well on a side note" someone on the Council.

"I was getting something to eat last night, and while I was at the bar, I overheard a couple of ladies talking about two handsome and in their words 'very sexy' Alex, and Peter. The ladies went on and on about how tall they were – Oh yes."

"Well, OK" someone in the Council joked, "Are we supposed to ask how tall they are? "No, not really" someone responded, "I don't think the ladies cared either, but they were making conversation about the boys.

They both stand six feet tall – and in the lady's words 'with piercing, deep chocolate eyes that with one look can melt your heart.' The women were going on about the way the boys' hair looked – short and black – just so dashing . . . so they said. Then, the two ladies took two shots and said 'OH MY GOD! Did you see those abdominal muscles! Talk about washboard stomachs with rippling packs?' Well, a few ladies wanted to take them home for the night!"

"Well," another responded "those ladies don't know these boys took off in their craft, while the two of them were just teenage boys, now they're innocent young men who haven't had a chance to kiss and tell. "Well, in any case, the boys have their whole lives ahead of them . . . and, of course, the pick of any lady they will want – to make a life with and fall in love." "Well, thanks for that interesting information, Bill. I think we'll all sleep a little better knowing the ladies in Grim Light City are dreaming about our two Earth boys!" someone laughed.

The rest of the Council members got up laughing – they pulled away from their chairs and retired from this long day. The Council members closed the doors for the night and agreed to keep an eye out on the delivery of the two prisoners that Harry T Bone were taking to the far side Sector 4. Also, keep an eye out on the work the boys are trying to discover. "Oh, one more thing, to get information on the whereabouts of the brother's parents. Good night, everyone" the head of the Council says as he closed the meeting.

The members leave the room, go home, and get sleep. Tomorrow is a new day hopefully it will be a day filled with answers to questions still lingering on everyone's mind. Meanwhile, Alex and Peter are still sitting outside on the ground, behind the cave near the platform that leads to the portal. The outside ring has not stopped moving in a circular motion. The boys are still waiting for the outside ring to line up with the portal. "Well, I guess it just might take all night. Since we are stuck here until it stops – we have no choice to bed down here and get sleep until the gateway opens,"

Peter says. "Yeah, you're right," responds Alex "OK let us find a guard to come and stand watch while we get some rest." The guards are over by the entrance to the cave" Peter replies. "I believe there are two guards there." "Let us give them their orders for the night" Alex says, "and make sure that they know to wake us up in the event the portal stops."

The boys walk to tell the guards their responsibilities for the evening. Afterwards, the guards leave, take their post, and stand guard – while the boys find a place inside the cave to crash and get sleep. Peter and Alex go take a walk around and find two cots to lie down on and grabbed blankets in a closet. As they wait to see, either what the night will bring, or the morning will offer them. As they lay their heads down, they will dream of what ifs and possibilities to come and exciting new adventures that will finally give them answers in their life. Round and round the portal go and where the gateway stops nobody knows.

As Peter and Alex lay sleeping on their cots – suddenly, the guards come rushing in to tell them the portal has stopped moving.

They get up and run outside to look – what they see is the outside rim has lined up with the portal. The gateway will open – at least they hope that, but then they both realize someone must enter the portal to see where it might take them.

They both stare at each other – then at the portal. "Well, OK I'm a little nervous," said Peter. "Yeah, me too!" said Alex. "Well – are we just going to walk through?" Peter asked. "No" answered Ales "let us send a message through first and then wait to see if we get an answer back." Yes – they both agreed. The message will say:

'We are Alex and Peter – for a day or forever they say we can stay – so they say. Don't you want the two of us to come in?' The brothers finish writing the message, send it through, and wait for a response. A few moments later, a message comes through, and it reads:

'For a minute, for an hour or a day won't you come and stay with us. Welcome home Peter and Alex! Your father and I have been waiting for an awfully long time, can't wait to see the two of you after all these years.' As they read the message, they both looked confused. "How can it be?" Peter asked. "Could it actually be Mom and Dad?" "I don't know, Peter" Alex answered "maybe - -

It could also be a trick – No!" said Peter. "I'm sure it must be! Why would they say they were our parents then?" "I don't know," said Alex "but things around here are not what they appear to be – this is the one thing that I'm sure of . . . and Peter – you should be aware of that fact too."

"Look another message is coming in – read it!" Peter implores Alex, who responds "OK Peter, but calm down! Keep it together!" "OK I promise" Peter responds. Peter looks at the message and reads it aloud. It says: 'Do you recall your favorite song of all when you were both small – twinkle, twinkle little star - - - how I wonder what you are - -

- up above the world so high - - - like a diamond in the sky.' Peter freaked out and scream – "I know it's Mom! Who else knows that?" Alex grabs his brother and says, "Look Peter, it might not be what you think." "Well, how can this be happening?" Peter asks. "Well, let's find out" Alex answers him. "OK, how?" asked Peter. "We will contact the Council and see if they know anything" Alex responds. "OK" Peter replies "but let us do it now."

The brothers go back to Grim Light City and to the Council room for an emergency meeting. They both enter the room and sit down - - - they were both shaken and terribly upset. The Council members entered the room and the Head Councilman said, "Yes, we are up to date and are aware of the situation." Peter and Alex respond "and what do you think? Do you have any information about our parents?" "Yes" the head of the Council responded, "we're aware they both went to Sector Five. This is where your father found the first portal that links with the one you two are working on.

He fixed it somehow and entered a code – both your parents went through." "Do you have the location code . . . the numbers he entered?" Alex asked. "Yes, but there is a problem" the Head Councilman replied. "What do you mean?" Alex asked. "The code he entered is no code we have ever seen. None of our engineers or scientists either." "So, what are you saying?" Someone else in the Council replied, "If he entered that precise code . . . he went to place marked with a red door."

The boys looked at each other "red door" they both said simultaneously. "Well – what does the red door mean?' asked Alex. "It's a red tag, of sorts – it means it's on the highest-level security there is in our world" the Council, responded. "So, you say . . ." Peter said – but was cut off by the Council "we're saying these portal doors are off limits to everyone." Alex responded "but why? What makes these doors so different from the rest?" "I can assure you both," the Council instructed them "you cannot go forward with this.

I would hate to arrest you both – believe me, I will hate it . . ., but you would leave the Council no choice. I will only say it is dangerous for all the worlds around us . . . if even one person tries to enter those red doors. I can tell you – it is not human! If even one thing from their world enters ours – we will all be destroyed. "I can tell you; they can't enter our world unless someone from our side enters their world.

It's how it works." "Well has it ever happened?" Alex asked. "Well, we've only heard stories. Years ago – before of us were even born. A red portal opened with a code no one had ever seen. They heard – so they said – a strange woman calling and saying things. One guard got curious and entered. He never came back, but a superhuman being – but not human at all – entered and killed people here before they were stopped and sent back to their world. Ever since then, those red doors and those codes were sealed.

If your parents went through and entered any one of the red sealed doors well then, I'm sorry for you both."

"But wait!" said Alex "our parents went through a portal – with a code that was different." "Yes" a Councilman said. "But maybe" Peter replied, "it was not a red door." "Well - - - your father's smart, but to say he's smarter than everyone in the universe and is able to find the one door that's a fantasy world and like earth. I am aware of the rumors and what he now looks for - - - but that is a legend. No one has ever found it – because it does not exist."

As Peter and Alex looked at each other . . . they now knew what their father was looking for. However, did he must go through a red sealed door to find it did? He uses that code to enter another portal – another gateway. Was it possible there were two doors side by side – one red and another one – and he entered that one and it took our parents to a dimensional world like our planet back home? We must get back - - - if we know our father - - - he would have left us a clue.

CHAPTER FORTY-TWO

SEARCHING FOR HOME

"Well, we know one thing for sure" Alex said. That is what?" asked the Council. "We already know it wasn't, in fact, a red door – and you know that now. You already told us . . . you it yourself! If one follows that line of thinking, enter – that was correct, wasn't it?" "Yes" the board said. "Well, then - - no one had entered.

Do not you see! Those things would've already been here - don't you think?" "Well," the board said, "brings in our engineers." "Yes sir, right away" the Guard replied. As the engineer entered the room, the board asked him have you found out any more information about the parents?"

"Yes, sir" the engineer answered. "Now we know the seal on the red door was torn. But somehow, it looked like it was repaired and fixed." "So, you are saying –

it does appear the father started to enter then realized it was the wrong door," the board said but not in time, whatever was on the other side got enough information about the boys to lure them in a trap. Anything else?" "Yes, sir" the board addressed him "one more thing, we discovered there was, in fact, another door – just like the boys had mentioned – beside the red door. We're now trying to find out more, but both the parents went through that door."

"It was not a sealed door, for sure – we do know that sir," the Guard reported. "Well - - - OMG, the father figured it out!" someone on the board said. "Well, if he hasn't - - - he's definitely on his way!" the Guard replied, "and it looks like he's one step closer to finding his sister home."

"OK" the board instructed, "go back to the portal – shut it down now! Seal off that portal connection now!" "Yes sir" the Guard said, "and I guess you'll both be going to Sector Five to do some investigation." "Yes, sir, we'll be leaving right now" Alex answered.

"OK" the board instructed them "we want you both to take a few people with you in your search – it just might help." "Well sir" Alex answered, "we prefer to do this alone, yes, but if anything were to happen – yes, we understand." "OK then" the board answered "please takes a few guards with you. If you like, you can take the same engineer with you." "OK sir, thank-you" Alex responded.

The boys walk out and get ready to make their way to Sector 5. The guards go to the portal, shut it down, and put a band on it, entering a code so no one could ever enter it again. Peter and Alex make their journey to Sector Five, they find the two portal doors and check to see if they can trace their father's steps and continue moving forward to find – not only their parents but a home called Earth.

"The boys approach Sector five, they move slowly and look around searching for the two doors. The area is large – open space with fields everywhere – overgrown grass. One could tell nothing had been there.

The guards moved forward, looking for a cave or a hidden entrance to the portals. The brothers are walking behind the guards . . . they take their time searching for the entrance. The moments turn into hours – still nothing. A guard says to the brothers "let's take a break." They all agree and see up ahead, a stream of flat boulders. They all sit for a while and rest.

The boys notice a funny looking stick poking out of the ground. Peter got up, walked over to the stick and as he started to exam it – he looks at Alex and says, "I think this is something more than just a stick." Just then, Alex walks over to it, pulls on it, and opens it up – it is an entrance to an underground cave. The boys call over the engineer and the guards to come over. They all gathered around the entrance.

Someone said, "Well, shall we enter the cave?" They begin to slowly enter the dark entrance of the cave   Peter noticed – up ahead, a light burning bright. They all walked toward it – it was a torch light stuck inside a holder on the wall.

Next to the light, on the left-hand side, was a door. In the middle – the light on the right-hand side . . . there was another door. It was there! This door was one door – they just knew their parents went through. Alex and Peter were so excited! "OK, which one is it?" Alex asked Peter. "Oh" said Alex "you mean the red door." "Yes" Peter answered. "Well let's see" Alex replied. "Look" Peter said "on the portal gateway! See if you can find any repairs it looks had Dad might have done."

"Oh, yeah very good idea" answered Alex. They examined the two carefully to find the right door. "Yes" said Peter "it looks like the door on the right had the outer ring around the door." "Well," observed Alex "it looks like Dad tried to remove the outer ring, so it wouldn't open and pull them both inside."

"Yeah, it looks like he pulled hard enough to stop just in time. before being sucked into their world," replied Peter. OK, so the door on the left let us see the engineer says, let us put the code into this door and see if it will open up."

"OK, let's begin" Alex answered. The brothers collaborate with the engineer to put the code into the portal gateway, wait to see if it will stop the outer ring around the door and see if they can open it up. As the rings around the door move around on the outside, everyone wants to see if it will line up and stop.

CHAPTER FORTY-THREE

A Place Called Earth

"Round and round, she goes, where she might stop . . . nobody knows," quipped Peter. "OK, Peter – not funny! Alex chided his brother. "Yeah OK – we better damn well know where it will stop" Peter replies. "It will finally bring us to a new world with Mom and Dad, it has been so long." "Well," Peter answered him "don't get your hopes up. Things are very strange here. We just must be in a wait mode for now."

They all wait for the gateway to stop and line up. The brothers, guards, and engineer sat down and had something to eat while they waited on the gateway and portal to line up. "We can't even begin to know what will happen or what is behind the door!

What world we will begin to see?" said Alex. "Yes" said Peter "since this is a code no one knows about.

" The gateway is still moving around – it slows down . . . slower and slower – the numbers line up. They all stared at the door – their eyes glued to the portal. It finally stops and lines up perfectly! The boys, guards and engineer all look at each other. "Well, are we ready?" asked the engineer.

"Yeah" said the boys "to go where no one has gone before!" "OK" snickers the engineer. Peter walks over to the portal and . . .. finally, Peter says, "I can't believe they have doors with the portal and gateways." "Well, it is very old," answered the engineer "it's before they did away with the doors, now we just have portals with the gateway."

"OK – here goes!" said Peter. Right then, Peter opens the door and sees a bright light coming from inside. Peter says, "Let's leave the door open." "Yeah, promising idea," said Alex.

As the guard and the engineer stayed behind, the boys took one giant step and went through the door, into the bright light, walking out onto the other side. Peter and Alex walked through and as they entered the other side, they see what looks like a man – yelling and looking at them both "tickets please, sorry you can't go through the gate to the other side without a ticket!"

The boys look at each other, and Peter finally says to the odd little man standing in front "we don't have any tickets, but I – Peter Bower, and my brother Alex Bower would like to purchase two please." The odd little man looks at the brothers and asks, "Are you Rob and Susan Bowers' two sons? "Yes" Peter says.

The man looks at them and Alex asks him "have you seen them – did they come this way?" The man spoke up, as he looked at them and says, "Oh, they left two tickets for you both. You may go through the gate." "Yes, thank you" Peter replies "but which way did they go – do you know?"

The man looked up at them once more and said to them "the tickets have all the information you will need." Then he yells "move along . . . next ticket please." Peter and Alex opened their tickets and read. The boys read their tickets – all it says is 'take the train all the way down to the last stop.' "Well, what do you think?" asked Peter. "I don't know" says Alex "but one thing for sure, if we don't go – we'll always wonder. So, let us get onboard . . . but wait. Let us go back – tell the guards and the engineer what we are planning to do – just in case there is a problem. "OK" Peter replied, "

We'll tell them, if they don't hear from us in one hour, send guards for help . . . because we'll be in trouble, and need assistance." "OK" Alex answered. The boys go back and inform the others about the situation. They then reenter, go through the gate, board the train, and wait for the last stop – to get off and hopefully see their parents for the first time in years.

They ride the train to the last stop. The train finally slows down – you can hear the conductor saying "Last stop! Last stop! All off." The brothers stepped down off the train steps and sees guards all around, as they are waiting. The guards approach the brothers and tell them "You will come with us now." The guards stood behind and in front circling them all around – so they could go nowhere.

The guards lead the boys away, to a location out of town. They arrive to a stairwell that spiral downwards to an underground city they called Star Sector Four. "Welcome" as a man comes close to them "yes, we know who you are – Peter and Alex." "Well, thank-you" they said. Peter asked, "Do you know our parents? I mean, have you seen them?" The man looked at them both and said, "Yes, they are here. Please come and I will take you to them." The boys grew excited after all these years they get to see their parents.

They walked up to an old train car, they stepped up the steps, grabbed the bar to pull themselves up to the finally step and stood in front of a door. Alex turns the knob, enters the car, and hears "Alex and Peter! Oh, my GOD!" "Mom is that you?" asked Alex. Susan and Rob Bower ran into the car, Susan picks her sons up off the ground, as were they still little children, and says, "Boys, we made it!" "Yes, Mom – we did" Alex answered.

Rob looks at his two precious sons and says, "thank goodness, I have two smart boys! Otherwise, I do not think we would be all together here at this moment. Then, they all smiled – and of course, Mom – started to shed tears of pure joy. They all were laughing and smiling! "Team Bower!" Peter said, "Is unstoppable!" "Yes" said Alex "just look at us now – see where we're going to be! Somewhere – somehow, we're almost there in finding our new world our new home called Earth."

"Well," Dad looks at his two sons and says, "It's called Star Light Earth Four, and we are almost there. This is a place where you must be a special guest or family to get an invitation to live here. I know you . . . can they, say – request a hearing to ask for an invitation? Your mother and I already did just that. We are waiting now to hear from them on their decision.

They have been informed and know everything about us – all of us. So, we just must see if we pass the test and get to live in a place that, for most part, does not exist and we'll never be able to figure out how to get here." A man approaches the car and says, "A decision has been made. You are to go to the far side and investigate the mirror wall.

"It's like a phone" Dad says, we'll be able to see the person who will be reading our decision." They all make their way to the mirror wall and stand before it. A man appears within the wall and reads the decision. "It has been decided. We do feel you are exceptional family, one worthy of entrance to our world.

However, we feel a test of courage is necessary to enter. We know just how extremely intelligent this family is. However, it is not enough! We want a test of courage. If you all pass this test – entrance will be granted for everyone." Rob got terribly upset; a man says to them "congratulations! This is certainly good news for you!" The family turns around and says to the man "what do you mean?" "Well," he answers, "no one – in probably centuries – have found this place. No one has been granted access ever! They are very hopeful you will all be with them soon. This place is amazing – no death, no sickness, no hunger – living out one's life in a place where the possibilities for whatever your heart desires is endless."

CHAPTER FORTY- FOUR

THE TEST OF COURAGE

"Well, what do we do now?" asked the boys. "We wait until we find out exactly what the test of courage will be" their father replied. "It makes no sense to worry, let us go, take a hot shower, change our clothes, and get something to eat. After all – we're guests here and we're safe for the time being" their mother said. The boys nodded 'yes' and Alex said, "That sounds good to us also." They left to go shower and get something to eat while they wait for their test to be revealed.

Days went by and still no word. They all seemed a little restless, until a man came rushing over to the train car. "It's time" he said, "They have your test ready. You all must go back over to the mirror wall to find out what exactly the test will be and how long you must complete it."

The Bower family got up from their chairs and left the train car once again back to the mirror wall.

They approached the wall and seemed a little nervous, but they were happy to finally find out. A man once again appeared on the wall and said, "Hello Bower family!" He said "We here at Star Light Earth Four have thought very carefully what type of test of courage to give to you. After thinking very carefully about this, our decision is as follows

You and your family will go back to Grim Light City and continue to the Sector 4 area.

There is a back door within Sector 4 – you will be given directions on how to find it. Peter spoke up right away and says, "What is the back door to?" "Well," the man explains, "you might know it has a red door." "Wait one minute . . .," says Alex. Those red doors are sealed off, it's illegal and punishable either by prison or death if you open or to enter a red door." "Yes" the man says, "we are aware of this.

I want you to continue to Sector 4 – within this area; you will find a back entrance to the red door. It has not sealed off but frowned upon if you enter this way. The area is only known by accessing to the back door. We want you to go inside – within the world of these giant superhuman robotic creatures. We want you to bring us back the head of one creature.

Afterwards, bring the head, go back through the back door, and seal it off. If you do not seal off the door, it could let them out. In doing so – I will tell you – it could well destroy Grim Light City's world. OK, you may ask questions if you like, but only on the task at hand. "OK" Rob Bower asks, "Why don't these creatures leave through the back door?

Do they know about the back door?" Someone says, "They are doomed and cursed – none of them can leave their world – unless someone enters their world. You must be careful, they are extremely intelligent and will stop at nothing to get someone to enter, be caught, and stay in their world. This would allow them access to a door, which will open and lead them to a portal.

This will allow all the creatures to destroy anything and everything in their path. Why would you want to risk having these creatures get out and allow them to kill and destroy everything? "I have to ask, and I want to know," asked Rob Bower "what's inside the heads of these creatures that you are willing to risk so much?" The man answered, "They have knowledge and information about all living things, creatures, and planets that haven't even been discovered yet.

You need figure out a way to get in the back door, go in the room where they keep their programed heads and bring one out with you – without being seen. Then well, you just should leave out the back door and seal it. I will welcome your entire family to our world if this can be conducted. You have 24 hours to decide to accept this offer or not. If you turn this down, you will not be granted access for the rest of your life . . . and every member of your family for the rest of their lives will not even be considered eligible for access to Star Light Earth Four." The man disappeared from the mirror wall, giving the Bower family just 24 hours to decide.

To risk everyone's lives for the reward of being given access to a world that would . . . fill you are every desire and comfort. This decision will not be an easy one for any of us to make. A man rushes over to the train car, hands a note to Rob Bower – it reads: 'One other thing you might want to know, you and your family will have 24 hours to plan and then one day to execute."

As they sit in the cab, they ponder their choices – if to accept this offer. Everyone sits in silence, finally, Alex says, "well, I'm not going to manage possibly starting a dimensional intergalactic war – that will start off small and spread like the plague, killing off and destroying everything in its path!

That is what we just might have to face if we are caught, and those things are released into the outside." "Well Peter" Dad asks, "What do you think? "I agree with Alex" Peter answers, "I don't really see how we can move forward with a plan that will assure our goal and keep those things under lock and key." "Well," Susan (Mom) says, "What do you think?

I think for me the deciding factor must be just how bad we all want to go and live in Star Light Earth Four. The second is the plan – it must be detailed to perfection."

"We would have to know for sure that we would be able to get in safely and out without disrupting or alarming anyone of those things" said Peter says. "So, we would need to have a blueprint, of sorts, of the inside of the building they're living in.

So, we can see for ourselves if it is even possible," said Alex. "Yes, I agree," Dad said, "even to make such a decision we need to have all the facts to base it on." "OK" says Alex "we'll go and send a message.

We'll ask for several things like well, for one a blueprint, information on just how many live there, their routine – of sorts – and how many are in or near the room we must enter." "Yes, that is excellent" Dad says "with this kind of information at our disposal – we can make a logical decision. OK – send the information request out. Now we wait for the information back."

The hours go by and still they receive no word. Everyone is concerned what he or she is asking for would not be allowed for them to see. More hours pass by, still no word. The Bower family has decided to decline. They all felt without valuable information, they would not have all the facts they must base their decision on. They send a message out explaining their decision. Hours pass by all the information they had requested was granted. With a note saying, 'we look forward to hearing your decision within 24 hours.' The family sits down and looks over the documents. "Well, OK" Dad says, let's see."

The brothers spread out the blueprints and then noticed the numbers of those robotic super beings living in their world. They could not believe their eyes . . . and what they are seeing. "OMG! this just can't be right! Peter says "Alex! Dad! Come here Mom . . . you had better have a look at these numbers. Then the boys just got so quiet. The two just sat down, just stared off in the distance, and blanked out.

"I can't believe this! It just can't be correct, Rob!" Mom said. "Yes, I know – I saw it just like you did" Dad, replies. "It can't be that there's millions upon millions living there!" Mom said. "Now we know why they are called super humans – it is not because of their strength Dad says, "It is because their brains are human, and their bodies are robotic. I think it might be possible to get in through the back door of that room – we just must go in when it's not being guarded." "OK" said Alex "what about inside the room . . . are there any of those things inside? You know we must find out.

We want no surprises; we risk being captured and letting those things out. "Well according to the paperwork, we have and looking at the blueprints, it seems to be an empty room, so we should be OK," Alex sees. "Well, how far is the room to the back door?" Peter asked. "It looks like, according to the blueprints, the room we need to go into is to the left of the back door. We enter the door and make a left turn. We should see the room right there.

We enter it – take the head and we are out. We leave through the back door, seal it and – no problem – that's it!" Dad told them. "I don't know," said the Alex "could it really be that simple?" "Or will we start something that just could turn into our worst nightmare . . . and not just for us" Peter replied. "We have to be sure this can be done - - - otherwise we could send millions of people to their death, and we'll be responsible.

Is this something we could live with?" Alex asked. "The risk is great, but the reward is unbelievable" Dad says, "I think we can do it without getting caught and without those killing human machines let loose. OK then, so have we decided. Are we all in agreement?" Dad asked. The boys were quiet and stood in silence as they nodded their heads to move forward, and all nodded their heads in favor. "OK then" Dad says, "Sends the decision to Star Light Earth Four to move forward, bring back the head of a superhuman killing machine and sent it to the leader of a planet where we all want to live."

CHAPTER FORTY-FIVE

ONE STICK OF DYAMITE

The time approaches, and the Bower family gets ready to leave and head to Sector 4. They must find the back door and to get back . . . since time is of the essence and the clock is ticking. They all head out of the train compartment and meet up with a guide who will show them the way to the entrance of the back door. He will not stay; his job ends when he gets the Bower family to the entrance of the back door.

They begin their journey and leave the haven behind. They realize they might not be coming back. Rob prays he has made the right decision for his family, one that will lead them into paradise – instead of being captured or killed. They keep moving along, finally after hours; the Bowers reach the back entrance to a world sealed off and entrance forbidden. "OK" Dad says, "let us gets ready.

People, we only have one shot at it. Peter – you and Alex stay behind at the back door. Stay close and get ready to seal the door. OK boys, get the equipment you must seal the door, as Susan and I get ready to enter." They slowly open the door and enter. Everything is quiet – they see none of the beings around. They get to the room – Rob grabs a head and high tails it out of there. He gets to the back door and they both exit.

Alex and Peter seal the door shut, then suddenly, they turn around and see a superhuman robotic machine staring them all down. "Get away!" yells Dad. Susan (Mom) screams. Rob grabs super veins – a plant that grows everywhere – luckily for them they were standing next bends down to take these super strong plants.

They look like ropes, and he throws it to the boys. Peter grabs a boulder and hits the robotic machine. The boulder knocks it down for only a second, then it loses its balance – the boys take the rope and bind its legs and hands.

After securing this strange superhuman machine, they all head back to the train station and to the underground city, where they were staying. They later, walking in with this creature bound and tied. The boys contact the leader on the mirror wall, informing him their mission succeeded – but with one exception. They have captured one creature.

The people all around saw – this thing – enters their underground world. They all panicked and scream. The father assured everyone everything was all right. They secured the creature by putting him in a locked room, chaining him to the wall. The leader of Star Light Earth Four told them bringing that creature to their underground city was a huge mistake.

They must dismantle it right away, before it gets free, head back to the door, breaks the seal and let us million and millions of those things out upon their world. The leader told the boys, their father, and mother they had completed their courage test! He then welcomed them to Star Light Earth Four. The family was overjoyed and excited.

Rob asked, "When do we get to enter?" He replied, "Now, if you like – go and get your things together and check on the creature before entering." They packed up their belongings and set them outside of the train cab. The boys and their father went into a secured room. As they open the door to check, it was gone somehow . . . got away! Now they knew it was heading to the back door to break the seal and let out millions of millions of those creatures.

A war to beat all wars was about to start – and they knew it would grow into a war that could not be stopped. "We have to go back and stop it!" Alex says. "NO!" yells the father "it's too late! We should protect ourselves now! Get your stuff and let us get to Star Light Earth Four."

The boys knew millions would be killed – they had no way of knowing what was about to happen to their world and others. Grim Light City and the other entire cities close by would be destroyed. They would not even know in time to prepare themselves a defense.

The boys said, "Sorry Father – we have to go back and lead the fight. We must stop this thing from letting out millions more of those robotic creatures. The boys run back and return to the back-door entrance. They found the human machine creature at the back door, trying to break the seal. They had a laser weapon and fired it at the creature – it had no effect. They got closer, trying again to hit the robotic creature with the laser – it turned around, picked them both up and threw them against the wall.

The boys were knocked down but got up. They took out the explosive they had – lit it and threw it at the robotic creature. The robotic creature was destroyed in thousands of little pieces thrown everywhere. The boys laughed - - "We did it!" they both said together. "We really managed to set things right! Look – the door is still sealed" Alex observed.

As they both got up . . . they knew they came close to starting an intergalactic war, which would have ended with all – or most – of humans erased.

The boys got up and headed back to the underground city to tell everyone what had happened. They were heroes - - - and everyone was smiling and overjoyed with them. The rest of the Bower family got prepared to enter their new world. The mirror wall opened –

finally, a greeting came across, it read: 'WELCOME WON'T YOU PLEASE COME IN AND STAY FOR AN HOUR OR A DAY. WON'T YOU PLEASE COME AND STAY. "No!" yelled the boys "we know now that it's a trick!" "What do you mean?" asked Dad. "It doesn't matter – Peter and I are not going inside!" Alex told him. Their father and mother both said, "OK, we are entering."

"NO! Please do not! Stay together, Dad. It took us so long to find each other!" Alex implored. As they were deciding to enter or not – the portal door opened and the parents looked at their sons and said, "I am sorry." Rob and Susan smiled at their two twin sons and entered the portal gateway. The boys felt they had no choice.

Peter grabs the last of his explosive sticks, lit it up, and threw it at the portal gateway. The two twin brothers from a long distant planet called Earth just turned around and walked away. Alex looks at his brother and says, "Now we have the head – let's find out what it knows." "Another adventure – To the Universe and beyond!"